One Deadly Game

A McCall / Malone Mystery

Glenn Harris

One Deadly Game is a work of fiction. Names, characters, places and incidents either are the product of the author's imagination or are used fictitiously. Any resemblance to actual persons, living or dead, or events is entirely coincidental. Portland, Oregon, of course actually exists. Major landmarks like Pioneer Courthouse Square and the Justice Center are where they belong, as are the streets and neighborhoods, but I have moved a few buildings around, put restaurants where none exist, erased houses that do exist, and generally wreaked minor havoc with reality for the purposes of my story.

One Deadly Game

CHAPTER ONE

She awoke knowing she was going to die. Worse, that she was probably going to get her daughter killed as well.

She didn't know where she was. Some kind of abandoned building, an upper floor from the faint sounds of traffic outside. Not a lot of vehicles but somewhere in town probably. She was bound tightly at her wrists and ankles, in a sitting position with her back wedged into one corner of a large space that, besides her, currently held only a stack of wooden pallets against a far wall. Otherwise it was bare wood, exposed rafters, and some high windows that were so dirty they barely let in the daylight.

There was no point in yelling and she couldn't anyway because her throat was too dry.

He'd taken her in the evening, after it was dark, so she must have been unconscious at least eight or ten hours.

She was thirsty. She was hungry. She was cold. The back of her dress was wet with urine. And none of that mattered. She deserved it all and worse for being so stupid, for allowing herself to be seduced into committing a crime so monstrous she still couldn't believe it.

Had she been insane? Did she contain some horrible flaw she hadn't even known about that he had recognized and tapped? She didn't know. She couldn't know. What she did know was that now her daughter was about to be used by this same terrible man and it was all her fault.

He was insane, for sure. At first, when she finally realized she was simply being used, that she wasn't loved, she assumed it was greed. Thirty million dollars was a lot of money. But he had the money now and could have easily gone..."in the wind," isn't that what they said on the TV cop shows? Yes, very far into the wind with access to that much money.

But he was still here and seemed to be obsessed with the idea

1

that he'd been betrayed by...somebody...and was endangered by, apparently, somebody else. Or somebody working with the first somebody. He'd taken time to torment her before injecting her with the drug that had put her to sleep. He'd rambled on for what seemed, in her initial terror, to be at least an hour but she didn't know who he was talking about or why. There was a "she" (the betrayer) and a "he" (the danger) and a "they" who might or might not have been them but...she didn't understand and it was useless to speculate.

The one thing he'd said clearly was that he was taking her to use as leverage. That his weapon would be her daughter, her lovely gentle daughter, and that the weapon would be wielded before she herself was dead. She would live to know he had been successful, he had promised her. It didn't sound like she would live much beyond that.

Through it all he also kept muttering about time, about needing more time, about being robbed of time.... But never once had he answered any of her questions, responded directly to any of her pleas. He had explained nothing about why the money wasn't enough. He hadn't even told her to shut up when she kept begging.

There was only one moment of absolute clarity and it was not welcome. As he pressed the needle against her arm he'd finally looked directly into her eyes.

"None of you," he said in a calm and confident voice that sounded deceptively sane, "had any idea who you were dealing with. I am the best and will always be the best. You are all pathetic fools."

Then he smiled and slipped the needle under her skin as tears rolled down her cheeks.

2

CHAPTER TWO

He had four inches and forty pounds on me, not to mention being at least thirty years younger and ridiculously robust. Even his frown had muscles. I was going to have to be careful not to hurt him.

Considering that it was a Saturday evening with a rare, late-winter snowstorm outside, attendance at the event was good. There were several dozen spectators seated on the folding chairs that lined three walls of Chejung's Northwest Martial Arts dojo and a few more standing against the east wall near the entrance and dressing rooms.

I had already determined that there were only two of us from outside the dojo participating in this tournament, the other being my accountant, Internet researcher and friend Eleanor Ivory who had invited me to the event to meet her new boyfriend, one of Chejung's black belts.

It had been my bright idea to join her in participating. I could have been one of those spectators. Contemplating my final opponent, I wished I had taken that option. I was tired, sore from a variety of kicks and punches that had gotten through to my poor old body in earlier bouts, and worried that defeating my current opponent without seriously injuring him was going to be a real test of my skills.

He meanwhile was probably not worried at all, glaring down as he was at a stocky, middle-aged (if I live to be 106) guy with thinning hair who looked like he might be a particularly fit college professor—which indeed I used to be. What the kid didn't know was that the old journalism prof had since become a private detective and fourth-degree black belt. He could see the black belt tied around my waist, of course, but didn't seem very worried about it; he had one of his own, along with those inches and pounds. Apparently the worrying was going to be my responsibility.

3

Thank goodness this wasn't Eleanor's boyfriend. I hadn't met the guy yet but she'd pointed him out when we first arrived.

The referee shouted to begin the match and my opponent's initial stance told me that he was about to deliver a right straight punch, that it was going to miss, and that he would probably leave me an opening for a straight-finger strike to the throat. Which is the sort of thing he should have been more concerned about, since in a real fight that would have meant he had about four seconds to live.

Another thing he didn't know about me: that I'd had to kill people in real fights.

He feinted with his left and launched the right punch straight at my chest. I blocked his arm outward with my left as my own right hand, fingers straight and stiff, exploded upward to stop with my fingertips touching his larynx. He made a gargling sound as he realized what had happened and the judges indicated a point for me by raising their white flags.

Compounding his error, the kid apparently decided the first point was a fluke and became even more aggressive, counting on youth, strength, and size to overwhelm his elderly opponent. Turned out that age, guile, and quickness were the better bet. I had the other two points I needed for victory within half-a-minute without either of us sustaining any notable injuries.

Ours was one of the final matches. Then we all had to sit through the closing ceremony and announcement of winners by Master Chejung, who looked a little more like a retired wrestler than a sixth degree black belt. He was a few inches over six feet tall, heavily muscled, almost stout, and pushing sixty by my estimation. His voice was harsh, as was his demeanor.

Not surprisingly, given that we were the outsiders, neither Eleanor nor I were among the over-all victors. As in most other highly specialized and closely-knit disciplines, there's a lot of politics in the martial arts. Chejung had not deigned to recognize our arrival and seemed determined to end our visit the same way. There was no way he had failed to notice our participation. My bet was that he didn't miss much.

I finally got to meet Eleanor's newest conquest as everyone (except Master Chejung) was shaking hands and socializing after the announcement of tournament results. Chet Findley was a big, good-looking guy with close-cropped blond hair and a hint of southern accent, probably in his late twenties or early thirties.

My just-turned-forty friend Eleanor is a classic blonde with a compact, athletic body and apparently the sexual stamina of a woman half her age. She usually went for the bad-boy types who were at least five years younger than her. Chet appeared to meet the age requirement but was more a corn-fed Dudley Do-Right by the looks of him. I shook his hand, guessing to myself that he'd not be in the picture for long.

I had no idea how true that would turn out to be.

CHAPTER THREE

We chatted for just a few minutes more. It wasn't a good time or place since most of the spectators had departed and the other participants were heading for the lockers to change back into street clothes. Eleanor, however, seemed determined that I get to know young Chet—whom she apparently had met herself just the week before. Maybe she was hoping I'd help her get to know him.

Anyway, she suddenly brightened as we were saying our good-byes. "Why don't you come over to my place Monday evening for dinner?" she asked. "Chet tells me that he makes a fine veal scaloppini and we'd enjoy having you join us."

From the transient grimace on Chet's face that Eleanor apparently missed, I was pretty sure the feeling was not mutual but I sensed that my friend was counting on me. I had no other plans and I was curious about *why* she was counting on me, so what the hell. "Sure," I said. "I've always been a fan of veal scaloppini."

Then she really surprised me. "Why don't you bring Devon along?"

My first impulse was to reply that I could think of numerous reasons right off hand, but that didn't seem entirely appropriate in front of the brand new boyfriend so I simply said, "I'll talk to her about it."

It was about then I became aware that standing behind Eleanor and Chet was at least one spectator who had not left, a petite young woman who looked like she might want to say something to us but was frightened to do so. She was staring straight at me, actually, gray-green eyes wide behind wire-framed glasses. I offered her a smile and raised my voice a little. "Can we help you?"

She seemed startled to be addressed. "Oh. Oh, no, I didn't mean to interrupt. I can...." She gestured in the direction of the spectator section, almost empty now. "I can wait over there until you've finished talking, Master McCall."

7

We all three laughed. "It's *Mister* McCall," I said. "Chejung is the only master in the place." I glanced at the other two. "See you later?"

"Nice to meet you," Chet said as he and Eleanor headed for the dressing rooms. I would have preferred to go with them and get on my way, but the young woman seemed anxious and no one was urging that the space be cleared.

"I can give you a minute," I said and escorted her over to the nearest chairs. Her reddish-brown hair was cut short, just long enough to frame her thin face. She was wearing jeans, snow boots and a heavy sweater. I put her at late teens or early twenties, though the wire-framed spectacles gave her an oddly old-fashioned look. We sat down and she took a moment to compose herself.

"My name is Libby Jance," she began. "I'm a journalism major at Portland State and I want to do an article about you."

"Really," I said, trying to identify why it was that I didn't quite believe her.

She was unduly nervous; no question about that. She kept adjusting her glasses and looking around the room rather than making eye contact. "Maybe a series of articles."

"I'm flattered. Why?"

She looked at me then, just for a moment. "You're talked about often in the journalism school. And you're in the news quite a bit. Not many of our professors go on to become famous private detectives. I thought it would be fun to do an in-depth profile."

There was intelligence in her eyes even as they skittered away again, along with fear and determination. Didn't look to me like she was anticipating a lot of fun. The kid was doing something really brave and I wanted to know why talking to me required such courage.

"I can give you an interview," I said. "What about my office at ten Monday morning?"

Her face almost crumpled. "We can't do it now? Or this weekend sometime?"

8

"No, let's keep it within business hours. Monday at ten. My office. It's only a few blocks from here."

"I know where it is. I can wait until Monday, I guess."

And why not? Very curious. "Fine. I'll see you then."

I watched her hurry away toward the entrance and listened to her boots clumping down the stairs. There was an urgency about it all that just didn't fit. Plus, it occurred to me, there was the most interesting question of all: How did this kid know I would be here in Chejung's dojo on a Saturday evening? Has she been following me around?

Must be one hell of a school project.

CHAPTER FOUR

"Eleanor Ivory wants me to come to dinner tonight? With you? To meet her boyfriend? What the hell?"

Devon Malone looked at me across the expanse of our partners desk, her left eyebrow cocked upward by an incredulity I'd become accustomed to in the last four months. Both my life and my friends often seem to amaze my partner.

She was wearing a blue pullover sweater, her usual form-fitting jeans and black boots. Her recently-trimmed short brunette hair was still recovering from the blue knit cap now hanging on a hook near the door. A woman of sharp features and strong temperament, her olive-toned skin was still glowing a little from the outdoor chill. She's not a classic beauty by any means but she has no trouble keeping my attention.

There was, as always when she was around, a hint of cinnamon in the air. I'd yet to determine whether it was shampoo or soap or her natural scent. And I was as always ignoring the little kick it always gave my pulse. That way lay madness. Or at least major disappointment.

"That was my first reaction, too," I said, playing my part. "You and she have yet to become good buddies despite the fact that she's practically a third member of the agency."

Malone sat back and dismissed that view with a "pfft."

"She's our accountant," my partner went on after a moment. "She does Internet searches that you could do yourself if you were willing to set foot in the 21st Century and learn how. It's not the McCall - Malone *and Ivory* Detective Agency."

Which was true enough. I was still trying to get used to the fact that it was the McCall - Malone Detective Agency. Said so right on the frosted glass in the upper half of our office door, on our business cards, on our letterhead, and on our new website—that was designed and maintained by none other than Eleanor Ivory. At least my name was first, thanks to a coin toss.

We'd been thrown together on a couple of cases before we decided—at my suggestion—to merge our two agencies into one. We'd been occupying the opposite sides of this partners desk since early November. We took separate clients as much as we could to maximize income, but it still amazed me how little personal information I had yet gleaned about Devon Malone.

She was of course willing to talk about our business. More than willing to talk about where to find her next meal. Even happy to talk sports or current news. She just didn't talk about herself. And I wasn't prepared to make a big deal out of the omission. I could wait. As far as I was concerned we were in this for the long haul and I had no doubt I'd learn everything I needed to know eventually.

"Eleanor is one of our back-up people, just like Johnny Crew or Hap Harbaugh," I responded. "I've been relying on them for a long time and now they're here for you as well."

Malone's mouth twitched in what might have been a slight grimace. "I'll accept the damned invitation. Maybe we'll be buddies after I've eaten her meal and met her boyfriend." She didn't look like she was optimistic about that outcome.

"Actually it's my understanding that the boyfriend will be cooking."

"Whatever. You got anything going on this morning?"

I surveyed the mostly empty surface of my desk in the hopes of seeing evidence of a new and lucrative case that I'd forgotten over the weekend. We'd had plenty of work in our new partnership so far, mostly from the publicity around the two cases we worked together before officially joining up. That had started to drop off lately, but not by much. "Reports to do," I said. "Bills to pay. Nothing pressing. There's a kid coming in at ten to interview me for some school project. That's about it."

"So she tracked you down?"

"I wondered how she knew where I was. You told her? How

did *you* know where I was?"

"I was sitting right damned here when Eleanor came in and invited you to the tournament or whatever it was, remember? The kid, if it's the same one, called late Friday after you'd left. She sounded pretty desperate to talk to you, so I told her she might find you at that martial arts place Saturday evening. Was that not okay?"

I shrugged. "Sure it was okay. She's just a student doing a project. Or so she says. She sounded 'desperate' when she talked to you?"

"I'd say so, yes."

"And she sounded pretty desperate when she talked to me as well. She really didn't want to wait until this morning for the interview."

"Sounds hinky."

"Or at least fishy."

"Ten you say? I don't have a full agenda this morning either. Maybe I'll be sitting here working away while she has her appointment."

"Shouldn't be a problem," I said.

14

CHAPTER FIVE

"You are not fucking going to believe what I heard on the news last night," Johnny Crew boomed at me through the static on his cell phone a few minutes later.

Reminded by the exchange with Malone that I did have at least one new (if not lucrative) case, I'd called Johnny to check on how he and his partner Hap Harbaugh were doing on their assignment, which was to check out one Joseph Imeson for his prospective bride. But first I would have to hear one of his stories. Johnny loved weird news stories even more than he loved dirty jokes and assumed that I never watched or read the news myself. Usually he was right.

"What did you hear?" I asked with only a hint of resignation.

"They're lookin' for a blind and deaf guy who got lost hiking in the woods."

"Don't tell me he went by himself."

"That's not the best part. He went with a deaf friend of his. They got separated, which probably wasn't that hard to do. Not much use yelling for each other, huh."

"I guess not."

"The poor bastard was blind, deaf and stupid, if you ask me. Probably dead now, too. All this happened yesterday and they still haven't found him. It was a fuckin' cold night out there. Can you believe people?"

"I often don't, as a matter of fact."

He laughed. "Yeah. Comes with the job."

"And speaking of the job...."

"I'm sittin' out in front of Imeson's office now. We lucked out on the parking space, good view of the front door. He just got in after breakfast at a Denny's."

"Where's Hap?"

"Gone to get us some more coffee and donuts. This guy is

15

probably staying put for the rest of the morning."

Johnny Crew and Hap Harbaugh are retired both from the Portland Police Bureau Detective Division and from the private agency they set up afterward, at which I did my own apprenticeship as a PI. They've been partners for almost forty years. Despite their ages—Hap is sixty nine and Johnny is seventy two—they were actively working yet again, partly from boredom but mostly because Hap recently got married and moved out of the spare room in Johnny's house where he had lived for years.

Although the Crew & Harbaugh Detective Agency was technically back in business they were, at least so far, primarily working for me as backup or to cover ongoing surveillance like this job. They had no office of their own this time around besides Johnny's living room.

Johnny Crew is a short and burly but very well-groomed fellow with a full head of thick gray hair. At the Justice Center he was known as "Dapper John." Hap Harbaugh has at least eighteen inches of height and a hundred pounds of weight on his partner. Johnny always looks immaculate while Hap is a total schlump who thinks nothing of wearing the same clothes a week at a time— though that seemed to be changing thanks to the former Wilma Wolfowitz. A completely bald mountain of a man, his nickname on the force had been "Hap the Hulk." He complains constantly about his back, bunions, knees, neck, and all the other parts of his body he can no longer reach; whereas Johnny never complains about anything. On the other hand, Johnny has an incredibly foul mouth among friends while Harbaugh never says anything more potent than "dang."

This was their second day of following Joe Imeson, the new fiancé of my new client Nora Hogan. Miss Hogan had a "gut feeling" that her future husband might be seeing someone else. She'd hired me to find out and I was still busy enough to justify subcontracting the boring part to Crew and Harbaugh. They'd started on Friday and skipped the weekend since Mrs. Hogan said she and Joe would be home together.

"Anything so far?" I asked. I assumed the answer would be no since I hadn't heard from them.

"Not much, but could be. He spent a good part of his lunch hour Friday trolling the blocks just off Burnside between Sandy and MLK. Ankeny, Ash. You know the ones."

I did indeed. Anything fast in that neighborhood wouldn't have been food.

"Could have been lookin' for a whore to pick up but nothing transpired. It ain't, as they say, probative."

"But it is, as they say, suggestive. Stay with him through the rest of this week, at least. The client's already covered that much. Maybe we'll get lucky."

"Ha! Maybe he will—or think he has, anyway. Oh, here comes Hap loaded down with crap. Shit, I think he cleaned 'em out and it ain't that long until lunch time. Gotta go."

I hung up. It seemed that Nora Hogan's gut had some potential talent. Or maybe her fiancé was just eccentric and liked to spend the occasional weekday lunch hour driving in circles. We'd see.

CHAPTER SIX

Malone and I spent the next hour or so catching up on reports, preparing some bills, writing a letter. Between us we had five active cases at the moment, but nothing much more exciting than keeping an eye on the possibly straying fiancé.

Our office (and that "our" still sounds funny to me) is at the corner of 2nd and Stark, on the second floor of an old two-story commercial building on the northeast edge of downtown Portland, Oregon. Previously Owned Books, a locally popular used bookstore owned and operated by our landlords, is downstairs. A single poorly lit stairwell provides the only access to our floor, from Stark.

The McCall - Malone Detective Agency is the first door on your right. Across from us is the agency's attorney Sam Bitterly. He lets us use his small conference room on the very rare occasions that Malone and I have clients in the office at the same time; one of us uses our office and the other Sam's conference room. Down the hall on the right is our insurance broker Raymond Witkowsky, with Eleanor Ivory's office across from him. A small telephone survey operation has the final two offices across from each other and the public restrooms are beyond them at the end of the hall. It was remarkably handy to have the agency's attorney, insurance agent, and accountant within shouting distance.

Besides the convenience, I liked this building because I imagined anyone approaching our door in the dimly lit, wood-paneled hallway would feel like they're in a 1940's detective movie. So I'm a romantic. So sue me.

Promptly at ten there came a firm knock on the glass upper panel of our office door.

In response to my invitation, Libby Jance opened the door and came in, pausing just inside as she registered Malone sitting across from me. She'd traded snow boots and heavy sweater for tennis shoes and light jacket; the jeans remained the same. Her short red-

19

toned hair was dripping and she shook it once, sharply, like a dog would.

She finally looked around the room and then focused on me. "This is neat," she said. "It looks just like a detective's office."

I couldn't help glancing around myself. The partners desk was the biggest change that Malone had brought with her and it certainly contributed to the old-fashioned detective office look. The elderly couch off to the side was the same. Each of us had two visitors' chairs. There was a second file cabinet. The coffeemaker and printer and other supplies on the counter were about the same. Soon after Malone moved in we purchased a larger office fridge. She likes to snack between meals. A lot.

It still didn't feel crowded because it had been a big office space for just me. It actually felt about right.

"Well," I said, sounding suitably blasé, "that's what it is. Come on in and sit down." I gestured across the partners desk. "This is my associate, Devon Malone."

Our young visitor clearly was trying hard to look relaxed as she ambled across to one of my visitor chairs and settled down, but the tension was palpable beneath the half-smile and carefully casual gestures. Fear? Or something else? I still couldn't tell.

She pulled a small digital recorder out of a jacket pocket and then looked from me to Malone. "Maybe we should do this somewhere else," she said hesitantly, more or less addressing my partner.

"No problem," Malone replied, waving it off and turning her attention back to her monitor. "I have excellent focusing skills."

Looking if anything even more discombobulated, Libby Jance leaned forward and set the recorder on the edge of the desk. "Okay if I use this?" she asked.

"Fine with me," I said. "But first, tell me what you have in mind."

A little eye-dart toward Malone again. "It's for my sophomore journalism class. I want to do a series of articles on Portland's most well-known private detective, especially considering that you used to be a professor in my department." Deep breath. "I'm sure there's a great story in how you got from one to the other."

"I'm afraid you may be disappointed," I played along, "but let's give it a go."

Her first genuine smile. "All right!" She turned on the recorder. "So...how *did* a Portland State journalism professor become a private eye?"

I had to laugh. "In three thousand words or less? Let's see.... I'd been an investigative reporter for *The Oregonian* before joining the faculty at PSU. I think I missed doing that kind of work. I'd gotten to know a couple of retired Portland cops who had a detective agency and, after my divorce, I was feeling kind of restless. Call it a mid-life crisis. I started working in my spare time with that agency and over the course of the next few years it became an official training period. I finally got my own license, resigned from the university, and set up my own business."

"Any regrets?"

"None at all."

"Uh, I'm going to need a lot of, you know, colorful detail for these articles. There are a few things I want to go into in depth. That history, for one thing. A few examples of what kind of work you do every day, *how* you work." Quick ragged breath. "For instance...I'm sure you do a lot of missing persons work. Tell me how you go about looking for someone who's missing. I want to hear every little step, beginning to end." Edging forward on her chair. "I'm sure our readers would find it fascinating."

Right. I was beginning to wonder if she could be one of those souls who simply like to hang around law enforcement. There are a lot of cop groupies, for instance, though not many private detective groupies. We're private, after all. Could it be fear of rejection that I was picking up? Afraid I wouldn't let her have the vicarious thrill of sharing a few cases? Nah. Everything about her demeanor since we'd first met told me it was more serious than that. I took a shot: "So who do you want to find, Miss Jance?"

21

This time it was a sharp intake of breath and her face fell into an almost comically-exaggerated expression of surprise. "What makes you ask that? I don't want to find anyone. I just thought our readers...." She was backing off, both literally and figuratively, so fast that I was afraid her chair would tip over backward.

I held up a hand in an effort to halt the retreat. "You may be a good reporter," I said, "but you're not a very good liar. Why don't you tell me what you're really after."

Meanwhile Malone just kept tapping away on her keyboard as if none of this conversation was happening three feet away. I did think I detected a slight smile in my peripheral vision.

Finally Libby Jance's shoulders slumped and she looked resigned. "Shit." She snapped off the recorder. "I knew I'd blow it."

CHAPTER SEVEN

I sat forward and put my elbows on the desk. Malone turned from her monitor, no longer pretending to ignore us. "It was a valiant effort," I said to the younger woman, "but you might try telling the truth now. You are looking for someone?"

She gave my partner a wary look, opened her mouth as if to object, closed it again. And then: "Someone, yes."

"Who?"

She dumped the recorder in her pocket and stirred in her seat as if to rise. "It doesn't matter. I can't afford you and my little ploy to get free advice didn't work...."

"Are you really a sophomore journalism student at Portland State?"

That stopped her for a moment. "Yes. I could even really do a series of articles about you, I suppose." Pause. "I was going to wait a while and then tell you the editor of the paper rejected the idea."

"Well, that would have saved you some work and taught me some humility."

"I'm sorry." Stirring again. "It was all a stupid idea. I won't bother you guys anymore." She stood up.

I couldn't help feeling sorry for her, her face flushed with embarrassment, eyes bright with welling tears, her already small stature seemingly diminished by disappointment. I mean, hell, she was about my daughter's age and she seemed to be in trouble.

"Sit down again for a minute," I urged. "Tell us who it is you want to find. Maybe we can help. Malone here used to work missing persons for the Portland Police and I'm no slouch at finding people myself."

She hesitated, looked toward the door and back, didn't sit. "It...it's my mother."

I sat up straighter, as did Malone. "Your mother? That sounds serious enough. How long has she been gone?"

23

Libby glanced back toward the door again and took a step. "I can't afford a private detective, much less two private detectives, so there's no use going into it."

"Miss Jance, I'm offering you some help at no charge." At which point I thought I heard a slight snort from Malone but I ignored it and went on. "I could at least give you the information you were after in the first place, about how to look for a missing person. Maybe even do a little nosing around myself."

Now she seemed impatient, almost irritable. This was one volatile young lady. "No, no," she said as she waved away my offer. "Not right now. Let me think about it. Good-bye." And just like that, she left.

We both sat there for a minute, looking at the door that had slammed behind her.

"Well," Malone finally said, "that was weird."

"No kidding."

"Not least that you offered her *our* free help with me sitting right here."

"Actually, if you were listening carefully you heard me switch to a singular pronoun at that point."

"I did hear that. Careful grammar, maybe, but not much business sense. As long as we're a partnership everything we do *pro bono* comes out of both our pockets."

"I believe it was syntax rather than grammar but point taken. I shouldn't have offered without consulting you first."

"Fucking English major." She started to turn back to her monitor but paused. "I'm not opposed to *pro bono*, as you well know. You think her mother's really missing?"

"If she is, there's obviously more to it. But I guess we'll never know."

CHAPTER EIGHT

I arrived at Eleanor's apartment right at seven with Malone only about two minutes behind me. We had, of course, come separately since we weren't together.

The apartment décor was seriously modern, much glass and stainless steel set off by other shiny materials in primary colors. The dinner was the promised veal scaloppini with steamed broccoli and fresh salad, preceded by hors d'oeuvres and followed by cheesecake. It was all delicious and nearly a tie between how proud Chet was of himself and Eleanor of him.

The conversation as we ate, on the other hand, was at times somewhat awkward. I was fine. Malone seemed to be her usual centered and utterly secure self. Eleanor clearly didn't know quite what to do with Malone and Chet seemed mystified by the relationship between me and my partner.

"You're just partners?" he asked at one point. "In the detective agency?" He sounded dubious, as if he found it hard to imagine a man and a woman working or even dining together without being romantically involved.

"Just partners," Malone agreed and I nodded in support.

"Surely you're at least friends by now," offered Eleanor, perhaps hoping to learn something about how to become Devon Malone's friend.

Malone held up a forefinger. "We've been sharing an office for four months and only today did I hear McCall talk about his past— previous careers, becoming a private detective, that sort of thing. And he wasn't even talking to me. He was answering a question from this college kid pretending to interview him."

"Pretending?" asked Chet with a slight frown.

"Long story. My point is that we're partners. Period."

I think, meanwhile, that my jaw had dropped. What I wanted to say was, "Are you fucking kidding me? You share almost nothing

25

personal in all the time we've worked together and you complain you haven't heard *my* story before?" What I did say, after a moment, was, "So far."

Malone shrugged, possibly in acquiescence.

At any rate our host and hostess had no such problems. Throughout the evening, Chet's enthusiasm for Eleanor was palpable. He'd apparently not encountered before such a combination of femininity and physical toughness. He seemed to like it. Quite a bit.

It was he, not Eleanor, for instance, who wanted to show off the extensive collection of martial arts weapons displayed in a glass case at one end of the living room.

"Can you believe this?" he inquired. "Look at all this stuff. She's even got real throwing stars in here. And a push knife! I don't think I've ever seen one of those in real life."

Malone's interest was definitely piqued. She carefully surveyed the whole collection and then looked up at Eleanor. "You know how to use all of these?"

Eleanor laughed as she raised the lid of the case and reached in. "No. I've played with them all, but trained with only a couple. I'm mostly a collector." She picked up the push knife. The serrated blade was three inches long with the two-and-a-half-inch handle forming a "T" rather than serving as an extension of the blade. She demonstrated by closing her fist over the handle so that only the blade projected from between her fingers. "I've trained with this a little, for instance, the push knife Chet was talking about. It's for really close-in fighting."

"I've seen them," Malone said. "Some prostitutes carry them because, as you say, they're effective in a small space—like a car."

That gave rise to a moment of silence. "Wow," Chet said. He gave Eleanor a possessive squeeze. "And this," announced Chet, "is one hell of a warrior woman." She leaned her head against his shoulder with a big grin. Which more or less got us to the end of the evening.

CHAPTER NINE

I awoke the next morning at five thirty to the awareness that there was a cat standing on my chest intently checking my breath, her nose right up against my lips.

"Good morning, Stella," I muttered. "Yes, I'm still alive and that means you'll be getting breakfast."

A moment later the bed shook slightly as Stella's much more tubby sister Maxine joined us—no doubt in response to the word "breakfast." Maxine was not interested in my breath.

My cats are tortoiseshell sisters who otherwise do not look at all alike. Stella is sleek and short-haired. Maxine is fat and fluffy, essentially a Maine Coon in appearance. I fear their mother may have been promiscuous.

They both jumped off as I climbed out of bed and followed me first to the bathroom, then back to the bedroom closet where I put on sweatpants and t-shirt, then to the kitchen to wait impatiently while I split a tin of Senior Diet Pacific Salmon Dinner between the two of them.

I had learned long ago to feed them before sitting down on my cushion for morning meditation; even at that, I usually ended up with Maxine snugging against me and purring away after she finished her meal. I meditate every morning for fifteen or twenty minutes before having my own breakfast. I don't claim it has any particular benefits, other than giving Maxine a place to snug. I just do it.

I finished my bacon and eggs around six thirty and had traded the sweatpants and t-shirt for my office-going khakis and polo shirt when I heard a buzzing. It took me a moment to realize it was my cell phone, still set on vibration from the evening before at Eleanor's.

Calls between six thirty and seven in the morning are rarely good news. This one was no exception. I could hear a tinny screech before the phone got near my ear. Someone was screaming, neither voice nor words recognizable. I tried to cut through the hysteria, hoping that it wasn't my daughter. "Colleen? Who is this? What's going on?"

There was a pause as the caller apparently tried to swallow air, seeming to choke on it and then recover. "He's dead!" It was Eleanor's voice. "My God, he's dead! I woke up and he was.... Oh God!"

What the hell? "Calm down," I said. "Take a deep breath. Tell me what happened. Where are you?"

Her breath was ragged but slower. "I'm here...at home, in the living room. He's...in there. There's so much blood...."

"Are you hurt?"

"No, no, I don't think so. I rolled over and...hugged...." Her words were overwhelmed by a dry retching sound.

I was on my feet now, reaching for my wallet and car keys with one hand even as I held the phone tightly to my ear with the other. "It's Chet? You're absolutely sure he's dead? Do you need paramedics?"

"He's ice cold, so cold, and...dead!"

"Okay, okay. Are you sure there isn't anyone still in the apartment?"

"Yes!" she howled. "I checked! The door's still locked! There's no one!"

"I'm on my way," I said. "Stay put and don't touch anything else. Don't open the door for anyone but me. Don't do anything. Just sit there and try to breathe slowly. Hang on. I can be there in fifteen minutes."

My house is on S.E. 37th three doors from the Marrakech Theater on the corner with Hawthorne. Eleanor's building is on S.E. 23rd just off McLoughlin near Westmoreland Park. I could shoot straight down Hawthorne and turn left on Grand, which then feeds into McLoughlin Boulevard. Five miles on wet surface streets at six thirty Tuesday morning. Easily done in a quarter-hour.

I hit one red light, at Grand, and took the occasion to press the speed dial for good friend and fellow black belt Portland Homicide Lieutenant Mike Whitehall on my phone. He was still at home and I briefly told him what little I knew, including Eleanor's address. By the time Mike could get there his day-shift would be starting and I wanted a good friend as the primary on this one. Our conversation was no more than thirty seconds; he said he'd meet me there and hung up.

The person who opened the door of Eleanor's apartment bore little resemblance to the happy, healthy woman I'd seen last evening. Now she was wearing a cream-colored satin robe, the chest area soaked with blood. Her long blond hair was disheveled, the tips on one side also blood-soaked. Her chalk-white face was twisted with anguish, her eyes almost as red as her chest. She reached out for me and I could see there was blood on her hands.

I hated like hell to do it, but I had to step back. I wanted with all my heart to take her in my arms and tell her she was safe, but right now she was evidence.

"I'm sorry, kiddo," I said, "but we can't touch until after the cops get here and check you out. You sure you aren't hurt?"

She looked down at herself and dropped her hands slowly. "No...yes, I'm sure." She stood aside to let me in. "I haven't called the police," she said apologetically. "You told me not to do anything...."

Stepping into the apartment, I was struck by the heavy odors of fear, fresh blood, and something else acrid I couldn't identify. "That's okay. I talked to Mike Whitehall. They're on their way. Is the.... Is he in the bedroom?"

"Yes," she answered so softly I could barely hear.

She indicated an open doorway at the end of a short hallway and I walked over to take a look. The bedroom was feminine without being girly, mostly in the blue spectrum without many frills. The covers of the queen-size bed were pulled down to Chet's knees and he was naked. Just from his relaxed, supine position, he could have been sleeping peacefully; there was no sign of a struggle. Between his neck and his waist, however, was a massive multicolored splash of blood and...vomit? Yes, that was the other smell. He was dead all right. Barely visible on the left side of his chest was what looked like the hilt of a push knife.

"I should.... I have to clean up. They shouldn't see him like that... I...."

I turned to find Eleanor close behind me, holding a large towel, her words running together as she babbled about making poor Chet presentable.

"You're not going in there," I said firmly. "We have to leave everything just as it is. Put the towel back and sit down."

Her face scrunched up like a small child denied a candy. "But I.... *I threw up on him!*" she cried. "I woke up and was...was snuggling when I felt the wet...and opened my eyes and...I threw up! We can't leave him with...."

I reached out and took the towel from her. "We have to," I said gently. "No one will blame you for throwing up. It's probably what I would have done under the circumstances. Now go sit down. You have to sit down and not touch anything else until Mike gets here. Please."

She hesitated, then finally shuffled over to the couch and weakly lowered herself onto it. I'd just had time to return the towel to the bathroom and casually wander over to her display case—her push knife was not there—when I heard a sharp rap on the door.

"Clint?" It was Mike Whitehall's voice and I was glad to have some company.

CHAPTER TEN

I opened the door and my friend stepped inside. "Where?" was all he said initially. Whitehall is extremely fit as you'd expect a fourth degree black belt to be, six three of solid muscle with short-cropped brown hair. He's also way smarter than the average cop and openly gay.

After a quick survey of the apartment and a look, from the doorway, at the body, Mike called it in. Within half an hour, the apartment was crowded with the medical examiner, three crime scene investigators, and a female uniform to escort Eleanor into the bathroom where she was allowed to clean up and put on some clothes.

After which she and I were both required to head for the Justice Center, she riding with Whitehall and me following in my Subaru Outback.

The Portland Justice Center takes up the entire block defined by 2nd, Madison, 3rd, and Main. It's just seven blocks from my office, straight down S.W. 2nd, and houses the city jail as well as the Portland Police Bureau. Mike had a spot for his vehicle and I managed to park only a block away, on the street. As I approached the building, I was surprised to see Devon Malone standing by the Police Department entrance.

"What are you doing here?" I asked as I came up to her.

"Waiting for you."

It took me a moment to process, but then I got it. "You put it together from what you heard on the scanner." In addition to the scanner we had in our office, Malone has one in her Jeep *and* one at home. I've never asked, but I suspect she sleeps with the damned thing on.

"I figured you and Eleanor would be showing up here pretty quick. Thought I'd check in to see what I could do. Her boyfriend is the DB?"

"I'm afraid so. With her push knife sticking out of him, it appears."

"Ouch. You think...?"

"No. I absolutely don't think she did it." I opened the heavy door and gestured her into the little waiting area in front of the desk sergeant. "Since you're here, might as well come upstairs with me. I have to give a statement but that won't take long. Then we wait to see what Eleanor's status is."

The Homicide Detail is at the rear of the Detective Division on the thirteenth floor. It's made up of a half-dozen low-walled cubicles with lots of light entering from the big picture windows. Reproductions of famous paintings hang on the walls and the workspaces are well-decorated with family photos and other mementos—a colorful, downright cheery-looking space.

After I'd spent a few minutes in one of the interview rooms off to the side of the detective area, Malone and I waited in Whitehall's office talking over what I'd seen in the apartment this morning and going back over what we'd both seen there the evening before.

I was pretty sure Eleanor wouldn't be arrested right away, both because evidence had yet to be processed and because Whitehall would not consider her a flight risk. I was absolutely sure that if the knife that killed Chet Findley was from her collection, she was in very deep trouble. From what I'd picked up before leaving the apartment, there was no evidence of forced entry and Eleanor had no memory of any disturbance during the night. She was going to need a good criminal lawyer.

"At least," Malone said after I finished thinking out loud, "she has a couple of good investigators on her side."

Okay, so my partner was still capable of surprising the hell out of me. "I thought you weren't a big Eleanor Ivory fan."

She shrugged. "We're not good buddies and we're probably not going to be, but she is part of our team. Like you were saying yesterday. Right?"

"Right," I answered, noting to myself that someday I would have to figure out how Malone managed to sound sarcastic and sincere at the same time.

A few minutes later Whitehall appeared with a still-free Eleanor in tow. He let us take her away with an only-half-kidding warning that she shouldn't leave town. She said nothing as we took the elevator and then passed through the building lobby. It had started raining while we were inside and the sky was now dark with ominous clouds. The mid-morning downtown traffic was heavy.

"I'm parked a block this way," I said to Eleanor as I tugged gently at her arm. "Did you drive?" I asked Malone.

She grimaced. "To the office, but then I walked over here. It *was* a nice day."

"Well, come on then. I'll drop Eleanor off at her place and get both of us back to the office." Meanwhile Eleanor seemed either unable or unwilling to move.

I was hoping we could get the damned travel arrangements settled quickly because we would soon be soaked if we just stood there. Eleanor finally turned to look at me, rain water trailing down her cheeks like tears. Or maybe they *were* tears.

"Take me to the office."

"Are you sure?"

She stood firm. "I can't go back home right now. I don't know how I ever can. What am I supposed to do? Get out some rags and scrub everything down while the sheets are in the laundry? Like spring cleaning or something?" She squeezed her eyes shut. "Oh, my God. How can I even live there anymore?"

Malone was the one who reached out for her arm this time. "Maybe you can't," she said. "That's something you'll have to think about. You certainly can't go back right now because they won't be done with the crime scene yet. Let's get out of the goddamned rain and I'll tell you all about crime scene clean-up services."

Eleanor looked up into the downpour as if aware of it for the first time. "Oh. Okay." We dashed for the Outback.

CHAPTER ELEVEN

"Maybe," I said as I pulled the vehicle into traffic, "you could stay in a hotel while you get some professionals to clean the apartment. You don't want to decide now how you're going to feel until after you've had some time to recover."

"I guess you're right," she said finally. She was riding in the passenger seat and Malone was in back. Then, abruptly: "I didn't kill Chet. I know I didn't."

"So what did happen?" Malone asked from behind us.

"Oh, God," Eleanor moaned, "I don't know. I can only tell you what I told Mike and the other detective. It's not much. We had a lot to drink, really a lot. I don't remember anything after we had sex. I don't remember *finishing* sex. The next thing I remember is...waking up." She was silent for a full minute. "You don't think I did it, do you?"

"Are you absolutely sure you didn't?" That was Malone again.

"Yes!"

"Then I don't think you did it. Clint?"

"Of course I don't."

Eleanor smoothed her wet hair back with both hands. "What can we do?" She included Malone in the question, apparently not as surprised as I was.

"Well," I answered, "we'll want to find out everything about Chet that we can. He'll have enemies. Everyone does. Also, you should make a list of all the people who might be pissed at you. Old boyfriends, clients—especially anybody who might have a key to your apartment."

"I don't give out keys to my apartment."

"Then focus on people who could have stolen or copied a key. Your apartment door has a high security lock. There was no evidence of tampering. Either somebody has a key or you're a killer—and, no, I don't think you're a killer."

35

"I'll make the list."

I pulled the Outback into the lot across from our building and eased it into my reserved spot. I shut off the engine and turned to make eye contact with Eleanor. "You're sure you feel like going to work?"

She grimaced. "I'd go nuts if I just sat around thinking about what's happened. Besides, I'm committed to trying to keep one of my clients out of bankruptcy today."

"Not your fault they're in trouble, is it?"

"No. It's a little old lady with a lampshade shop. Great at finding lampshades, not so great at turning a profit. I don't think she's mad at me."

"Well, don't forget to make your list."

"I won't. Thanks, Clint—and Devon. I owe both of you."

"Don't worry: We'll take it out in trade." I put my hand on her shoulder as she moved to open the passenger side door. "One more question. Just curiosity. Probably irrelevant. Why was it so important to you that I get to know Chet? You didn't seem to care with any previous boyfriends."

Tears welled up in her eyes. "I guess.... I guess it was because he was such a nice guy. I wanted you to see me with a nice guy. It was stupid."

I still wasn't sure what to make of that, but I gave her shoulder a squeeze before letting go. "He was a nice guy," I said, "and I'm glad I got to know him a little."

The three of us hurried together across 2nd, around the corner, and into the shelter of the stairwell. Eleanor headed on down the hall to her office as I unlocked ours.

"You're her father figure," Malone said as soon as she closed the door behind us. "I had no idea."

I thought about that while I hung up my jacket and unhooked the holster from my belt, stowing the Smith and Wesson in my top right-hand drawer as always. "I'm a little young to be her father," I finally said.

Malone dumped her Glock in her top right-hand drawer and sat down. "It's got nothing to do with biology. She works for you, works *with* you, and on top of that you're her martial arts teacher, right? She respects you and wants your approval. You think she favors bad boys and she knows that; she wanted you to see her with a good boy, like she said."

I wasn't sure I cared for the idea of being a father figure to a forty-year-old woman, but it was as good an explanation as any. "And instead she ends up with a dead boy," I said as I took my own chair.

"Yeah, we need to make a plan—but first I see I've got at least one message waiting here." She picked up her phone.

My message light was blinking as well and I had three, it turned out, two that could be ignored for now because the callers didn't actually indicate they were looking to hire me, only that they were shopping around. The third was from Libby Jance.

"I've been thinking about your offer," her message said, "and I do need your help. Thank you. Not free: I'll find a way to pay you, both of you, but I can't do this alone. I think Mom.... Call me and I'll tell you everything." She sounded resolved, focused, determined. Everything that I no longer was when it came to her situation.

I needed some time to think about it. I'd call her back after I had a chance to take a breath, talk to Malone, maybe eat lunch if I could find an appetite. I still didn't really know what was going on with the kid and wasn't sure I'd have the time or energy to find out.

Malone was busy tapping away on her keyboard, so I decided to call Mike Whitehall. Whatever Malone and I were going to do, it would go better if it did not duplicate or interfere with the Portland PD investigation. Which was going to require some coordination.

"We've talked to his immediate family and are about to start working our way through the friends," Mike reported. "So far no enemies, nobody even mildly pissed off. Mr. Findley was a fine fellow, according to his parents and brother. Not surprising."

"Garden variety nice guy. Of course."

"We'll see what the friends have to say. You onto anything?"

"Haven't even started. I was thinking I'd go visit his dojo, get a feel for that part of his life."

"Okay. We'll be going over there later to get a list of students and do individual interviews. Okay with me if you want to get your take on the place first."

"Will do," I agreed and hung up to find Malone focused on me again.

"So who's the nice guy?"

"Chet Findley, so far. Not a critic in the world much less an enemy, according to his family." I retrieved the Smith and Wesson from the drawer and stood up, holstering it as I moved toward the hall tree.

Malone also stood. "Mind if I go along?"

"To the dojo? No."

She must have heard the question in my voice. "Just curious what one of those places looks like. I hear you talking about your martial arts stuff all the time and I don't have a picture really." Slight grin. "Unless it's like the movies."

I smiled back. "Depends on the movie. Some of them are pretty accurate." We both grabbed our jackets. "Come along and see. Maybe we'll get some useful information about our victim besides."

CHAPTER TWELVE

Chejung's Northwest Martial Arts occupied the first floor of a gray two-story box on 82nd between Powell and Division, the name painted in bold black letters across the glass front. This time I registered curtains on the windows of the second floor and wondered if that might be where the master himself lived.

Inside there was just a scattering of white uniforms sparring or working out, all of them brown or black belts. Clearly no formal class was in session. The folding chairs off to the side for spectators were all empty. It was just a large open space with polished wood flooring and the flags of Korea and the United States prominently displayed on the wall opposite the entrance. Not that different from my own dojang.

I recognized Master Chejung standing in a far corner with two black belts, deep in conversation.

They saw us before we were halfway across the floor and one of the black belts came to meet us. We stopped at a distance of about six feet and bowed to each other, bowing at the waist with arms bent at the elbow and fists forward, head up so that we made eye contact with each other, simultaneously an expression of respect and wariness.

And, apparently, for Malone an occasion of wonderment. "Wow," I heard her mutter under her breath.

"You were at the competition Saturday," Chejung's black belt said as he came closer. He was ignoring Malone entirely.

I didn't recognize him. He was mid-twenties, dark hair in a crew cut, average height, very fit; there must have been a dozen guys who looked just like him at the event.

"Yes," I said, "but that's not why I'm here." I pulled out my ID and flipped it open, as did my partner. "I'm Clint McCall and this is Devon Malone. We're private investigators. Are you aware your fellow student, Chet Findley, has been killed?"

"Yes." He stepped back, eyes narrowing. "One of *your* fellow students killed him."

Well. They had excellent sources of information—and an obvious willingness to jump to conclusions. They'd not only connected Eleanor to Findley's death but also to our dojang. This wasn't going to go well.

"That's not been established," I replied firmly. "We're looking into it on her behalf. We'd like to talk to Master Chejung."

He finally shifted his attention to Malone and looked her up and down as if wondering whether she too was a member of the dojang. Then: "Wait here," he replied brusquely and returned to the far corner.

After a brief exchange, the same black belt returned to where we were standing, his expression grim. "The master will not speak with you," he announced.

"Then I'd like...."

"None of us will speak with you. Master Chejung holds your entire...group...responsible for the death of his student and there will be no further talk until that debt is settled."

"What? We had nothing...."

"Please leave at once." He turned and stalked away, leaving me with my mouth hanging open.

"What was that about?" Malone asked as we exited to the sidewalk. "Your *group*?"

"You know that I belong to a small dojang. 'Dojang' is the same thing as 'dojo,' by the way; we use the Korean word because we do taekwondo. We aren't a formal school like his, just some black belts who rented a space to keep in practice together, a group of friends. That's the group he's talking about. Apparently he blames all of us for Findley's death just because Eleanor is a suspect."

"That's weird. Talk about jumping to broad conclusions. And they got a hell of a lot of information in a hell of a hurry. Which is interesting."

"It is," I agreed with both points, and punched Mike Whitehall's number into my phone as soon as we were settled back in the car.

CHAPTER THIRTEEN

I briefly described to Mike what had just happened. "Thought you'd better know before you get over here," I concluded. "They seem to have good info, but surely they wouldn't know that you're also a member of the dojang. So you've got the option of provoking them or not."

"Hmm. Might be interesting to piss the master off. He can't refuse to talk to me. It sounds like he's translated this into a matter of personal honor—or wants to give that appearance, anyway. You get any impression of how sincere he was?"

"From observing him yesterday and today, I'd have to say pretty sincere. He looks like he's straight out of an old samurai movie. Maybe he thinks he is."

"Well, I'll try not to piss him off so much that he comes to visit our place."

"That would be good. There are only seven of us and a lot more of them. You have anything new?"

He sighed. "No. I have to tell you, so far the only person of interest is Eleanor. I'll keep her out of the system as long as I can, but...."

"Do your best. Meanwhile, I'm going to talk to her again when I get back to the office. I asked her to make a list of everyone who could have stolen or copied a key. That seems like the only explanation."

"Only *other* explanation."

"Give me a break, Mike."

"Okay, okay. Anybody interesting turns up on that list, remember to share."

"I will. See you."

"This whole martial arts scene is awash in testosterone, huh," Malone observed dryly as I put my phone away and started the car.

"You could say that." I pulled into traffic, mulling over my priorities.

"Eleanor is still Whitehall's only suspect?"

"Yep. I'm going to have to tell the Jance kid that I can't help her. We've got to focus on this."

"I'm not sure I agree. It's not in my nature to ignore a possible missing person's case." Not surprising, given her last assignment before leaving the Portland Police Bureau under a cloud, thanks partly to yours truly. "What do you say to seeing her one more time? There's something weird there."

"Maybe. Let me think about it."

We were silent the rest of the way back to the office. Then I caught an inquiring look from Malone as we were settling on the opposite sides of our partners desk. "Okay, okay," I said. "We'll take another look at it. But the priority has to be Eleanor. Definite murder versus maybe missing."

"Agreed."

I punched in Jance's number on my desk phone and she picked up about three milliseconds into the first ring. She must have been sitting there with her hand poised over the receiver.

"Yes?"

"This is Clint McCall...."

"Mr. McCall! Thank God. You'll help me then?"

I had the sense yet again that there was something not quite right. I couldn't tell if she was overplaying a role, desperately in trouble or just plain nuts, but her reaction was not ringing true. It did ring some more warning bells.

"We want to talk with you again," I replied cautiously. "How about ten o'clock in the morning at my office?"

I caught a brief hesitation. "That's great, but could you come here? I have a hard time getting downtown."

This was very odd. "You mean, come to your home?"

"Yes. Please."

I could see from Malone's frown that she also thought the request strange. She was making some kind of gesture toward my phone but I couldn't interpret it. In any event, there was no way were we going to Libby Jance. She got downtown a couple of times before without apparent difficulty and she could do it again.

"No," I said firmly. "We have to meet in the office again. Can you make it at ten?"

Resignation in her voice. "Yes, I can be there."

"Okay, We'll see...."

"Could we do it this afternoon? My mother is...could be in great danger. I...I think she stole some money. A lot of money. I can be in your office in a half-hour. Are you there now?"

Okay, so we'd gone from a hard time getting downtown to no problem making it in thirty minutes. We'd also gone from Mom may be missing but I don't want your help to...Mom is a thief in danger and I have to talk to you right now. I'd had enough of this bullshit for the day. Whatever was going on, Eleanor had precedence.

"No," I said again. "I'm sorry, but we're already booked up this afternoon. We'll see you at ten in the morning. That's the best I can do. There are other private detectives in Portland, you know."

"I.... All right. I'll be there." She hung up.

I put my own handset down and looked at Malone. "What were you trying to tell me by waving your hands around?"

"That you should put her on speaker so I could hear both sides of the conversation."

"Oh. Sorry. I'm a bit of a technophobe. But even I know these are two-button phones. You could have picked up and listened on my line."

"I'm not going to jump in uninvited. Try to remember next time. It's not rocket science. Anyway, I heard enough to know we've got a weird situation there. Very weird."

"True enough. But let's worry about it in the morning—if she even shows up. I'm going to go see if Eleanor has that list done."

CHAPTER FOURTEEN

I walked down the hall and rapped on the frosted glass of Eleanor's office door. No response. I knocked again and was about to open the door without invitation when: "Come in," she called, sounding very business-like.

Eleanor Ivory Accountancy is a single room like mine and Malone's, though smaller. Eleanor's decorating touches are somewhat more elaborate, including a doll collection and numerous pictures of herself in various exotic locales, usually with whichever past boyfriend had paid for the trip. (You could call them both doll collections, I suppose.) There are colorful knickknacks and even a small mobile of papier-mâché birds hanging from the ceiling.

All those cheery touches were offset today by Eleanor herself, grimly ensconced behind her desk, calculator, computer, printer, and several stacks of folders. She sat ramrod straight, hands flat on the desktop as if to hold herself in place. Then she recognized me and relaxed—or, more accurately, collapsed.

"You okay?" I asked as I closed the door behind me and took one of the visitor's chairs.

"Yes, I guess so. I needed a few seconds to get myself together." She smiled weakly. "If I'd known it was you, I wouldn't have bothered." She pushed her hair back on either side as if she might make it into a ponytail, but then dropped her hands again. "I keep drifting back into the nightmare. Or maybe I'm trying to wake up. But it's not a nightmare, is it? Not a dream."

"No," I said, "it's not. Did you make that list?"

She picked up a piece of paper and handed it across to me. "This is everyone I can think of that I've dated in the last two months. They're the only ones I can think of who have had a chance to get at my keys. They've all been to the apartment. You want me to go back further."

"No, this will do for now." I looked at the names. Seven in a couple of months. Not too bad, except... "This reads like a list of terrorist suspects," I said.

She snorted. "Don't be a bigot."

"Sorry. Just making a bad joke, trying to lighten the atmosphere. Big fail. Let's see.... Martin Idris, Ahmad Sadat, Oliver Spengler, James Ibrahim, Rodian Rospovich, Daniel Habash, Siddig El Fadil.... Come on. You made that last one up."

"No, I met him through Daniel. We just had one date. He had to go back home."

"When was that?"

"Week or so ago."

"So now he's...."

"Somewhere in the United Arab Emirates, as far as I know."

"So we can probably cross him off the list."

"Probably. He could have come back, I guess, but he was a nice enough guy. An actor. We certainly didn't have any trouble."

"Did you have trouble with any of these guys? Which one did you go out with most?"

"Daniel. I guess he's the answer to both questions. He's the only one on the list I had more than two dates with. We were together, like, seven or eight nights in a row and he wasn't happy when I broke it off. He didn't threaten me or anything...."

"Why did you break it off?"

She shrugged. "He was getting a little strange."

"Strange?"

"He started hinting about some big plan he had for us. It didn't sound like he was talking about a vacation. And it was like he didn't want to let me out of his sight.... He just got *strange*."

"Sounds like maybe he got in love."

This time it was more of a shudder. "I don't think so."

"Well, I'll check him out. Anybody else?"

She thought for a minute. "Ollie Spengler was kind of different, too. He spent the evening telling me about all the women he hated."

48

"Really. Do you think you got added to *his* list?"

"I think he was just really neurotic, but who knows? I couldn't tell why he hated any of them. If it was because they didn't go out with him again, I could certainly be on his list, yes."

"I'll check him out, too." I rose to go. "I'll check them all out, but give special attention to Spengler and Habash. If you think of anybody or anything else, let me know."

"I will."

"And take care."

"I will."

I gently closed the door behind me and went back to my own office.

After briefly updating Malone on what Eleanor had said, I checked my phone to find that I had one voicemail, from Johnny Crew, reporting that Joseph Imeson had once again patrolled the blocks off Burnside during lunch hour without making any connections worth photographing. In addition Johnny had to describe in some detail the food Hap had consumed as they drove, each item with its own accompanying obscenity.

Finally he offered, on behalf of himself and his wife Gerry, to take Eleanor in for a few days while the apartment was cleaned up or she found a new place, whatever she wanted to do. He was checking with me first because he didn't want to give her the impression he thought she couldn't handle it.

It's a good thing we have a voicemail service that permits very long messages. It's also a good thing to have friends. I had a hunch Eleanor would take Johnny and Gerry up on their offer. It would be better than a hotel.

CHAPTER FIFTEEN

The next morning, a wet and gray Wednesday, Malone and I were both in the office by nine. Libby Jance knocked on the door promptly at ten.

She'd chosen a very different look this time. The short red-brown hair was the same, as were the gray-green eyes peering at me through fashionable glasses, but she was wearing an expensive leather jacket over a light tan top with dark brown slacks and shiny leather dress boots. She carried a leather satchel and a black umbrella. She left the umbrella leaning against the wall just inside the door. No jeans, sweatshirts or tennis shoes today.

She shrugged the jacket off as she crossed the room and dropped it on one of my visitor chairs while she sat in the other. She shifted subtly so that she was facing the two of us equally. The top she was wearing looked like a body shirt of some kind, shiny and a very snug fit. Perhaps my young visitor was petite, but her nipples were not. I was gonna have to keep my eyes on those glasses, especially with Malone across the desk monitoring.

As soon as the hellos were out of the way, I got straight to the point. "I'm afraid this may be a short meeting," I said. "I have to tell you that we aren't inclined to take your case at this time."

She practically left the chair as her body surged forward. "No!"

"Miss Jance, we already have a client who is in very serious trouble and requires all our attention. I can recommend another...."

"You have to help me! It has to be you!" Now she was focused literally and intensely on me, not Malone. "I...don't trust anyone else to do it."

Bells and more bells, but Malone spoke up first. "You have no reason to trust us, either," she said quietly, emphasizing the "us."

Our young visitor switched her attention to my partner and stared at her for a good five seconds. "Of course I do. There's all the stories on TV, Mr. McCall's reputation at school...."

"Nevertheless...," I started to say.

She scooted to the very front edge of the chair and leaned forward from there, very intense, back to addressing us both. "Please listen. My mom has always had lots of problems, men and alcohol mostly, but she's never just disappeared before. She didn't show up at work last Thursday and nobody's seen her since. She's an accountant at Ecotopia Venture Capital." She pulled a file folder out of the satchel and opened it. "I found some financial records at her house that makes me think...."

She frowned as she inspected the contents more closely. "Oh shit! I picked up the wrong file." She looked up at me, a helpless expression on her face. "I left the papers at home. You have to see them. At least give me some advice about what to do. Please!"

My first impulse was to say, "Oh, come on," and I heard a little snort from Malone that I knew meant exactly that. But then I hesitated. Libby Jance looked so much like my daughter Colleen does when she's making one last desperate try to get me to do something I've already said no to. It appeared that this kid was definitely in trouble—either because what she was telling me now was true or because it wasn't. Something was pushing her to extremes.

"So," I asked carefully, "are you planning to go back home, get them, and bring them back here?"

"Won't you be going out later today? You could stop by and look at them. I'm afraid.... Mom's last boyfriend, the one she's probably with now, he's a dangerous man and I'm afraid he might hurt her. Please come."

I sat back and gathered my thoughts for a few seconds. Now I had to come to her home because there might be a dangerous boyfriend involved. What or who was at her place that she needed me to see? The forgotten files? Fat chance.

"Where do you live?"

"An apartment building near the corner of Elm and S.W. 18th, upstairs, number five."

I didn't bother to remind her of her claim yesterday that she has a hard time getting downtown. The location she described was on the other side of the Portland State campus, true, but still a walk of no more than thirty minutes to city center—not to mention other available transportation.

Was she trying to seduce me? It didn't have that feel, even considering the sexy outfit. Unlikely anyway, given our age difference. Did she have an unusual interest in getting me to her home? Obviously. But why, if not for purposes of seduction? All I knew for sure was that she was out of her depth, attempting deceptions she couldn't pull off. Unless I wanted to just abandon her in distress, which I now found myself deciding I couldn't do, I was going to have to find out more—and it looked like that meant going where she wanted me to go.

"Okay," I said. "Okay. Are you going to be home the rest of the day? I can't say when I'll have a chance to stop by."

She leaned back in the chair with a deep sigh. "Don't worry. I'll be there." She gathered her jacket and stood up. We shook hands, she nodded at Malone, and she left, stopping in my doorway to pick up her umbrella and one last assurance that I would be at her apartment before the day was over.

"Well," Malone said after the door had closed. "Maybe she likes *really* older men."

"Ha. It crossed my mind but I don't think so. There's something else going on."

"So...you're going to go find out?"

"That's the plan."

"You want company?" She was grinning when she asked.

I grinned back. "Come along if you want, but I can probably handle the kid by myself."

Malone turned back to her monitor. "I'm sure you can. I've got one more report to write—damn it—and a couple of follow-ups to do on other cases. I can keep busy while you go visit your groupie."

CHAPTER SIXTEEN

I spent the next couple of hours doing what research I could on Eleanor's seven guys, Idris through El Fadil. Of course my "research" didn't extend far beyond looking in the phone directory and plugging their names into a couple of basic Internet search engines. I found Idris, Sadat, Rospovich and Habash in the Portland directory. The Internet searches of course brought up half the people on the planet with the names on her list, but I focused on some addresses in Vancouver, Washington, that likely belonged to the right Spengler and Ibrahim. No local address for an El Fadil, but maybe he was just passing through on his way home if she really hadn't made him up. Nothing else on any of the seven.

The irony was not lost on me that normally it would be Eleanor herself doing this kind of work, much more effectively, but of course it wouldn't be appropriate in this case. Her case.

I resorted to another resource, one with whom I had even more history than with Eleanor: Joy Castle, the civilian manager of the Portland Police Bureau Records Division. I'd been dating Joy when my ex-wife, Colleen's mother, disappeared—which is a story in itself. The relationship with Joy did not survive my obsessive but unsuccessful search for my missing ex and I didn't handle the breakup well, given all the other stresses of the time. However, we'd run into each other occasionally since then and at least we were still speaking.

She answered her phone on the first ring and I asked her to run the list of names and addresses through her databases to see if any of them had criminal records. She said she would look into it when she had time and hung up without inquiring about my health. Maybe not a lot of speaking.

Malone and I had a late lunch, hamburger and fries, at the Home Run Sports Bar across the street and I came back to the office while she headed off on her follow-ups. My intention was to collect my good jacket and start interviewing Eleanor's gentlemen friends.

But, as they say about the best-laid plans.... The phone was ringing as I opened the door. I got to my desk in a couple of long strides and picked up the receiver.

"McCall."

Johnny Crew's stentorian voice blasted out at me: "Clint! Jesus H. Christ, you ain't gonna believe it!"

I jerked the phone away from my head and yelled at it: "Johnny! You almost blew out my eardrum!" I brought the phone back to my ear. "Now tell me what I won't believe. Quietly, goddamn it."

"Sorry," he grated in a very poor attempt at *sotto voce*. "We got a big fuckin' problem here. Imeson's gone."

"Gone?"

"And there's a girl dead."

"What girl? Where the hell are you?"

"Mid-Town Motel on Burnside. Mike Whitehall's here, too."

What the hell? I took a deep breath. "Start at the beginning," I said. "What's going on?"

"We were following Imeson on another noon-time cruise and this time he found himself a girl. Picked her up on Ankeny and came around the block to the Mid-Town where they got themselves a room."

"Okay."

"Yeah, that was all about what you'd expect but then this other guy came along."

"Who?"

"Don't know. It was raining and he had a hood up over his head. He knocks on the door of Imeson's room. The girl opens the door and he goes in. Then he don't come out. Imeson don't come out. Nobody comes out, so after about an hour we go to check."

"And?"

"The girl's dead and Imeson's gone. No sign of the other guy. There's a sliding glass door open in the back; that must have been the way out. We weren't watchin' the back. No reason to watch the back...."

"No, of course not. I'll be right down there. You say Mike is on the scene?"

"Yeah, he's runnin' the show."

"That's good, at least. I'll see you in a few minutes." I hung up and headed for the door cursing all the gods I could think of. One more crisis and I was not going to be able to keep all the balls in the air.

CHAPTER SEVENTEEN

Wishing (for no particularly good reason) that I had Malone along, I parked a block away from the Mid-Town Motel, which was already surrounded by police and news vehicles. I approached cautiously while I surveyed the TV vans. None of them belonged to the small independent station that employed Alison Roberts, so I was probably safe from immediate media harassment. I had a feeling my reprieve would be short.

It was obvious which room was the center of attention. I identified myself to a uniformed officer manning the crime scene tape and he called for Mike Whitehall, who appeared almost immediately. His eyebrows went up when he saw me, but he repressed a smile of greeting as we shook hands. There were at least three news cameras pointed at us.

"Come on in," he said. "Just watch where you step."

We entered the room no further than was necessary, just inside the doorway and off to the left almost against the wall. It was a small, cheap motel room, dimly lit even with all the lights on and the curtain on the sliding door partly pulled back to reveal that the door was open. I couldn't see a body on the floor on the other side of the bed, but that's where all the activity was focused. It was the same crime scene crew as at Eleanor's apartment yesterday morning. I got several appraising glances when they noticed me standing there.

Whitehall ran a hand through his short-cropped brown hair as he grimly surveyed the room. "We have to stop meeting like this," he said dryly.

"Do you believe it?" I responded. "What happened? Where are Johnny and Hap?"

"I stashed them out back. We already got their statements. They're basically just waiting for you to show up." He looked at me as he pulled a notebook out of his sport coat. "The guy who rented the room, Imeson, has a suspicious fiancée, is that right?"

"Right. Her name's Nora Hogan. She thought he might be seeing someone else, so I put Johnny and Hap on it."

He wrote it down. "I'll want her address, whatever else you have."

"No problem."

"You told her yet that she was on to something? Any chance she hired someone else to look in on the boyfriend?"

I thought back on the small, tight-lipped woman who'd come to my office. "She might be capable, but I hadn't reported anything of interest yet. This was his first activity since we started the surveillance."

Whitehall again surveyed the room. "It was a doozy."

The CSI team had finished taking photos and were getting ready to bag the body. "How did the vic die?" I asked.

"Looks like she was strangled. Fair amount of struggle. Can't tell which side Imeson was on. Given that your guys saw the woman let the second man in, it might have been a set-up that went wrong. I'm not exactly clear on how. You wouldn't expect the john *and* the assailant to be gone."

"Kidnapping?"

He shrugged. "Could be. Or maybe they were in it together—which, yes, would be unlikely." He put the notebook away. "I'll want to talk to your client before I start constructing a theory. No contact until after we've interviewed her, okay?"

I wanted to be the one to tell her I'd lost her fiancé, but I understood. "Sure," I said.

Whitehall left me where I was standing for a moment as he consulted with the crime scene people on whether there was a clear path between me and the sliding door. Having established that there was, he let me go check on my surveillance team.

The sliding door opened into a partially enclosed courtyard with, I noted, several exits to the surrounding streets. Sitting—and smoking—together on a park bench in the middle of the grass were Johnny Crew and Hap Harbaugh. Johnny looked angry, his burly torso pressed back against the seat as he gestured with his cigarette, his thick gray hair unusually mussed. Hap was clearly dejected, his mountainous body leaned forward, hands on knees and cigarette dangling from one side of his mouth, his bald head gleaming with the misty rain. More than I'd ever noticed before, they looked like two old men.

"You guys okay?" I called as I approached.

Johnny waved his cigarette at me. "Just fucking fine!" he boomed. "We're standing around with our thumbs up our asses while a girl gets killed and our subject disappears, but, what the hell, that's no fuckin' big deal."

Hap meanwhile raised his head enough to give me a hang-dog expression and said nothing.

I stopped just outside the cloud of heavy smoke surrounding the bench. "It wasn't your fault and you know it," I said. "You need to get on home and get some rest." I leaned in a little closer, suppressing a cough. "One question before you go: Is there anything you saw or did that you didn't tell Mike?"

Johnny roused himself, poked Hap in the arm, and started to get up. "Nope. Not this time. Not a thing."

"Okay then," I said. "Go home. See your wives. I'll talk to you tomorrow."

They left without another word. Never easy when somebody gets away or dies on your watch. Even worse when it's both.

CHAPTER EIGHTEEN

From the motel, I swung by the office first to phone in the information on Nora Hogan I'd promised Whitehall. It took all my willpower not to call her next. Actually, once I had sat down behind my desk, it took all my willpower to get up again. It was too late in the day now to track down any of Eleanor's old boyfriends. There was nothing I could do on the Imeson case until I heard from Mike, because my first step—just like his—was going to be talking to my client.

No sign that Malone had returned while I was gone. I was a little surprised she hadn't shown up at the motel, devotee of the police scanner that she was. Maybe none of the transmissions mentioned names. More than likely she'd gone on home herself. So I hiked down the hall to the one bathroom shared by all the tenants on my floor, noting as I passed that Eleanor's office was already locked and dark, then left to fulfill my final commitment to Libby Jance.

The drive to the corner of Elm and S.W. 18th took five minutes, reminding me once again of the young woman's claim that it was difficult to get downtown. Her apartment building was small, four units down and four up, probably built in the sixties and painted generic beige most recently sometime in the eighties.

I took the interior stairs, found number five and knocked.

She opened the door wearing a short denim skirt, light blue blouse, and sickly smile. There was a new bruise blossoming on her upper left arm. I didn't even bother with hello. "What happened to your arm?" I asked.

She glanced down at it, almost guiltily, and forced a laugh. "Oh, nothing. I slipped in the bathroom and bashed it on the sink."

Didn't look like that to me. Looked more like someone had grabbed her hard. "Am I interrupting something? Are you alone?"

Wide-eyed. "No, not at all. I mean, yes, I'm alone and you

63

aren't interrupting. Come in."

It was a nice little apartment, sparingly furnished with what looked like relatively good-quality flea market furniture and decorated about the same. No sign of anything wrong. The kitchen and living room were one big space with a waist-high divider. The doors to the bedroom and bathroom stood open with good views beyond.

She led me to a spot near the small couch. "The papers are in the bedroom," she said quickly. "I'll go get them." She pointed to a lamp sitting on one of the end tables. "You might be interested to look at that. I'll be right back."

I was getting used to the weirdness so I dutifully turned to look down at the lamp. It was a goddamned lamp. Brass base, cream-colored slightly frilly shade. Why in the world was I supposed to be interested in that?

Behind me I heard a muffled sob and the words "I'm sorry." I'd just started to turn when the right side of my head exploded with blinding pain, then oblivion.

CHAPTER NINETEEN

Light. Voices. Urgent voices. Should I be doing something? Yes: Opening my eyes. White shirts. Young guys in white shirts looking down at me. Paramedics? "How long has he been out?" That was one of them. "I don't know, since I called, ten minutes I guess." A female voice. Malone? No. Is that a cop? Other voices, other lights, all blurring out....

Back again, with one mother of a headache. Same young guys, definitely paramedics. "Do you know where you are?" one of them asks. Hmm, that's a tough one. Visiting, visiting.... She said something and then wham. Ah.

"Libby Jance's apartment," I replied groggily, not even sure I'd gotten it out loud until the guy nodded in agreement.

"Good," he said. He held up a finger. "Follow my finger." He moved it from side to side and I followed it, taking in a couple of uniforms and a couple more guys in plainclothes that I recognized as police detectives. Didn't know either one of them personally. What the hell had happened? "Good," said the paramedic again.

"What happened?" I asked somewhat plaintively.

"Try sitting up," he replied.

I groaned my way into a sitting position, head throbbing.

"How do you feel?" he asked me.

"Like shit," I replied. "What happened?"

He didn't answer that time, either, instead going off to confer with the detectives. Now that I was upright, my head began to settle into a manageable agony. I found I could even move it from side to side. There was no sign of Libby Jance, though it seemed as if I had heard her voice earlier.

A commotion brought my attention back to the apartment door where the detectives and paramedic were talking. Mike Whitehall had joined them and it looked like the conversation was getting pretty animated.... Mike Whitehall. Crap! Had Libby been killed now? Had I missed that there was a goddamned killer in the apartment and let him knock me out? Oh god. My headache got worse again.

I was trying, with no immediate success, to get to my feet when the other two detectives suddenly left and Whitehall hurried in my direction. I eased back down on my butt.

He squatted next to me, his expression intent and concerned. "You okay?"

"Just wonderful. Mike, what's going on? What are those guys doing here? Is Libby Jance all right?"

"She's all right. The other detectives are from Sex Crimes. But they're going to let me have this one. I told them it could be related to the murder of Chet Findley, which is bullshit, but there's no serious injury or alleged rape so they're willing to go back to the shop."

Boy, I had a headache. "Rape? What are you talking about?"

"What do you remember?"

It took a minute, but I found I could concentrate and reduce the dizziness and pain to a steady dull throb.

"Libby Jance, the girl who lives here, wanted me to look at some papers," I said slowly. "She insisted I come here to see them. I'd just arrived and...she told me to look at the lamp. I turned away from her, heard her say...'I'm sorry'...I think that's what she said. Then something hit me."

Whitehall's face was scrunched up like he was the one who'd been cold-cocked. "She told you to look at a lamp? Which one?"

I was able to turn my head and point, alert enough now to be feeling a little embarrassed.

Whitehall considered the frilly shade, then looked quizzically back at me. "And she said she was sorry?"

"I'm pretty sure that's what she said."

He let out an almost explosive snort. "Well, it ain't what she's saying now." He stood up and held out a hand. "You okay to get up? We should talk somewhere else so she can have her apartment back."

The throb held steady as he helped me rise and I took another look around the room. Only one uniformed policeman in sight, standing near the now-closed bedroom door. "Where is she? What's her story? I want to talk to her."

Whitehall gestured in the direction of the closed door. "Not today. There's a female officer with her in the bedroom. They aren't coming out until you're gone. So..." He gently took me by the arm. "Let's go. You want to get checked out at the ER? The medics said you might have a mild concussion."

I was able to take the stairs without a great deal of extra focus, so I declined further medical attention. My head was feeling no worse now than after a good punch. A very good punch.

CHAPTER TWENTY

We crossed the street to my vehicle. The sky was dark gray but it wasn't raining and the chilly air felt fresh in my nostrils. I led Whitehall around to the passenger side, out of the street, and stopped. "You still haven't told me: What's her story?"

"Yeah," piped up a familiar voice from the sidewalk a couple of cars back. "What's her story?"

I spun around to see Devon Malone striding up to us. I couldn't believe I hadn't spotted her; maybe the head injury was worse than I thought. Not so bad, though, that I couldn't deduce *how* Malone came to be here at this moment.

"You heard my name on your police scanner," I said.

"That I did. The cops couldn't wait to share with one another that our famous local PI was the suspect in a sex crime. I'm not sure they all like you."

What the fuck? I turned back to Whitehall. "Sex crime?"

He leaned against the rig, arms crossed, watching me intently. "Libby Jance is claiming that you sexually assaulted her."

I'd swear my spine froze solid. "You have to be kidding me."

"According to the other detectives, she says that you were at her place for an interview, that she was doing a story about you for her college paper and you said you wanted to talk where there was some privacy. As soon as you arrived, she says, you attacked her. She does have a prominent bruise on her arm and her top is torn, but she claims that's as far as you got. She picked up a heavy candlestick and popped you with it."

I rubbed the tender side of my head. "Jesus. That last part might be true; I don't think there was anyone else in the apartment. But the rest of it is bullshit. She was trying to get me to take her on as a client, said her mother was in trouble and missing." I looked at him in utter perplexity. "What's going on?"

He opened his arms wide to the dusk. "Beats me. You guys got

69

a client file on this girl, notes, anything like that?"

I glanced over at Malone, who could only offer a little negative head shake. "Crap," I said. "No, we don't. I wasn't planning to take the case, so I hadn't made a file or any notes. Malone had no reason to, either. Jance was at our office twice. Malone was there with us both times and she can testify at least that it was Jance who asked me to come to her apartment, not the other way around." I met Whitehall's gaze, headache pounding harder. "But it still doesn't look good, does it?"

He glanced back over at the apartment building. The last two cops were leaving and Libby Jance was with them, probably going downtown to file charges. She didn't look in our direction.

"Not particularly," Whitehall said finally. "I'll talk to her myself, of course; I'll see what she says about your and Malone's version. We'll interview the people in her building. Find out if anybody knows anything. I'm not going to be able to keep you out of the system for long." He paused. "Huh. Wasn't I just saying that about Eleanor?"

I sagged against the rig and rubbed both sides of my head this time. "Yeah," I said. "Hell of a note, isn't it?" My hands fell to my sides and I straightened up again. "I don't have a clue why she's doing this, but I'm going to get one."

"You know if she files charges you can't talk to her."

Malone stepped in closer to us, almost between us. "But I can," she said to Mike.

I had been trying not to imagine just how hideous my life would become if Libby Jance filed attempted rape charges against me, but Malone's determined tone brought me back to the moment. "There are a lot of other people I can talk to," I said.

Whitehall reached past Malone to clap me on the arm. "And I'll do what I can to help." He actually grinned. "I knew you were innocent when I heard her story of how she clipped you. If somebody does take you out face to face, it won't be the young woman in the living room with the candlestick."

70

"Thanks," I said. "How'd you get here so fast, by the way?"

"Same way as your partner here. Heard your name and the location on the scanner."

It was really starting to sink in now. "Oh shit," I groaned. "Everyone knows."

He shrugged. "Not everyone. We haven't had a shift change yet."

"Great," I muttered. "Just great."

Malone, being Malone, laughed.

CHAPTER TWENTY-ONE

Maybe to make up for that, Malone insisted on driving me home after Mike relayed that the paramedics had said I shouldn't be alone for a few hours because of the possible concussion.

I did still have a hell of headache, though I'm sure I could have focused sufficiently to get myself home. Nevertheless, between the two of them I was coerced into the passenger seat of her Jeep.

"So," she said, as she pulled out into the traffic flow, "I guess we were both wrong about you being able to handle her."

"I guess so," I agreed and closed my eyes in an attempt to shut off further discussion. It worked. Malone drove us the rest of the way to my house in silence.

I was half-asleep, or felt like it, by the time she pulled into my driveway—so sluggish that I actually stumbled a little after getting out of the vehicle.

She came around to my side and took my arm. "Give me your key," she said.

I wasn't going to be treated like an invalid and tried to pull away. Which I wasn't able to do. So much for not being an invalid. I dug in my pocket and handed her my keys. She more or less steered me to my front door, unlocked it, and we both went inside.

I guess I was a little disoriented. It felt like I'd last been home weeks rather than hours before. Stella seemed to agree, as she was in the kitchen grumbling at her empty food dish. I'm sure her sister would have been with her if Malone hadn't been present. Not even hunger would overcome Maxine's avoidance of everyone other than me.

I managed, with a little help from Malone, to refresh their kibble and water, downed four aspirin for myself, and then collapsed on the couch.

She sat down in the recliner but didn't tilt it back.

"You don't have to stay," I said. "I appreciate your concern, but...."

"As instructed by medical personnel, I'm going to stick around for a few hours," she announced firmly, "and during that time you are *not* going to sleep. How do you feel?"

I considered the question. "Fucking bewildered," I finally replied.

"What the hell happened at Jance's apartment?"

I took a breath, noted that the aspirin was beginning to ease the headache a bit, and laid it all out for her just as I had for Whitehall. "What really gets me," I concluded, "is the way her voice sounded when she apologized. It was almost like she didn't want to do it."

"You're absolutely sure no one else was there."

"Well, not absolutely. I didn't have a chance to clear the whole place. Didn't even know I needed to. Didn't have time. Hello, look at the lamp, lights out."

"So now your case is our number one priority."

Shifting uncomfortably, I protested. "We owe Eleanor...."

"We owe Eleanor the best effort we can make while keeping you out of jail. You can't help her much if you're behind bars for sexual assault."

I rested my elbows on my knees and lowered my still-aching head to my hands. I must have looked pitiful but I couldn't help it. "Don't forget the dead woman in the motel and our missing surveillance subject," I said, my voice muffled by my hands.

I felt a slight impact against my leg and looked up to see that Malone was perched far enough forward on the recliner that she could reach me with her foot. With which she had just gently kicked me.

"Our plate runneth over," she said with some asperity, "no question. So maybe you should stop feeling sorry for yourself and try focusing."

Beyond her I saw Maxine hurrying along the far wall toward the kitchen, no doubt hoping to join her sister for dinner without confronting my guest. Life in the McCall household was going on

74

whether I felt overwhelmed or not. Malone was right: time to focus.

"Okay," I said. "It looks like tomorrow is going to be a very busy day, assuming I don't spend it in jail."

CHAPTER TWENTY-TWO

I never sleep in, but that Thursday morning the cell phone woke me up at eight-thirty. Malone had insisted I stay on the couch while she put together something to eat—which turned out to be chicken noodle soup from a can. Or should I say, "cans." I had a half. She had one-and-a-half. She'd finally left after the obligatory couple of hours without our having made any progress on any of our new cases. At which point I toddled off to bed and dreamless sleep.

At least, I realized as I finally found the damned phone and pushed TALK, my head didn't hurt nearly as much.

Mike Whitehall was the caller and his news was good, or at least as good as could be expected: Libby Jance's charges were being treated—for now—as assault four and they wouldn't come after me as long as I stopped by the Justice Center today to be booked. I winced even at that. If I couldn't prove my innocence and get the record expunged, my PI license would be in jeopardy. Not to mention my looking at possible jail time.

"You pick up any hint of why Jance is doing this?" I asked Mike.

"Not a one," he replied. "She's badly shaken up by something. Downtown she was acting guilty as much as traumatized, which is consistent with her lying about what happened—but it doesn't help explain it. She's sticking to her story about the interview and the assault. Says her mother is out of town and can't be reached."

"Ha," I said. "You'll be looking for her?"

"For Mom and at Jance herself. A lot closer than we normally would, sure."

"Anything on Imeson?"

"I talked to your client Nora Hogan, but she had nothing useful. I got the impression she didn't know her true love all that well."

"Could be," I said. "You don't usually hire a PI to shadow

somebody you trust."

"We're running down everything we can on Imeson himself. Maybe he was into some other risky behavior that caught up with him."

"Anything interesting on the dead girl?"

"No. Her street name was Brandy Wine. Real name Heather Lipinski, twenty years old, family in Grand Rapids, Michigan. She'd only been in Portland a couple of months, no tracks on her body, no known connections beyond her pimp.... So far she looks like a plain vanilla whore."

"Reuben Keys wasn't her pimp, was he?"

"No, it was Big Avenue."

Reuben and Big had both been informants of mine in the past and in Reuben's case at times even more like an assistant detective. Reuben had been my first client's last pimp, the one who got her off drugs and gave her a chance to escape the life. It was his most prominent eccentricity, that he insisted his "girls" be clean of drugs. Big Avenue's reputed eccentricity, on the other hand, was killing the women who gave him too much trouble. Never proven and I wasn't sure I could see it in him myself, but I did not often seek out his assistance and was sorry to hear the dead prostitute was his.

"Crap," I said. "What did he have to say for himself?"

"About what you'd expect. He was pissed off that somebody besides him hurt one of his girls but otherwise he didn't know nothin' about nothin'."

"I'll check with Reuben anyway, see what he's heard. Maybe talk to Big myself."

"Let me know if you come up with anything," answered Mike. "But first take it easy some more. You have a head injury."

"I will," I agreed, and we hung up.

CHAPTER TWENTY-THREE

Once I got to moving around I was surprised to see my car was in my driveway. I assumed Malone had seen to it somehow or another. I finally got to the office at ten minutes after ten, having fed myself and the cats then done a few minutes of meditation. My partner was well settled in by then.

"I was getting ready to call and see if you were all right," she greeted me. "How's the head?"

"Feels fine this morning. I went straight to bed after you left and slept late. I'm good. And thanks for getting the car back to me."

"No problem."

Scanning my desk as I hung up my jacket, I saw nothing new or pressing. Not even a blinking message light on the phone. I wanted to sit down and start trying to put all the puzzles together before I went over to the Justice Center for booking. (Hell of a thing to look forward to.) But first, I decided, I would check in with Eleanor to see how she was. She had no idea how totally distracted from her case I'd been in the past twenty-four hours.

Her door was closed but I could see through the frosted glass that her light was on. I rapped on the glass and opened the door a couple of inches, ready to excuse myself and back off if I saw she was with a client.

She was alone, sitting at her desk and looking worse than she had at her apartment right after Chet Findley's death: face pale, hair in some disarray, and expression almost dazed as she looked at me standing in the doorway. She was wearing a relatively conservative business suit, but it was wrinkled as if she'd worn it several times without cleaning. Her PC monitor was blank. Apparently she'd just been sitting there.

I stepped in and closed the door behind me. "What's the matter, kiddo? Bad news from the cops?"

She hesitated. "No."

I helped myself to one of the guest chairs, concern growing. This was not like Eleanor at all. "What's going on?"

She looked away from me. "I've...I've decided I need to handle this by myself."

I know my look must have been really quizzical. "Handle what by yourself? What are you talking about?"

Still that vacant, off-center stare. An aura of total misery. "My...case. There's no point in your trying to help me."

My gut was tightening up by the millisecond. "Eleanor, what's happened? Why are you saying this?"

She looked at me now, eyes welling with tears. "I don't have any choice. It's...it's what I have to do. You have to let me handle this on my own. Please."

What the hell? This was one mind-boggle too many. "I can't do that," I finally said. "You have to tell me what's going on. What are you afraid of?"

Her lips set in a firm line as she blinked back the tears. "Nothing. I'm not afraid. I'm telling you to leave me alone and let me handle it. It's not your case. I haven't hired you and I don't want your help. I'm not saying any more."

I sat forward, feeling like I should reach across the desk and shake her. "This is nuts," I said urgently. "Absolutely nuts. I don't care what is going on with you, you have to let me help you."

"No. No, I don't." She pushed herself back from the desk as if to get maximum distance from me. "Go back to your office now. You have plenty of other problems to worry about." Her voice kept getting louder. "Leave me alone!"

I was getting desperate. "How...?"

She stood up suddenly and stepped around behind her chair, setting it as another barrier between us. "Get out! I mean it!" She was shouting now, nearly screaming. "Leave me alone!"

We stared wide-eyed at each other for a long moment and I finally forced myself to get up and go to the door. I opened it and turned back to look at her one more time. She hadn't moved. "I don't know what's going on," I said, "but I'm going to find out. You have my help whether you want it or not."

All the energy and anger seemed to go out of her again. "Just leave me alone," she said quietly.

I closed the door, paused, and then headed back for my office —so perplexed that the hallway looked momentarily unfamiliar to me. One more shock and I would begin to have out-of-body experiences.

What did Malone say last night, that our plate was running over? Which should have been a cup, come to think of it. Cup or plate, the damned thing was about to shatter, as far as I could tell.

CHAPTER TWENTY-FOUR

Confusion pisses me off. And apparently it shows.

"What happened to you?" Malone asked before I even got across the room to my desk chair. "Somebody try to mug you on the way back from the bathroom?"

"I wasn't in the bathroom," I said as I sat down. "I was talking to Eleanor—who has now decided that she doesn't want our help."

That shot my partner's eyebrows up. "She's hiring somebody else?"

"No. She's going to handle it herself, she says. And she looks like she's scared shitless when she's saying it. Something changed big time for her in the last twenty-four hours and we need to find out what."

Malone processed that with a frown and then sat back a little. "I want to say that's very weird but what really strikes me is that I've been saying that too damned much lately. Is it a full moon or something? Your karma come home to roost?"

"I don't know. I just don't know." I put my hand on the desk phone. "All I can do is keep trying to figure it out. I'm going to start by calling Johnny Crew and see if he or Gerry know anything about what's going on with Eleanor."

"How about using the speaker this time?"

"You got it." I punched the appropriate button, got the loud dial tone, and entered Johnny's home number.

He picked up on the second ring. "Crew."

"Johnny, it's Clint. I've got you on speaker and Devon is here. How are you guys doing?"

"Tired of sitting around, I'll tell you that. Hey, Devon. How about *you*, Clint? I heard some chickadee filed rape charges. What the fuck is that about?"

I sighed. Yes, there'd been a couple of shift changes by now.

"Assault charges," I replied. "Just a kid I was trying to help out, some kind of set-up that I don't understand yet. We're working on it."

"How can me and the big guy help?"

"You can't right now. You and Hap have to lay low until we get a better handle on how everything relates."

"Shit."

"Here's a question. Did something happen last night or this morning that might have upset Eleanor even more?"

He was silent for a moment. "Nah, not that I know of. I was thinkin' she seemed a little better this morning, in fact. Why? Has she gone and got herself more problems?"

"I'm not sure, but I have a hunch."

"You want to talk to Gerry? She'd be more likely to notice somethin' like that."

"Yeah, put her on, would you?"

He called his wife to the phone and I asked her the same question.

"No," she answered slowly after saying hello to Malone, "I don't believe so. No surprise she's not happy to be kind of homeless right now. There hasn't been anything special happen that I know of. She was pretty much okay when she left this morning. There was just that one call."

"What call?"

"Some friend of hers, she said. Called while we were having breakfast. I didn't hear the conversation, but it was real short and she didn't seem upset by it. Maybe a little miffed."

"Miffed?"

"Oh, you know. Impatient. A little irritated. Like it was a friend she didn't want to bother with right then. You know, when you got a lot of problems of your own you don't want to hear about other people's."

"So this friend wanted to tell her about problems?"

"I don't know that for sure. It's just how it looked to me, from how she was when she came back to the table."

"Okay. Thanks, Gerry."

"You take care of that girl now. Both of you."

"We will."

I hung up.

"Miffed," said Malone. "Not much to go on. Maybe nothing."

"Maybe something," I responded. There was a feeling nagging at me now, a feeling I'd developed while I was talking to Gerry that there was something I should have noticed or something I already knew that I should think about...but I couldn't put a finger on it yet so I let it go.

I looked at my watch. Eleven-thirty. "Time to head down to the Justice Center before they decide I'm in the wind."

"Have a good time."

"Right."

CHAPTER TWENTY-FIVE

The weather had turned more cheery than I, sunlight streaming through the clouds as I drove south on 3rd Avenue. I found a spot on Madison and walked around the corner toward the Police Bureau entrance on 2nd. I was anticipating a lot of quick glances, a few whispers, and some awkwardness.

I did not anticipate the Channel 11 news van sitting across the street from the entrance.

I stopped cold and a teenage punk who must have been skateboarding right on my heels whipped around me with an angry mutter, his orange Mohawk glowing in a stray sunbeam. Hadn't even heard him, which meant I was way too preoccupied.

That, however, was not my biggest problem at the moment.

After giving a few seconds' serious consideration to running like hell, I kept going straight. The Justice Center is a fifteen-story building covering an entire city block and Channel 11 has other news crews. Even if it was Alison Roberts, I thought to myself as I entered the lobby, she could be anywhere in here.

For instance, she could be just exiting the elevator and heading straight for me, a huge gotcha-grin on her face and cameraman Murray Kravitz in tow.

Amazing how abruptly a headache can return.

"Clint McCall! Fancy meeting you here. Come to turn yourself in? Set up a shot, Murray."

Alison Roberts is about five-nine with shoulder-length black hair and an athletic build. In her late twenties, young to have her own late-night show, even on a small independent station, but with a good face for TV—pretty but not too spectacular. She's talented, very intense, perfectly suited to the ambush journalism she practiced so well—and so often on me.

Kravitz was her regular cameraman, a big, beefy old guy with a goatee and long gray hair pulled into a ponytail who looked like he'd probably been carrying a camera since Berkeley in the sixties.

She marched forward with an extended hand as Murray stepped aside, lifting the camera to his shoulder and turning on the flood.

Meanwhile my mind was racing. My frequent response to Alison Roberts was to use however many obscenities it took to make her give up and have the camera turned off. I was not exactly a good interview, though it never kept her from trying. This time, however, she certainly had the sexual assault charge and probably the motel murder, maybe even my association with the Findley killing. She'd be happy to run a clip of me being obscene and hostile along with *that* story no matter how many bleeps were required.

I smiled through gritted teeth and held out my hand to take hers.

She didn't waste any time, raising her microphone as she let go of my hand. "Mr. McCall, is it true that you assaulted a young female client of yours at her home yesterday?"

Oh, Jesus H. Christ in a bucket. That took care of the phony smile. "No," I replied, "it is not true. Not true that I assaulted her and not true that she was a client of mine."

"Then why were you at her apartment?"

"As part of an ongoing investigation that I can't discuss."

"Why would she make up an accusation of sexual assault?"

I could see the lens turning on Kravitz' camera. He was zooming in for a close-up.

"I have no idea," I said firmly.

"Two detectives who work for you were involved in the murder of a prostitute and the disappearance of a man named Joseph Imeson—also yesterday. Is that related?"

"The detectives were not 'involved.' They were performing a surveillance of Mr. Imeson and were some distance from the actual crime scene which was indoors and out of their view. They don't know what happened, nor do I."

"So it's not related to the sexual assault."

Bitch. "There was no sexual or any other kind of assault."

"Why were your people following Mr. Imeson?"

"As part of an ongoing investigation that I can't discuss."

"But not the *same* investigation."

"That's correct. Not the same investigation."

"Nevertheless, you seem to have had quite a bad day yesterday."

"That's a fair statement."

She paused for a beat, then lowered the mike with a satisfied smile. "That's it, Murray." She looked up at me. "Thanks, McCall. You must *really* be in trouble to be willing to talk that much. Are they going to book you on the assault charge?"

"No comment."

She laughed. "Well, that didn't last long. Okay, let's go, Murray. Good luck, McCall. Keep those ratings points coming."

I said nothing in reply. At least she was leaving. Time to check in with the front desk.

CHAPTER TWENTY-SIX

The booking experience wasn't that interesting. Whitehall came down to escort me to the processing area for the fingerprints and photo. Normally I would have had to follow up with an appearance in court and pay a small bail to be on my way, but he'd arranged to have me recorded as out on my own recognizance. Sometimes it's especially helpful to have a friend in Homicide.

He didn't have anything new on Findley, Imeson, or Jance, however. I didn't share with him the latest mystery concerning Eleanor.

The only good thing about the day so far was that Alison Roberts apparently wasn't connecting the Findley murder to the other dots. That would keep Eleanor out of her news segment tonight.

Despite a compelling desire to flee the building, I decided to go up to the eleventh floor and stop by Records to see what Joy Castle had come up with. The day was already in the toilet; I wouldn't make it any worse by visiting a semi-hostile ex-lover.

Joy is a civilian employee of the Portland Police Bureau, not a member of the force. Just over five feet tall, fiftyish, with short blond hair, gloriously blue eyes, and a mean temper. She was hunched forward, focused intently on her PC monitor when I walked up to her desk. "Yes?" she inquired without looking up.

"Just thought I'd stop by to see how you were doing," I said.

She sat back and gave me a long, appraising look. "Well, if it isn't our newest sexual predator. What a lucky girl am I."

"Good to see you, too. Have you had a chance to check those names I gave you?"

"Yes." She started shuffling through the hills of paper on her desk. "Sit down. It's here somewhere."

I sat down just as she triumphantly retrieved a print-out from one of the piles. She scanned the page.

91

"Four out of seven with records. Your friend Eleanor likes the bad boys."

"Great," I said with resignation and pulled a notebook and pen from my jacket pocket. "*How* bad are these boys?"

She grinned a crooked little grin. "Not that bad, most of them. Nothing on Sadat, Spengler, or Ibrahim. Rospovich has two speeding violations in the past five years and El Fadil has numerous—like more than fifty—unpaid parking tickets."

"Which will remain unpaid," I interjected. "I understand he's gone home to the United Arab Emirates."

She made a note. "If that's so, I'll change his status. Let's see. Habash was wanted as a material witness in California. The warrant was issued two years ago in what looks like an identity theft case. Either the case was resolved or they let it go cold because the warrant's been canceled. I'd say Idris is your best bet."

"Yeah?"

"He has a domestic violence a decade ago in Ohio. Must have been pretty bad; he spent thirty days at county. Nothing since, though."

I glanced over my brief notes. So Martin Idris and Daniel Habash were the ones to check out first. Spengler might hate a lot of women, as he told Eleanor, but he had no record to indicate he did anything about it. "Thanks," I said as I stowed the notebook. I started to get up and Joy stopped me with a gesture.

She hunched forward just as she had been while peering at her monitor. "You know I think you're an asshole."

"Yes."

"But I *don't* think you attacked that girl. You're an asshole with some moral standards." She sat back. "Anything I can do to help on that one, give me a call."

I got up and offered my hand. "I will," I said. "Thanks again."

She shook it lightly, quickly. "You're welcome."

The grudging vote of confidence was almost enough to give me an appetite, but not quite. I went straight back to the office.

CHAPTER TWENTY-SEVEN

As soon as I got back, Malone of course suggested we go to lunch and compare some more notes. It occurred to me that maybe I *could* stand to eat a burger over at the Home Run. Lots of work to do and I would need some energy.

First, though, I wanted to call my one paying client in all this current mess—though she might not be paying any more now that I'd lost her fiancé.

Malone agreed to wait but wandered toward the fridge, probably looking for a snack to tide her over the couple of minutes my call would take. The woman's appetite never ceased to amaze me.

I should have called Nora Hogan sooner. Whitehall would have had her interviewed, at least initially, right after I called him yesterday with the contact information. I'd planned to call her when I left Libby Jance's apartment. Then I got kind of distracted.

She picked up on the fifth ring and I identified myself.

"Mr. McCall." Her voice on the phone was as tight as her lips had been in my office. "I'm glad you called. I need to know how much I owe you."

Yep, just what I was afraid of. "I'm sorry I didn't call yesterday," I said, "but the police wanted to talk to you first. They have been in touch with you, I assume."

"Oh yes, of course. They did want to let me know my fiancé had disappeared while in the company of a prostitute and that possibly he was involved in her murder. Do you have anything to add?"

"Only that I'm determined to find Mr. Imeson and learn what happened."

"Well, that's nice—if you plan to do it as a matter of personal curiosity. I'm certainly not going to pay for it. I've learned quite enough about Joe Imeson. I'm only angry because I should have known. All men are bastards, Mr. McCall. That's the lesson I take away from this. Again. How much do I owe you?"

I sighed silently to myself, did a couple of quick calculations, and gave her a number.

"I'll put a check in the mail today," she snapped. "Goodbye."

I hung up the phone and adjusted my thinking for what must have been the twenty-fifth time in the past twenty-hour hours. Okay, I couldn't just let the Imeson case go but now I had zero paying clients. I was pretty sure Malone still had two or three, so we weren't entirely without income...but me? Three major cases I was working *pro bono* and/or in self-defense, a few accounts receivable, and that was it. Very depressing.

Despite Nora Hogan's lack of curiosity about what happened to her bastard fiancé (or, most likely, ex-fiancé), I was going to find out—for my own sake as well as Johnny Crew's and Hap Harbaugh's. I might even discover Ms. Hogan had something to do with it. Wouldn't *that* be interesting.

Before solving the Ivory, Imeson, and Jance cases, however, I was going to go get that burger with Malone and compare those notes.

CHAPTER TWENTY-EIGHT

I brought her up to speed on what I'd been doing and thinking as I enjoyed my double burger and fries. She clearly savored her status as the agency's only current breadwinner even more than she did her ample lunch order. Which was saying something.

Tracking down Martin Idris, he of the domestic violence conviction, had been number one on my list of chores, but I wanted to stop by Reuben Keys' apartment while the icy indifference of Nora Hogan was fresh in my mind. I never knew how to find Big Avenue. He liked to keep moving. But Reuben could probably tell me where he was even though they were fierce rivals who hated each other's guts. Or maybe because of that. Maybe finding out more about Brandy Wine would give me a lead to Joseph Imeson.

Since Malone had just wrapped up two of her current cases (a skip trace and a straying husband), she volunteered to take Idris. Sounded like a good plan to me.

Reuben at this time lived about a mile east of the Burnside Bridge in a dilapidated two-story apartment building near the corner of 21st and Ash. I parked on the street a couple of doors down and took the outside metal stairway up to the second floor balcony that ran the length of the building. I knocked on the door of apartment 2B. It was early afternoon, so I figured he'd be up by now.

The peephole was shadowed for a moment as he checked me out and then I heard multiple locks being unlocked. He opened the door and glared at me, his outfit of red gym shorts and pink tank top practically glowing against his black skin. I was reminded again that there are even more scars on his shoulders and upper arms than on his face and throat.

"What the fuck you want?"

Apparently he hadn't had his coffee yet. "To come in, to start with."

He stood aside. "All right," he growled, "come the fuck in."

95

Reuben Keys was Portland's most media-friendly pimp, thanks to his prominent role in my first client's best-selling story of escaping her life on the streets. His second eccentricity, besides denying drugs to his girls, was what you might call excessive flamboyancy. He drove a classic pink pimpmobile and dressed in garish colors, which only enhanced the attention that he loved so much. None of which made him less dangerous. You did not want to cross Reuben when he was in a bad mood. Or a good mood for that matter.

Notoriety had not improved his housing or housekeeping skills. Clearly he cared a great deal more about his clothes and his car than he did his residence. In this current apartment, there were only two rooms visible, the small living room with a fold-out couch and a kitchen that barely qualified as a nook. Clothes, magazines, discarded fast food packaging and a number of unidentifiable items littered every square foot. The odors of stale French fries and pot hung in the air.

I had to push several empty potato chip bags off one of the frayed couch cushions before I could sit down. The sofa still crunched under me.

"How's Eleanor?" he asked as he took a seat on the only up-holstered chair. Yet another oddity of my pimp friend, that he had a terrible crush on my accountant. But, alas for him, he was way too bad even for her.

"She's fine."

He thought about that a moment and apparently decided it wasn't worth pursuing. "You want a beer?"

Obviously, if I did, I'd have to get it myself. "No," I said, "I need some information."

"'Bout what?"

"You know where to find Big Avenue lately?"

His scarred face took on a sour expression. "Maybe. Why?"

"One of his girls was killed yesterday and my surveillance subject went missing at the same time. I'm wondering if he might know what happened."

Reuben dug under one side of the seat cushion and came up with a slightly mangled cigarette. He retrieved a book of matches from the floor and lit up. "I heard about that," he said as he exhaled the first puff. "That stupid shit's losin' girls all over the place lately. But I'd have to bet he don't know what happened—yet."

"Why?"

"'Cause what I heard was that he was tryin' to find out. He's got a hit out on whoever did the girl, providin' you can prove you popped the right guy."

"How much?"

"I don't know. Small shit. Two, three thousand. I didn't pay that much attention. Not like I give a fuck."

"Well, I want to talk to him anyway."

That brought him to the edge of his seat. "What? I done told you he doesn't know nothin'. I can find out more shit about his girl than that fat island fuck can, you believe it."

Big Avenue is ethnic Samoan, thus the "island" reference. Reuben really likes the idea of playing assistant detective—and really doesn't like the idea of Big Avenue doing it.

"I'd appreciate anything you can find out," I said, "but I'm still going to talk to Big if I can find him. Brandy Wine was the girl's street name. Ever heard of her?"

"Nah, but I will."

"I want every rumor and theory that's out there, especially anything that has to do with another woman being involved."

"You think one of Big's other girls did it?"

"No. I'm interested in a woman named Nora Hogan."

"Who's she?"

"Just keep an ear out for her."

Another contemplative drag and exhalation. "I can do that."

"And, once more: Any idea where Big is right now?"

Big grin. "Not a fuckin' clue."

Which was a big lie, but there wasn't much I could do about it. And I could find Big Avenue on my own.

CHAPTER TWENTY-NINE

She was determined not to worry about McCall. He was a grown up and could take care of himself. Still, they were partners now...whatever that was supposed to mean, if anything, besides sharing the agency.... Let it go. Right now she had little Miss Accountant/Hacker to worry about. Or at least one of her apparently many boyfriends.

The Portland directory said Martin Idris lived on Killingsworth in Northeast Portland. The address turned out to be a medium-sized shabby-looking apartment building. At least the stairs and hallway were clean and well-maintained; Devon Malone saw no one as she made her way to the third floor and found apartment D.

She'd just knocked a second time when she heard a door open behind her and turned to see an elderly woman looking out of the apartment across the hall. The woman was small, frail, and dressed in a very unfortunate outfit of matching light blue tube top and slacks. A much younger woman's platinum blond hair cascaded in curls over her bony shoulders. She peered at Malone with rheumy eyes.

"Martin's at work."

Malone stepped over to her. "Martin Idris?"

"Yeah."

"Do you know where he works?"

She squinted up at me. "You ain't after money, are you, honey?"

"No. And the name's not 'Honey.' It's Malone. Why? He have a lot of bill collectors after him?"

A bony shrug. "Not a lot, but there was one last week Martin chased him off pretty good. He got a temper, Martin does. He's Jamaican, you know."

"No, I didn't know that. I just need to ask him a few questions."

"You a cop?"

Malone pulled out her ID and flashed it. "Private."

"Martin in trouble?"

"Not that I know of."

"It's always Martin with him. Never Marty. I had a nephew named Marty and it took some getting used to." She gave it a few more seconds thought. "Well...he works at Daily Storage. It's just a few blocks over, on Greeley." She stepped back and started to shut the door, then paused. "Don't tell him it was me that said so, honey."

"I won't," Malone assured the closing door.

Daily Storage turned out to be exactly what it sounded like, a half-acre of large, bright green storage units in which to store all the stuff your garage won't hold. The clerk in the front office told Malone that Martin Idris was the maintenance man and that she'd find him somewhere on the property. "Or he'll find you, you bein' a good-lookin' woman and all," the clerk added with a grin.

Malone gave him an inquiring eyebrow. The clerk's grin grew wider. "You'll see. He don't look like no maintenance man."

Curious now, Malone set off among the storage buildings and had the explanation as soon as she got a good look at her quarry. He could have stepped straight out of a European art house film—though he was in fact stepping out of one of the green buildings when she came around the corner and first saw him.

Late thirties or early forties, six two, very fit, longish black hair, classically chiseled features, wearing a brown uniform that contrasted nicely with the emerald background of the building but very little with his rich mocha skin tone.

They made eye contact and she stopped about five feet away. "Martin Idris?"

She watched him shift into ladies' man mode: widening smile, elevating eyebrows, arms opening slightly. Nothing subtle about it.

"Who are *you*?" he asked. His voice was deep, the tone cultivated. Definite Jamaican accent. Even more definite come-on.

She pulled out her ID and held it open for him to see. "My name is Devon Malone. I'm a private investigator. Are you Martin Idris?"

And just that fast he started making readjustments into a defensive posture, knees slightly bent, shoulders forward, and right foot back a couple of inches for balance. She noted that he was carrying a long, hefty wrench in his right hand. It hadn't been so relevant during the seductive phase.

"What do you want?" he asked with a frown. "If you're after money...."

"I'm not. I have some questions about Eleanor Ivory."

That put one of his eyebrows back up. "Eleanor? I haven't seen her since last month. If she's in trouble, it has nothing to do with me."

Which at least established for sure that he was Idris—and that he was very quick to deny involvement in any trouble that might be about. Trouble he assumed was about. If it was an assumption.

"Are you sure? You haven't seen her since last month?"

His frown deepened and he took a step toward her. He didn't exactly brandish the wrench, but it noticeably bounced in his grip. "I'm sure. I don't have to answer any more of your questions, woman. Go away."

Apparently he didn't like information collectors any more than bill collectors—perhaps especially female ones. Loser.

She maintained eye contact but made sure that wrench was well within her peripheral vision. "It's true you don't have to answer," she said, "but if I go away without any answers then I'll get what I need in some other way—and who knows what else I might get at the same time? You could save yourself a lot of trouble by talking to me now."

"I have done nothing." Bounce, bounce, bounce.

So much for that threat. She stepped back and held up her hands palms out.

"I understand," she said. "I'll leave you alone for now. If you're

101

lying about the last time you saw Eleanor, we'll be speaking again."

She turned and walked away from him, listening very carefully for following footsteps but there were none.

Maybe this asshole was just a somewhat paranoid individual with poor spending habits. Maybe he was an insanely jealous killer. Either way or in between, Martin Idris needed some more checking out.

CHAPTER THIRTY

Spengler having dropped further down my list because he had no criminal record, I went for Daniel Habash. Per my Portland directory, he lived in an apartment complex covering a square block just northwest of downtown. It comprised four six-story, cream-colored buildings trimmed in tasteful purple. The grass, what there was of it, was neatly cut, the foundations of the buildings lined with flowering plants that were entirely bare this time of year.

The complex was classy enough to have individual building directories, but not enough to have even medium security. Habash was listed as residing on the top floor of the northeast building. I took the elevator up and knocked on the door.

It opened to reveal a man around six feet, thin but wiry and looking very fit, black hair short and styled, features soft-edged with a middle-Eastern cast.

"Daniel Habash?"

"Yes. Can I help you?" He appeared to be getting ready to go out. He was wearing dark slacks with highly polished black dress shoes, well-pressed white shirt with collar open and waiting for a tie to be added. Nevertheless his voice was patient and polite, a mellifluous tenor.

I pulled out my ID and presented it. "My name is Clint McCall and I'd like to ask you a few questions. Can I come in?"

He handed back the card with an expression of sly amusement. "A private detective, just like on TV. I'm preparing for an engagement but, yes, certainly I can give you some time while I finish dressing." He stood aside with a theatrical sweep of the hand inviting me in. "You don't mind if I continue getting ready, do you?"

A slick customer, this one. "Not at all," I replied as I entered the apartment.

The living room, dining area and kitchen were all one spacious layout, kitchen set off by a waist-high counter with a small dining

103

table on this side. The other end of the room held a large couch and several comfortable-looking chairs oriented around a huge widescreen TV. The decoration was of the art-clearance generic variety, faux-impressionist oils and bucolic landscapes in water-color. Either Habash had no artistic taste or he'd run out of money before he got to the walls.

"Would you care for a drink?" he asked as he picked up a nearly empty wine glass from the counter.

"No thanks," I said. "Nice place."

He downed the remaining red liquid. "Yes." He moved toward an open door, through which I could see a jacket and tie laid out on a king-size bed. "Have a seat," he called over his shoulder. "What is this about?"

Taking any of the available seats would have cut off my view of the bedroom. "I'll stand, if you don't mind. I just have a few questions about Eleanor Ivory."

He picked up the tie with one hand as he flipped his collar up with the other, turning to look at me as he used both hands to bring the tie over his head and against the back of the collar. "Eleanor? I hope she's all right." He started constructing what looked like a classic Windsor knot.

"Not exactly," I answered. "Someone's trying to frame her for a murder."

That stopped his hands for a moment and he let go a short, sharp laugh. "You're joking."

"No joke," I said.

"That's terrible." He finished the knot, shoved it up tight against his neck and leaned down to pick up the jacket. "What can I do to help?" he asked as he carried it into the living room over one arm.

"When was the last time you saw Eleanor?"

He gave that some consideration as he put on the jacket. "It's been several weeks. We are not together anymore."

He said it as if it had been his idea, but Eleanor had told me *she* broke it off because Habash was getting weird. Something he was bugging her about, a big plan she said. Worth a stab.

"The plan didn't work out?"

It was like watching a hyper-fast chameleon. There was just a flash, a millisecond of surprise and anger, and then he resumed the colors of his background.

"My only plan was the same one I have for this evening," he said with the slightest of smirks, "and it worked out just fine for as long as I was interested."

He was very good. "She says she was the one who broke it off."

He carefully buttoned one button of the jacket. "If it makes her feel better."

"And you haven't seen her since?"

"As I said." He checked his watch. "I really must be going now. I'm sorry I couldn't be of more help."

"Don't apologize," I said. "It's been interesting. I'll show myself out."

Which I proceeded to do.

The street outside was just darkening with the beginning of February's early dusk. The air was chill and smelled of rain.

Speaking of cool, Daniel Habash would definitely qualify as such. He hadn't even asked what murder Eleanor was being framed for. Was it a lack of curiosity or the presence of prior knowledge? And that one fleeting reaction.... Was he angry because I caught him lying about being rejected—or because there really was a plan? I certainly couldn't dismiss the latter possibility.

I looked at my own watch. Quarter to five. Very early to be leaving for a date.

About the right time, however, to go home and do some thinking. I remembered also that I'd promised Mike Whitehall I'd share with him anyone interesting from Eleanor's list.

I'd definitely be sharing Daniel Habash.

CHAPTER THIRTY-ONE

I got downtown just after eight the next morning, Friday, very curious to hear if Malone's interview had been as provocative as mine.

Before entering my own office, where I saw the light was already on, I checked Eleanor's office. Her door was locked and no light shone through the frosted glass. I walked back down the hall to my door, resolved that if she weren't in by nine I would call the Crew homestead to see if she was all right.

Malone was on her side of the partner desk, typing away.

"Good morning," I said. "How'd it go with Martin Idris?"

She held up a finger, typed a little more, and then sat back as I was settling into my own chair across from her.

"I was just writing it up," she said, "but I'll give you the short version: Martin Idris is a very good-looking, smooth-talking customer who doesn't like cops and is hiding something. Claims he hasn't seen or been concerned about Eleanor since they broke up. What about Daniel Habash?"

I had to laugh. "Just make two copies of your report and you've got him covered."

She grinned and shook her head. "Our Eleanor really does have questionable taste in men. Idris almost came at me with a wrench."

"Really? That sounds like it will be good reading. Habash was smoother than that, no open hostility, but smirky. Very smirky."

"And..." Malone paused dramatically. "Speaking of smirky, were you watching TV last night?"

I didn't like the sound of that. "No. Why?"

"Your buddy Alison Roberts featured you on her little news show. There you were in the lobby of the Justice Center with a big phony smile on your face like some corporate honcho caught with his hand in the till while her voice-over explained that our local hero had recently been tripping badly over his own clay feet."

I know I sagged a little. "Oh shit. The sexual assault charge and the whole nine yards?"

"Ten yards at least."

"Shit."

"The price of fame, my friend, the price of fame."

"Oh well," I said finally, resolving to soldier on, "at least I've got something more for Whitehall to look at. I'll give him a call so he can add Martin Idris to his list of people to check out."

"You already told him about Habash?"

"Yeah, he called me last night, actually, about some trouble at our dojang and I told him then."

"What kind of trouble? Something to do with Chet Findley's murder?"

"That's a good guess. You know how Master Chejung was going on about it being 'one of us' who killed his student? Well, Mike says that despite his best efforts not to provoke them the other day Chejung and two of his senior students showed up last night to 'watch' the workout. Eleanor wasn't there, thank goodness. According to Mike, the three visitors just stood stiff and frowning against the wall with arms folded. Didn't say a word beyond hello when he greeted them. Left when the workout was over. I gather that it weirded everybody out."

"Calculated intimidation."

"And probably just the beginning. If Chejung has decided he needs to satisfy his honor, they'll keep coming back until there's *real* trouble and somebody gets hurt." I sat back and looked out the window at the gray day. "Just what I need on top of everything else: a crazed black belt looking to take on me or my friends." I sighed, deeply. "I guess I'd better be there this evening just in case."

"You haven't been doing that much lately, have you? You were going most evenings, I thought."

"I was. I usually do. I've been a little distracted the last few days."

She smiled a little, for some reason. "Well, it'll be good for you to get in the workout. Don't want to get out of shape at your age."

"Huh. Thanks for your concern."

"You're my backup. I don't want to see you sloughing off on the conditioning."

That damned grin was very irritating. Time to move on.

"Mike's got nothing new on the Findley murder. He has forensics looking for something, anything, that would tie to somebody besides Eleanor—but *nada* so far. Ditto on Libby Jance. He told me he spent a large part of the day interviewing her teachers, friends, and relatives with no hint she'd do anything like frame me for sexual assault. Also no hint of where her mother might be."

At least Malone had lost her grin by the time I finished. "Well," she said, "that was just a bunch of bad news, wasn't it? So what next?"

I checked the time. "I'm going to go see if Eleanor is in her office now. She wasn't when I first got here. I want to chat with her some more about old boyfriends—and also see what her attitude is this morning."

Malone stirred in her chair. "Want me to come along?"

I shook my head. "No, not this time. If she's still antsy and evasive, I'll have a better shot by myself."

"Okay. Good luck."

"Yeah," I said as I headed for the door. "That's something we could use more of all around."

CHAPTER THIRTY-TWO

I went back down the hall to Eleanor's office and this time there was a light inside, plus the sound of a keyboard in vigorous use. I knocked and, after a moment, heard her voice.

"Yes?"

I didn't announce myself; I opened the door and went in. She looked a little better than the last time I'd seen her, but there were bags under her eyes that couldn't be concealed by make-up. Her hair was pulled back tight in a ponytail and she was wearing a plain white blouse ironed with military precision, creases still showing. My impression was of someone held tight in an invisible vise.

Her monitor was again blank. Either she'd been typing blind or she turned it off before responding to my knock.

She made a feeble attempt at a smile of greeting. "Clint, good to see you...but I'm really busy right now. Could you come back later?"

I sat down even as she was speaking. "Not a chance," I replied calmly.

The smile flickered and died. "I...I'm *really* very busy...."

"I can see that," I cut in with a gesture at the blank screen.

She looked at it as if it had just appeared out of thin air. "Oh. I was working on something confidential."

Yeah, right. "Malone talked to Martin Idris and I had a chat with Daniel Habash," I said. "Interesting couple of guys."

Her eyes went wide and she stiffened even more. "I told you to drop the case. You said you would." Sudden frown. "And *she's* interviewing my ex-boyfriends now?"

"I didn't say I'd drop the case. On the contrary, I said I was going to help you whether you wanted me to or not—and since she's my partner, that means Devon Malone might help out as well."

Eleanor slumped back in her chair, her features sagging for a moment as if tired of holding up. "You guys can't help. Believe me, you'll just make it worse."

I sat forward. "What?" I asked urgently. "What is *it*?"

She took a deep breath and sat up straight. "*It*," she said firmly, "is my problem. Not yours. You and your *partner* shouldn't be talking to my old boyfriends, anyway." Pause. "Especially Martin. He could be dangerous if you push him. Please, just let it go."

"So why would you go out with a guy like that?"

"I don't anymore."

Time for the question I'd come to ask. "You told me Habash had a plan. What was it?"

Whoa. That cranked the vise a couple of turns tighter. She paled noticeably and her voice grew raspy, as if her throat was closing off. "I have no idea. He never told me and I didn't want to know. Please!"

Speaking of pushing, maybe I'd done about enough of that to my old friend for the moment. Something had her by the throat and she couldn't tell me what it was, but she'd given me some information despite herself. Enough for the moment.

"Okay," I said gently as I got up. "I'll try not to make it any worse."

She attempted the smile again, failed. "Don't try anything at all. Not when it comes to me. You have your own stuff to deal with. I'll be all right."

CHAPTER THIRTY-THREE

"So," said Malone as she idly stared out the window at the gray February day, "Martin Idris is supposed to be dangerous."

"So Eleanor warned me. Did he seem dangerous to you?"

"Well, he was carrying a big wrench and I think he intended it to be threatening. But basically he was just a misogynistic jerk, as far as I could tell."

"Hmmm," was all I could think to say.

Malone focused back on me. "You think this Habash guy has a plan and our girl knows what it is."

"That's my theory, given the reactions I got from both him and Eleanor."

"But what you don't have is any clue what this plan might be. Maybe he was planning to propose."

"I don't think so. That's not what my gut says. It was a damned scary proposal he had in mind, if that's it. We've still got the other four on her list to talk to but I'm betting Habash and Idris are the ones we stay focused on."

And there was *still* something nagging at me, damn it, something I felt I should be seeing but wasn't. No point in mentioning that to Malone, not until I could figure out what it was.

I realized she was looking out the window again.

"What?" I inquired. "You have something else?"

She took a breath and looked back at me. "Mike Whitehall called while you were down the hall."

Uh oh. "And?"

"I told him about Martin Idris, so you don't have to."

"And?"

"He still hasn't come up with anything new on Jance."

"And?"

"Sex Crimes wants to go with assault three and pick you up again. He said he could hold them off for another twenty-four

113

hours, maybe thirty-six, but that's it. Sounds like that's got to be our first priority."

"Shit." I hated to sound so discouraged but I was really feeling jerked around here. Much as I wanted to help Eleanor, I was going to have to re-focus on the Jance case. I took my own deep breath and joined Malone in looking out the window while I gave it some thought.

The cops were checking out Libby and her story; it wouldn't pay many dividends to re-trace their steps, but....

"Why don't we check out her mother ourselves?" I said finally. "That's what Libby wanted us to do in the first place. If Whitehall doesn't have anything, maybe we can at least get a better idea how much of her original story was true."

Malone nodded. "Sounds like a plan."

CHAPTER THIRTY-FOUR

I swung back around and quickly went through my notes. Where did Mom—Rebecca was her name—work? Accountant at Ecotopia Venture Capital, according to our erstwhile client. Right downtown here, probably within a dozen blocks. It wasn't raining. We walked.

Turned out to be just over a dozen blocks, on the third floor of an office building on the far edge of Broadway's theater district. The wood-paneled reception area smelled too heavily of lilac, an air freshener of some sort that was either just used or over-used. Otherwise the small area was tastefully appointed. A petite blonde in her mid-twenties awaited us behind the desk.

"Can I help you?" she inquired with a nice professional smile.

I pulled out my wallet as I crossed the room. "My name's Clint McCall. This is Devon Malone. We're private investigators. We'd like to speak to the person in charge if he or she is free."

She looked at my ID, at Malone's, and then back up at me. "Oh my," she said. "I'll be right back."

There were only two doors besides the one we had entered, one to her left and one to her right. She went to the one on the right and knocked. I heard a muffled response, whereupon she went inside and closed the door behind her.

She reappeared in thirty seconds and stood by the open door. "Mr. Johansson can see you right now," she said. She pronounced the name aggressively, "Yohanzen" with emphasis on the second syllable, and I guessed she was trying to capture her boss's accent. I was right.

Thomas (long "o" as he introduced himself) Johansson looked to be in his late thirties, six one, broad shoulders and trim waist, well-groomed and expensively dressed head to foot. Another good-looking non-native guy. We were on a roll.

Malone and I accepted his invitation to sit, the chairs covered in fine leather, and we both declined his offer of something to drink from the small bar in the corner. The entire wall behind his desk was glass looking out on Broadway.

He took his own chair, steepled his hands on the shiny desktop, and looked from one to the other of us curiously. "Private detectives," he said. "What are you investigating?"

"Do you employ a woman named Rebecca Jance?" I asked.

He sat back. "Becky? She's our accountant—or possibly *was* our accountant. She hasn't come in for the past week and we haven't been able to get in touch with her. My secretary even stopped by her home, but there appeared to be no one there. It's been quite worrisome. Is she in trouble? Is that whom you're investigating?"

He spoke very good English, even considering the accent. Few people, even native speakers, use "whom" correctly anymore.

"There's a possibility she has disappeared," Malone replied. "We're looking into it at the request of her daughter. Do you know her daughter, Libby?"

He shook his head. "No. I knew she had a daughter, but that's all. I don't believe I've ever met the girl."

I took up the questioning again. "What did Mrs. Jance do for you, exactly?"

He shrugged. "She's our in-house accountant. She keeps the books straight—not an unimportant job when investing is your business. We provide capital, Mr. McCall, for start-ups and product development that I believe will provide a good return. It's a risky endeavor, especially in the current economy, but it pays very well if you're good at it." He smiled more than a little smugly. "We're good at it."

"What about this past week?" Malone again, with nice rhythm. "Has no one been keeping track of the money?"

"We have an agency that provides a person when Becky's sick or on vacation. They've been covering this week. What do you think has happened?"

Me again. "We don't know, Mr. Johansson. Has the temp accountant mentioned anything about a problem? Anything in the books that appears to be incorrect or suspicious?"

That got his attention. "No," he said with a frown, "nothing at all. Should we be looking for something like that? Becky's been with us for several years and has been completely trustworthy. Surely you don't...."

"We're not accusing anyone," I interjected, "of anything. When someone is possibly missing, however, you have to look at all the angles."

"Hmm. Well, at least the timing is fortunate."

"Oh? In what way?" Malone asked.

"Our interim audit is scheduled for this coming Monday. If there has been any misappropriation, we'll find out then."

"That's good," I said. "I'd appreciate it if you'd let us know if you do discover anything." I handed him one of our cards.

"Of course. You *and* the police."

"Meanwhile, are you aware of any other unusual problem or concern Rebecca Jance might have had recently?"

He shook his head again. "No, nothing. I wish I could help you. If you find out what's happened to her, please give us a call."

"One of us will," I agreed as I got up. We shook hands and we left to walk back to our office.

CHAPTER THIRTY-FIVE

The day was still gray and now there was a light mist in the air. Foot traffic was heavy as lunch-time approached, no one paying any more attention to the moisture than I was. Umbrellas don't appear in the Pacific Northwest unless there's a major downpour and even then they protect mostly tourists and newcomers.

I barely noticed the marquees of the theater district on Broadway as Malone and I strode quickly through what was even more quickly becoming an outright drizzle.

"So," I said, "we've confirmed some of Jance's original story. Her mother worked for Ecotopia and is missing—from work, at least. If that Monday audit turns up evidence of embezzlement, then that's more of the truth."

"In which case, why the hell would she set you up on a sexual assault charge? If her mother's really in trouble and she really needs our help, that seems a tad counter-productive, don't you think?"

My cell phone started to vibrate. "I think," I said as I retrieved the phone from my jacket pocket, "that's something I really need to discuss with her." I punched the TALK button. "McCall."

"Big Avenue."

Whoa. Another surprise. I nudged Malone, who was already looking sour about my last comment, and gestured that we should take a detour under the awning of the next storefront. Then I put the cell phone on speaker and held it up between us.

"How are you doing, Big?" I said into the air and her eyes widened with surprise.

"I'm up too fuckin' early. Not even noon yet, but I heard you was workin' on my girl getting' killed and I figured you'd want to know somethin' I found out. If you're fuckin' still in bed or something, I can call back later."

"No, that's fine. I'm standing out on Stark near my office at the moment. Devon Malone is here, too, and you're on speaker. What have you got?"

"You're out on the street?"

"Cell phone, remember? Wonders of technology. You're probably talking on one right now."

"Fuck off. You wanna hear what I got or not?"

"I just asked you, didn't I?"

There was a sound something like a growl. "Okay. There was another one of my girls at the motel, in a room the other side of that courtyard there in the middle."

I exchanged a look with Malone. "At the time of the killing?"

"Yeah, at the time of the killing. Why the fuck would you care elsewise?"

"That's interesting," I said. "You only found this out now? Don't you know where your girls are when they have dates?"

A definite growl this time. "Not when they're on their own time, tryin' to rip me off, I don't."

"Ah. I'm surprised she told you at all, then."

"Dead girl a friend of hers."

"I hope she survived the confession."

"She's alive, if that's what you mean. She ain't gonna rip me off again."

I really didn't want to know the details. "And?"

A slight pause, I guess while he refocused from her pain to his story. "She saw two guys leavin' the room through the back door, goin' through the yard."

Very interesting. "We need to talk to the witness." And maybe check on her condition at the same time.

"Fuck no. You don't need to talk to her. I can tell you what she saw."

Malone shrugged and I thought I knew what she meant. Big Avenue was very protective of his "girls" except when hurting them himself—and he wouldn't want us to see evidence of the latter. If he had good detail, it wouldn't be worth the time and effort to get past him to the woman. He said she'd survived. There wasn't much we could do for her.

"Okay. Let's hear it, exactly what she saw."

"A businessman-type and another guy, tall guy, wearing a stocking cap pulled down over his ears. Both white. The businessman looked scared, she said. She thought maybe he was bein' mugged by the other guy but then they kept goin' together out to the street."

"So maybe the businessman was being kidnapped."

"Could be. She said the other guy had ahold of him all the way."

"Anything else? Like her name and where she is right now?"

"Not a chance." He hung up.

CHAPTER THIRTY-SIX

It was mid-afternoon when I finally parked near the corner of Elm and S.W. 18th. I spent a few minutes watching Jance's small brown apartment building and thinking how nuts it was to do this alone. I was about to visit a woman who'd accused me of sexual assault; I really should have a witness, but that would reduce the chances of her telling me anything to zero.

Malone had objected strenuously to my latest plan, pointing out that appearing to harass Libby Jance would only make me look more guilty. I insisted that it was time to get some kind of damned explanations and that I had to do it alone. If I did get deeper in trouble as a result, I would need Devon out in the world and free.

She very grudgingly conceded the point and said she would see if she could track down some info on Big Avenue's source. Apparently she wasn't quite as sanguine as I'd thought and wanted to reassure herself if she could that the woman was at least relatively okay. That sounded good to me, so we parted ways on the corner in front of the office. She didn't even suggest we have lunch first, though I was betting she'd grab something pretty soon. I wasn't hungry at all, myself.

As I took the outside stairs to the second floor balcony, I found myself growing intensely curious about how Jance would react, assuming she was home. After all, I hadn't in fact assaulted her; it was the other way around. And I'd swear I heard her say she was sorry before she bashed me in the head. If I could just get her talking, surely I'd learn something. That was, however, a very big if.

My plan was simple, totally illegal, and hardly foolproof. I was going to impersonate a police officer and hope she was willing to open the door sight unseen. I'd manage the sight-unseen part by holding a fake badge up to the peephole, close enough that she couldn't see past it. The badge came from my glove compartment, where I've long kept it in case I needed a simple and illegal plan.

I positioned the badge and knocked on the door of Apartment 5. As if in response, the door of Apartment 6 opened and an elderly gentleman with a felt hat and umbrella emerged. He bustled off toward the stairs as I heard Libby Jance's voice from behind her door, asking who it was.

I wiggled the badge. "Detective Whitehall," I said, doing the best imitation I could. "I have a few more questions."

Long pause. She was thinking. Stop thinking, I thought. I heard the lock click open and saw the knob turn. I pushed gently from my side as she began to open it and made it across the threshold before she really saw me.

Her gray-green eyes were the size of small saucers behind her glasses. "You!"

I closed the door. "Me," I said.

A petite young woman the first time I saw her, she seemed even smaller now, her short hair flat against her head as if she hadn't washed it recently. Barefoot, dressed in jeans and a Portland State sweatshirt, she was backing away as fast as those bare feet would carry her.

"Calm down," I said, holding my hands up and palms out. "You know I'm not going to hurt you. I just want to talk."

She stopped in the vicinity of a small writing desk with a phone sitting on it. She gave the instrument a hard look.

"Talk first," I said. "Phone later." Hopefully without a tale of my attacking her again. Hmm, this could be a really dumb idea.

"What do you want?" Her voice was shaking and she looked like she might pass out.

"Just to talk," I said again as gently as I could. "Please, sit down. There's nothing to worry about."

To my surprise, she choked out what might have been a short laugh. Then she sat down in an armchair across from the couch. I lowered myself onto the couch and cocked my eye at the frilly cream-colored shade to my right.

"Nice lamp."

She grimaced. "I'm really sorry."

"Let me cut to the chase. What the hell is going on, Libby?"

Now her lower lip was trembling and she was tearing up. "I can't tell you. Please leave me alone."

"Leave you alone?" I hunched forward and gave her my best you've-got-to-be-kidding-me stare. "You're framing me for attempted rape, endangering my license and livelihood, not to mention my freedom...and you want me to leave you alone? That's it?"

She bit the trembling lip and stared right back. "Yes. That's it."

"It's obvious that you're in some kind of trouble," I said. "Let me help you." Meanwhile I'm thinking to myself I've had this conversation almost word-for-word very recently, with Eleanor.

Libby Jance was the one who leaned forward this time, her voice tight. "You can't help me—and I can't help you. It's my mo...." She waved a hand in the air as if to erase the last sound. "No. You have to leave now." She looked around the room as if seeking some reason I should go. Then she took a deep breath and literally gritted her teeth. "You'd be in a lot more trouble if I called the police and said you tried to attack me again," she grated, the words seemingly forced past her lips, "or I could start screaming right now and let one of the neighbors call. I'll do it, I will, unless you leave *now*. Please!"

I looked at her pale, pinched face and her intense gray-green eyes. She meant it. Shit. Helpless again. I got up and left without even saying good-bye.

The frustration was already starting to ease by the time I got back to my car. Perhaps I had a few new pieces. For one thing, I was almost certain that the unfinished sentence would have been, "It's my mother who needs help." If so, Libby Jance had no vendetta against me; she was somebody's pawn. We were both in the same jam—and that was a very important piece.

On top of that was how much she'd reminded me of my recent conversations with Eleanor. Could that possibly be coincidence? If not, how could they possibly be related? Again some-

125

thing was nagging at me, something I felt I should know or at least suspect; my gut was telling me to pay attention.

Malone was not in the office when I got back. There were no messages on my voicemail, no e-mails beyond the normal and unending spam, and no lights on in Eleanor's office.

I reviewed the bills I didn't want to pay yet. I tried, but failed yet again to come up with some coherent theory of how and why everything seemed to be crashing in on me at once. Otherwise I puttered, watched a new rainstorm develop, and nursed a steadily worsening tension headache. Malone never did show up.

Finally I headed across the street to the Home Run in the hope that the first food I'd eaten since breakfast would help ease the pain before I headed to the dojang. If I hadn't already had a headache, I could anticipate getting one when Chejung showed up looking for trouble. On the other hand, if we were really lucky and he didn't show, maybe losing myself in a good workout would give my subconscious a chance to do a little productive work.

CHAPTER THIRTY-SEVEN

The dojang is only three blocks from my office, a pleasant walk even in the rain.

Six of us, all advanced black belts, had pooled our resources to rent the space when our teacher decided to retire. We don't advertise, we don't take students, we don't even have a name for the dojang. The space is strictly for our own training and workouts.

Mike Whitehall and I are fourth-degree black belts. Daisy Mansfield, Carmen Gonzales, Roger Arbuckle, and Bobby Brewster are third degree black belts. By my special request, second-degree black belt Eleanor Ivory had become the seventh member of the group. I'd been her teacher even before she was my accountant and resident hacker; plus she was very skilled for her belt level.

I topped the stairs and stepped onto the highly polished floor of the dojang at six-fifteen. It's one large room with attached office that comprises the second floor of an old warehouse at the corner of Second and Pine. We'd sanded and polished the wood floor, hung some heavy canvas bags along one side, brought the plumbing in the single bathroom up to code, and installed lockers in the office space to create a dressing room. There was no spectator seating and it wasn't decorated with flags like Chejung's more public dojo but otherwise it had the same ambience.

So far there had never been an evening without at least two of us in attendance, and usually there were four or more. Whoever was senior each evening led the workout. Which would be me this evening because I'd been promoted to fourth degree six months ahead of Mike. Which also meant it would be my responsibility this time to confront Chejung if he appeared again. Which made me wish dinner had done more to ease my headache.

The evening was already unusual. With my arrival, all were in attendance except Eleanor. Even more unusual, unprecedented in fact, Devon Malone was here—standing off to the side looking a little bemused at all the activity. Apparently everyone knew that there might be trouble with Chejung.

Roger, a 53-year-old retired Army colonel, was in the corner stretching and warming up. Mike was practicing some advanced forms with his domestic partner, Bobby, a successful corporate lawyer somewhere in his thirties. Carmen, a compactly-muscled 38-year-old veterinarian, and Daisy, an independently wealthy 21-year-old who was the quickest of us all, were sparring with each other in the middle of the floor.

It was the two women who had Malone's attention when I walked over to ask her what she was doing here.

"Didn't expect to see you here," I said as I positioned myself against the wall next to her and watched the women spar.

"I thought I might as well get an idea of what you do in the evenings," she said. "Plus it sounded like it could be quite a show if that other guy shows up."

I glanced over at her with a sly grin. "And you wanted to be here to make sure your partner didn't get hurt, right?"

She tossed a little grimace back at me and returned her focus to the sparring. "Yeah, that was it. You bet."

I pushed away from the wall. "Well, enjoy the spectacle if there is one. I have to go change."

An hour later, an hour with much sparring and no spectacle, Malone was looking a little restless when suddenly there was the sound of rapid tramping coming up the steps. I glanced over at Malone and she mouthed the words "show time."

And she was right.

I'll say this for Master Chejung: he knows how to make an entrance. He and two of the senior students I'd seen with him before cleared the stairs and came to a stop about ten feet inside the room, well into the practice area, Chejung in the center. They were all three in their dobaks (the standard white uniforms, much like ours) with arms folded and expressions grim. They were soaking wet and literally steaming, mist rising from their heads and uniforms. They

128

were *very* hot despite the winter weather outside and, knowing the mentality, my guess was that they'd run, barefoot and in the rain, all the way from Chejung's dojang on 82nd—a distance of probably eight miles. Making the point that they were extremely tough warriors clearly not intending to just watch this time.

There was some contrast among our three visitors. Chejung was absolutely focused, standing like a rock, yet seeming to radiate energy—and hostility. One of the accompanying black belts was trying hard to imitate his master but was standing stiff and tight rather than solid, face frozen rather than calm, eyes darting rather than fixed. Even his crew cut looked unusually rigid. The other black belt, short and stocky with a mop of red hair, was trying to remain expressionless but I could see as he surveyed the room that he was sizing up the odds and couldn't help smirking a bit. More fool he.

I had called a halt to the current round of sparring when the three stepped beyond spectator distance. As senior black belt, it was my responsibility to greet the new arrivals, so I walked toward them from the center of the training area.

I stopped six feet in front of them and bowed. "You are welcome," I said pleasantly.

Master Chejung frowned mightily but had no choice but to lead the three in a return bow. Rigid Boy barely managed, a flush climbing the back of his neck, and Mop Head almost grinned.

Once everyone was standing straight again, Mike moved in behind me to my right and Roger Arbuckle similarly to my left. No doubt the other three were ranged right behind us. Six to three but two of us were female and two of the men were in their fifties. The red-headed kid was fully grinning by now.

Chejung never took his piercing black eyes from my face. He leaned his heavily muscled body ever so slightly forward, trying to tower over me from six feet away. "We must fight," he said simply. No accusations, no explanations; he wanted to re-establish his dominance.

Well, I thought to myself, isn't this a fine kettle of fish? I'd just go with the flow and see what happened. So: "Of course," I said cheerily. "We enjoy observing the styles of other schools. A short demonstration would be most appropriate."

I could see Chejung's brain racing and his teeth wanting to grind. It appeared I had successfully put him in a hell of a spot. He could hardly throw a hissy fit and scream that that wasn't what he meant—but if he acquiesced to a demo, his honor wouldn't allow him to purposely harm his opponent.

Unfortunately, his honor also wouldn't allow him to hesitate and his brain wasn't racing quite fast enough. He stepped toward me as if accepting the invitation even as he said, "We must fight." It was a lame compromise and he immediately knew it, his own face becoming almost as frozen as Rigid Boy's had been before.

I could see, meanwhile, that Rigid Boy looked to be approaching a snapping point. Mop Head continued to smirk at the turn of events, but this other guy was profoundly angry that his master had been out-maneuvered. I was glad I had my breath back, just in case.

You spend enough time in martial arts training and you develop a sixth sense, really just a heightened awareness of what little sounds, little changes in air pressure, might mean.

I had just turned my back to them as if everyone were in agreement and begun to lead the way to the center of the dojang when I heard the faint slap of a bare foot on the floor behind me. I couldn't believe that Chejung would dishonor himself by attacking me now, but someone was coming.

I executed a back kick in the direction of the sound before I even started to turn. When my head did come around, I wasn't very surprised to see my foot about to impact the chest of the high-strung student. He'd apparently lost it and blown right past his master to take me on, in the midst of his own flying kick when I first saw him.

It was unfortunate for him to be off the ground at that moment. In addition to my back kick, Master Chejung came up with

130

an excellent roundhouse kick and Mike Whitehall managed a jumping side kick. We all three hit him while he was still in the air. He landed very hard and not on his feet as he'd no doubt intended.

He moaned loudly as Master Chejung leaned down, grabbed him by the front of his dobak, and jerked him to his feet so that their noses were almost touching. "You have shamed me," he said fiercely, and shoved the young man away from him. As the student staggered to a stop, barely able to stay on his feet, Chejung pointed at his waist. "Give me the belt."

The young man's face twisted up as if he were going to cry, and probably also from the pain of multiple injuries, but then he got control of himself. He was by now as white as his uniform even though standing a little more steadily. I didn't blame him. He'd lost control, gotten himself knocked six ways from Sunday, and now was being "defrocked" as it were, asked to give up his black belt because he'd dishonored it. His name would be erased from the rolls of the school and it would be as if he'd never trained. The martial arts equivalent of a death sentence. His hands trembled as he untied the belt and handed it to his master with a bow. A bow that Chejung did not return.

Chejung did, however, turn and bow with great dignity to me. Then, without another word, he left with both his former and his remaining student in tow.

Just about the time his head disappeared below the landing, I realized that Malone had come up to stand beside me.

"That was every bit as good as promised," she said. "I'm impressed."

"It's not something you see every day," I said, practically weak with relief that a huge brawl had been avoided. I glanced over at her. "You're welcome to come and train with us," I offered impulsively.

She gave me a kind of wry look. "Not that impressed."

Which was a further relief, since I had no idea how we could have fit in a beginning student.

Malone excused herself and the rest of us went back to sparring, everybody needing to work off some adrenaline before we hit the showers.

And I had maybe a little more adrenaline than the others, because I now knew what my next step would be in Eleanor's case.

CHAPTER THIRTY-EIGHT

It was nearly nine-thirty the next morning before I got to moving much around the house; last evening's confrontation had taken a lot of energy, so I'd slept in until awakened by anticipation of the plan I'd come up with. Even the two cats had apparently been unable to bother me. I'm sure they tried.

I fed them, ignoring the loud complaints about the meal being late, meditated, and then prepared my own breakfast—if you consider peeling a banana and opening a box of cereal "preparation." By the time I finished the banana and cereal, my plan for the rest of the morning was fairly well-developed.

I rinsed the cereal bowl, set it in the drying rack, and dialed the Crew residence. Johnny answered the phone and I casually asked what was going on.

"Not much. I was just tellin' Gerry how much I miss football already."

"Yeah, it's too bad the season has to end."

"You know what I don't miss, though?"

"What's that?"

"Them goddamned erection malfunction ads. What is with that? They got some new research that shows the average sports fan can't get it up?"

"Maybe. They do seem to come on every few minutes during a game."

"Gerry hates the damned things even more than I do. She's afraid I'll buy some of the stuff."

I laughed. "I hope you've reassured her about that."

"Damned straight—or maybe that's not the best way to put it."

The man almost always cheers me up. But I hadn't gotten to my business yet: "How's Eleanor doing?"

"Gone back home."

"Back to her apartment?"

"Yeah, said she imposed on us enough and Gerry couldn't hug her out of it. She did go with her, though, to help the kid finish straightening up the place and buy some new stuff. The crime scene cleaners were done yesterday."

I took a moment to process the pronouns. "So Eleanor and Gerry are together."

"My wife wouldn't be denied. You know her. Eleanor said she could handle it by herself, but Gerry insisted. I mean, shit, even with the blood and crap cleaned up, it's probably still a mess. You can't leave the kid to face that alone."

"I'm sure Eleanor appreciates it."

"Well, she wasn't appreciating it when they left—not that that was slowing Gerry down at all."

"Maybe I'll check over there later. Gotta go now. Talk to you soon, Johnny."

I hung up and contemplated my good luck. Despite any demurrals from the object of her benevolence, I could count on Gerry to stick by Eleanor's side for most of the rest of the day. The apartment would be totally refurbished and re-stocked before she let go. My perfect window of opportunity.

I was going to need still more luck, but this was an excellent start.

CHAPTER THIRTY-NINE

Picking the lock on Eleanor's office door took only a moment, for which I was grateful. I'd been surprised to find Malone in the office on a Saturday morning; apparently she was just as bothered about everything going on. Said she was doing research. She had no objection to my breaking into our accountant's place of business in the meantime. Whatever works seems to be her typical attitude about such things. I promised I would explain if my hunch turned out to have any validity.

At some point during class last evening a couple of things had added up. I don't know when exactly, only that the resolution was there by the time I watched Chejung disappear down the stairs.

For one thing, I realized what had been nagging me about my recent conversations with Eleanor. She'd referred, twice, to my "other problems" in a tone that clearly indicated she meant more than day-to-day irritations. She seemed to have definite knowledge of my growing difficulties, which she shouldn't have, given that—at the time—there'd been nothing on TV and I'd mentioned nothing myself.

Then there was that remarkable similarity between her demeanor and Libby Jance's, the eerie parallel in their denials and evasions. I'd gotten no help from either of them and it appeared I was not going to get any—but it was no help in exactly the same way and for apparently similar reasons.

I needed to help myself, first to whatever information I could find in Eleanor's office that might explain why she'd suddenly decided she had to go it alone. It might also confirm my hunch.

I shut the door quietly behind me, locked it, and flicked on the light.

There were papers left scattered across the desktop, a half-full paper coffee cup sitting perilously near the edge on one corner, and her chair pushed back against the shelves behind the desk—hard enough to knock over several dolls. Usually Eleanor left her office very tidy; this time it looked like she'd simply jumped up and left it.

I pulled the chair back to the desk and sat down, feeling distinctly odd to be viewing the office from this vantage point. There was nothing of interest in the papers on the desk, mostly having to do with the tax problems of a local bottling company.

The drawers were equally unproductive of evidence—unless I needed evidence that my accountant was hiding a serious junk food habit. The bottom right drawer contained far more salty, high-preservative snacks than it did files.

The PC had been left running, so I turned on the monitor and waited for it to brighten. She had remembered to log off, of course, but long ago she'd given me her password because I needed some of my records while she was out of town. If I was really lucky, she hadn't changed it. If I wasn't, I'd have to hope I could find something in the file cabinets and I did not want to spend the rest of my day going through her file cabinets.

I brought up the log-in window, typed CURVGIRL, crossed my fingers, and hit Enter.

The machine played a little melody and displayed a quick variety of messages...none of which said the password was bad. After another minute everything settled down and I was looking at the high-resolution image of a shiny red Corvette she uses as her desktop background. I have an ink drawing of Japan's Mount Fuji on my PC. Whatever turns your crank.

There wasn't much else visible; apparently Eleanor likes a tidy computer screen as well. There were no icons, much less one labeled "evidence." Not necessarily a problem. I called up the main directory and went from there.

There were financial and tax programs, of course. Bookkeeping. Word processing. I hesitated, not knowing where to begin and beset with growing doubts. I could be reading more into Eleanor's comments about my troubles than I should, the same with the similarities between her demeanor and Libby Jance's....

136

Then again, I was already sitting here. Might as well click on something—and it might as well be her calendar. It came up showing nothing scheduled for today—not surprising for a Saturday.

I brought up the weekly view and found myself looking at the past week. Monday through Wednesday appeared to be pretty busy, with meetings and conference calls scheduled throughout the day. Thursday and Friday almost everything was cancelled. That fit with when Eleanor pulled back from me. So something happened on Wednesday of last week. I went to the full-day view of last Wednesday. Nothing unusual, no names that rang a bell. I clicked on tomorrow, Sunday. Nothing, of course. This coming Monday. And eureka.

Chills chased each other up and down my spine as I stared at her one appointment for the day, at ten in the morning: *Ecotopia audit*.

Let's hear it for hunches.

Thomas Johansson had said he wasn't worried about a misappropriation of funds going undiscovered because there was an interim audit coming up on Monday. It hadn't occurred to me at that moment to ask him who the auditor was and now I didn't need to.

I sat back and took a very, very deep breath.

Becky Jance was the in-house accountant for Ecotopia Venture Capital and Eleanor Ivory the auditor. Libby Jance said she thought her mother had stolen money. The audit of Ecotopia's books would reveal such a theft...unless the auditor had been intimidated, say by her boyfriend being murdered in her bed and her being framed for the crime.

Talk about the plot thickening.

CHAPTER FORTY

We turned off McLoughlin onto S.E. 23rd and pulled into a visitor's space at Eleanor's apartment building. The sight of a familiar Ford hatchback in the next slot over brought me back to the problem at hand.

"That's Gerry Crew's car," I said to Malone. "Step one is going to have to be persuading her to vacate the premises."

There had been no way I was going to keep Malone in the office while I went to pursue this newest revelation. Nor did I want to. Dragging the full story out of Eleanor was not going to be easy and I needed all the help I could get.

"Shouldn't be that hard," Malone responded as she opened her door. "Just tell her to go home."

I also got out of the car. "Maybe. You haven't seen Gerry in full mothering mode." We stood surveying the building for a moment. It was a middle-aged, five-story brick box with old-fashioned wrought-iron fire escapes. It didn't look like it should contain an apartment so starkly modern as Eleanor's. I shivered. The air had chilled to a point I'd call outright cold and it felt like it might snow, a rare occurrence in Portland even in February.

"Let's do it," said Malone. "I'm freezing my ass off standing here."

We went upstairs and knocked on Eleanor's door, which was opened by Gerry.

Gerry Crew is a stout woman, an inch or so shorter than her husband Johnny and with the same aura of immaculateness. She greeted me with every hair in place and her dress unwrinkled despite all the clean-up work she'd undoubtedly been doing.

"Clint! We could use some muscle to...." Her smile widened as she registered that there were two of us. "and Devon came along to help. Even better."

I leaned in toward her slightly. "We need to talk to Eleanor," I said. "Alone."

She looked a little dismayed. "Right now? We're in the middle...."

"It's really important," Malone said. "We need to talk to her right now."

"Go on home, Gerry," I chimed in as firmly as I could. She was already looking a little stubborn. "Eleanor will be fine. It's not more bad news, but it is very important."

She considered, looked from one of us to the other, then nodded her head. "Just give me a minute." She stepped back and pulled the door open wider. "Come on in."

We entered the apartment and saw Eleanor standing in the doorway of the bedroom. She was wearing loose-fitting blue jeans, sneakers, and a pink sweatshirt, her hair pulled back with a red bandana. She appeared stunned to see us in her living room, which wasn't entirely surprising.

"What are you guys doing here?" she finally asked, her voice barely audible.

"We need to talk," I said.

Meanwhile Gerry was gathering up her coat and purse. "I'll be getting out of the way, honey," she told Eleanor. "I can come back later to help you finish. Just give me a call."

At that Eleanor's face took on an expression of panic. "Don't leave, Gerry! I need you to stay." She glanced at me and pinned her gaze back on her older friend. "I... I can't talk to these guys right now. We... We still have lots of work to do here. Don't go."

Gerry stopped, coat and purse in hand, looking from one of us to the other, bewilderment and indecision playing over her features.

"We have to do this, Gerry," I assured her again. "Eleanor will be all right. Trust me."

One more look and then her mouth firmed up in decision. "I'm sorry, honey," she said to Eleanor as she started for the door. "I'll come back just as soon as you call."

Eleanor didn't plead anymore and a moment later I heard the

door open and close behind me and Malone.

We were all silent, motionless for what seemed like a full minute. Eleanor wasn't looking at either of us, her eyes focused somewhere in the middle distance off to our right. Dressed as she was and so distracted, she appeared out of place in these surroundings of modern glass, stainless steel, and primary colors.

Finally her head turned and her eyes met mine. She repeated her initial question: "What are you doing here?"

"We know about the Ecotopia audit," I said portentously, hoping to give the impression that we already had everything I hoped she was about to give us.

She looked appropriately shocked. "How?"

"We're private detectives, Eleanor," put in Malone, playing her part perfectly. "It's what we do."

Just that fast, tears welled up. "Oh shit." A sob. "Oh shit. I'm sorry." She left the doorway and half-staggered toward her couch, pulling off the kerchief as she went, her hair falling in a tangle on her neck. "I'm sorry, I'm sorry." She collapsed on the couch.

I followed quickly and sat on one side of her. Malone perched on the armrest of the couch on her other side. "It's okay," I said. "I know you were scared." Still winging it, trying to sound like we knew everything.

She was leaning forward, elbows on knees, and used the kerchief to wipe her eyes. "What are we going to do now?" she asked finally.

"What you're going to do now is tell us the rest. Then we can make some decisions."

She sat staring at the living room rug as her trembling lips slowly firmed up. Finally she said, in a whisper, "So you know it's Daniel."

Whoa. The clever girl had tried to put us onto Martin Idris by saying he was dangerous. Not so, apparently. I flashed on the tall, well-dressed middle-Eastern ex-boyfriend I'd visited on Thursday. I made eye contact with Malone who was frowning slightly. She, of course, had not seen him. "Habash?" I inquired for confirmation.

"Yes." Eleanor offered her own little frown. "You did know that, didn't you?"

I realized I'd been holding my breath and let it go. Maybe at last I was going to get some truth—and probably more if I reverted to the truth myself. "We know you're doing the Ecotopia audit and we deduced that it was related to your being framed." I paused.

"But that's it," Malone finished for me. "We need to know the rest if we're going to help you."

Eleanor's face flushed, with embarrassment or anger or some combination, and she jumped up, stomping partway across the room and then turning to face us. "You tricked me!" More tears were welling from her eyes. "You're going to get all of us in even deeper trouble!"

CHAPTER FORTY-ONE

While I was wasting a moment feeling a little guilty, Malone just went for it: "You're telling us that all of this, your boyfriend's murder, Clint being accused of sexual assault, a client maybe being kidnapped, are all somehow related?"

Eleanor looked at her like she'd suddenly grown a second head. "What kidnapping?"

"Okay. Forget the kidnapping. You and Clint both being framed. They are related, right?"

Eleanor paled and looked down at the rug as she answered. "Yes, I think so."

"You think so," I said. "You don't know?"

She looked up at me, showing a spark of defiance. "Well, I mean I don't know *how* Daniel has done it—or what else he might have in mind. He hasn't shared all of the details with me." While she was saying this, she returned to the couch.

I put my hand on her arm as soon as she was settled and squeezed gently, trying to be as reassuring as I could. "You need to share with us," I said. "Whatever he has told you."

She sat back, glanced up at Malone who was still perched above her, and then down at her lap.

"I didn't know what he was after." Her mouth twitched in what could have been a wry smile. "I thought I did, I thought it was me, but I was wrong." Deep breath. "There's a cash transfer scheduled for later next week. I'm supposed to not find it when I perform my audit. He says he can clear you and me both if I do that." She let go a short, dry laugh. "The funny thing is that I probably wouldn't have found it anyway. I tried to tell Daniel that, but...."

"Wait a minute," I interrupted. "The transfer hasn't happened yet?"

"No, not according to Daniel. Why?"

"Never mind," I said. Libby Jance had even fewer details about what was really going on or she'd lied again. Her mother hadn't stolen any money; she was apparently helping Daniel Habash steal money. "Start at the beginning. When we were going over that list of guys, you said you broke it off with Habash because he got weird on you. Was that true?"

She almost glanced at me. "Yes."

"Then when did all this about the audit happen? You and I were going over that list on Tuesday, just four days ago."

"He called the next day."

"Which is why you started trying to put me off when I saw you on Thursday? Because he called you? Threatened you?"

"Yes. Both of us, yes."

"He told you that he killed Chet Findley and framed me for sexual assault?"

Her hands twisted together. "No. No, he didn't say any of that exactly. He just said he knew we were both in bad trouble and I had two choices. If I went along, he could get us out of trouble; if I didn't, the trouble would get worse." She looked over at me finally, her eyes red and glistening. "He said that if I kept you out of it, didn't tell you anything, we'd all be okay. I'm sorry."

"Wait a minute," Malone interrupted. "Just for the record: Did he ever threaten me?"

"No. He never mentioned you."

Malone frowned almost as if she were disappointed about that but said nothing more.

I tried another tack. "Are you the regular auditor for Ecotopia Venture Capital?"

"Not really. Ernst & Young does the annual audit for tax and reporting purposes. The CEO, Tom Johansson, hired me to come in and do a very superficial interim audit around this time of year as a precaution, a kind of backup." She snorted. "It's really just so he can advertise that he's audited twice a year. I don't spend more than a few hours going over the books, very broad brush, not what you'd properly call an audit at all."

144

"How long have you been doing it?"

"A couple of years." Her mouth twisted in that wry almost-smile again. "I dated Tom for a while. That's why I got the job." Her expression drooped. "When I told Daniel it was just a farce, that I probably wouldn't have caught the phony transfer anyway, he didn't believe me. He thought I was just trying to get out of it."

"Not surprising," I said. "Do you know Becky Jance?"

She frowned. "Becky? Their accountant? Sure. It's primarily her work I'll be auditing."

"Ever heard of a man named Joseph Imeson?"

Deeper frown and longer pause. "No. Doesn't ring any bells. Why?"

"Never mind. Just checking. What do you know about Habash? Why, for instance, is he going to all this trouble? If he was able to get this transfer set up, why hasn't he already executed it and disappeared along with money?"

Eleanor was beginning to relax, sitting gingerly forward, making occasional eye contact with me at least. "He told me that doing it this way he would have an extra six months or so before Ernst & Young discovers the money is gone. That's a lot of time to cover your tracks—and I guess he must be pretty good at covering tracks."

"Why do you say that?"

"He told me he used to work for an intelligence agency in the Middle East. Lebanon, I think."

"He was a spy?" I exchanged another significant glance with Malone. The good news just kept on coming.

"That's what he said. He warned me that he'd know if I told anybody." She shuddered and looked around the apartment as if he might be hiding in a corner.

I looked around too, because if he wasn't bullshitting her he certainly could have planted a bug at some point—and might as well be sitting in the damned corner. I managed not to shudder along with her.

No point in searching for such a device. Nowadays they were far too sophisticated to be found by visual inspection. Also, no point in panicking Eleanor further. She'd already blown it if he was listening. I could only hope that he was either exaggerating his résumé or hadn't had the opportunity to plant something.

"He's probably just trying to scare you," I said to try to ease her mind.

"He's doing a hell of a good job," she answered with another wide-eyed survey of the room.

I sat back for a minute and tried to take it all in. Meanwhile, Malone asked, "How much money are we talking about?"

"Thirty million."

I think she and I whistled simultaneously. "Shit," I said.

"That's a lot of money," Malone responded. "Could his plan work? Even if you don't report the scheduled transaction, won't Johansson or somebody else notice a missing thirty million dollars in the next six months? Hell, in the next six days?"

A little shrug from Eleanor. "It can work. Thirty million *isn't* really a lot of money; it's a tiny percentage of Ecotopia's cash flow and you have to remember, we're not talking about real money disappearing out of a vault or something like that. It's just a computer record saying the money was here and now it's there."

"Nevertheless," I said after some more reflection on everyone's part, "he couldn't have planned all this ahead of time. It's both too pat and too complicated. There would have been no reason to kill your boyfriend or set me up, not just to steal some money, even thirty million."

"I think," she said slowly, "his plan was just to seduce me into helping him. Daniel seems to have a very high opinion of his power over women. He must have been hinting when he started talking about having a big plan for us, but I wasn't going along—and I guess...I guess I talked about you too much."

I didn't know what to make of that and I could tell Malone

didn't, either. "Me?"

Eleanor actually blushed. "Well, I guess I brag sometimes about this private detective who lets me help out on some of his cases."

Any other time I would have laughed out loud. "Really?"

"He told me later that that was why he decided he needed some...'leverage,' he called it. I'll bet he still believes he could have seduced me otherwise, the pathetic jerk."

Malone jumped in again. "So he thought Clint was a threat and that's why he set him up?"

"I think so, yes."

"So what's he planning for me?"

Again Eleanor gave Malone the you've-got-two-heads look. "Nothing. He's not planning anything for you. I don't think he even knows about you."

Malone leaned forward and squinted at Eleanor as if she were trying to understand. "You mean...you talked all that much about Clint and never mentioned me at all? Never told Habash that Clint has a partner?"

Eleanor had the grace to look even more embarrassed. "It...never came up."

Malone sat back. "I'll be fucked."

"Actually," I chimed in, "it sounds like Eleanor saved you from that. *I'm* the one who's fucked."

"Humph," was all I got in response to that observation. By this time I was really hoping that Habash wasn't listening.

Time to cut this off, in any case. "We need to think all this over," I told Eleanor. "We're going back to the office and later I'll call you when we've decided what we should do. Meanwhile stay put, keep your door locked, and don't make any calls. Okay?"

She nodded. "Okay."

We all three rose and moved together toward the door, then Eleanor stopped me with a hand on my arm. "How *did* you find out?" she asked. "About Ecotopia? Did Tom tell you?"

"No, I saw it on your schedule, on your PC."

She stepped back. "On my PC? How did you see that?"

"I broke into your office, logged onto your computer, and looked at it."

A flush started creeping up her neck and it wasn't embarrassment this time. "You...you broke.... How could you do that?"

I figured she must be feeling a little better if she could get so scandalized over a minor case of trespass. "I needed to know what was going on," I said simply, "and you weren't in the mood to share."

She opened her mouth and then closed it again. "Well," she said finally, "I'm going to change my password."

CHAPTER FORTY-TWO

We got into the Subaru and just sat for a moment. I needed to absorb all we'd just learned and I imagine Malone did, too.

"Office or cop shop?" Malone finally asked. I understood what she was really asking: Should we tell Mike Whitehall right away or not?

Since I'd already been considering that very question, I had an answer ready. "The office. If—and it's still a big if—Daniel Habash really is a well-trained intelligence agent, the Portland cops might not be a good match for him."

Malone made a little throat noise. "And we are?"

I literally threw up my hands, as best I could in the small car interior. "I don't know. But I don't fancy sitting in the middle of police headquarters trying to explain all this. Not without some thought first, at least. Don't you think it's going to sound like the dumbest alibi ever? I didn't do it. My accuser is lying because this international spy my accountant was dating has set me up as part of an incredibly elaborate scheme to cover a huge theft."

"Good point and a good reason not to do it in the Justice Center, but I think Mike needs to know. You've got to get covered somehow."

"I agree. I think. I'll give him a call soon and set up a meet somewhere else."

I started the car and pulled out into traffic. "Meanwhile, we've got to be very careful," I said—and just that fast spotted what might be a tail pulling out behind us.

It was a plain brown sedan staying three vehicles back, edging to the side of the lane once in a while to keep me in sight. I changed lanes a couple of times and it stayed with me. Then it followed me onto the Morrison Bridge heading downtown.

"I think we might have somebody with us," I said to Malone.

She didn't turn her head to look back but she did check the side mirror.

"How far back?"

"Three."

"The brown one?"

"Yep. It pulled out right behind us when we left Eleanor's and it's still there."

"Could be."

"I want to be sure. Hang on."

The traffic was heavy on the bridge, but I had room to do a little maneuvering. I hit the accelerator and managed to put another five cars between us. That was enough for me to drop out of the sedan's line of sight as I approached the foot of the bridge. I hit the surface street, Washington, and pulled abruptly into the parking lot located to my right. I sat idling at a spot where we could see the vehicles coming off the bridge. The lot had entrances at both the bridge egress on Washington and on 2nd, which was the one-way cross street. I could follow the sedan whichever way it went.

It appeared about ten seconds after I stopped, slowing as it approached 2nd, dropping to a crawl as it pulled even with me. I made eye contact with the driver just as several horns honked at his slow pace.

"Shit! That's Habash, right there."

As if cued by my announcement, his vehicle jumped forward and squealed around the corner onto 2nd right in front of me. It started weaving through traffic in the direction of Burnside. I peeled out of the lot just behind it, heart racing and palms sweaty, hoping my pursuer-turned-fugitive crashed into somebody before I did.

"Yahoo!" yelled my passenger. It very briefly crossed my mind that I could love this woman. Then I focused on keeping both of us alive while staying on the brown sedan's back bumper.

CHAPTER FORTY-THREE

Ever attempted a high speed chase in heavy downtown traffic without a movie director to choreograph the other vehicles? No? Wise choice.

In the first place, the chase isn't high speed; more like slow and jerky. You do a zig and hit the brakes; he does a zag and hits the brakes. The other drivers look at both of you as if you were nuts. It probably doesn't even occur to them they're witnessing a chase.

We maneuvered like that northeast on 2nd, me a couple of cars behind Habash, both of us managing to catch green lights all the way to Burnside where he turned left, literally heading for the hills. I ran a yellow to stay with him and, Burnside being a broader thoroughfare, we both sped up significantly—until he hit a red light at 10th just short of Powell's Bookstore.

We sat there. He was in the right lane at the intersection and I was four cars back in the left lane. Malone meanwhile drolly observed that Powell's appeared to be having some kind of event. Just wanted to be sure I knew she was cool, I guess. I knew that.

I was focused on Habash and could almost see him thinking through what to do next: Bail out? No. That would be ridiculous. Keep heading west toward the heights? Not promising; some very heavy traffic ahead on Burnside. But there's not much traffic on 10th. Plus, the stupid PI is stuck in the left lane and there's a warehouse district seven or eight blocks to the right.

I must have been correct about his conclusions because he peeled around the corner just as the light changed and was out of sight beyond a building before I could even hit my right turn signal.

It is not easy to change lanes in three car-lengths when both lanes are packed and traffic is starting from a dead stop. The process involves lots of honking, cursing, and intimidation by various participants, including the middle finger of my passenger. I provided most of the intimidation; the other drivers did most of the honking and cursing. It took a very long thirty seconds to get over there and around the corner; I caught just a glimpse of Habash's sedan in the distance making a left four blocks down. There was a stop sign and a green light between me and him, meaning he must have run the first and lucked out on the second.

I, on the other hand, had to stop at the sign and caught a red. Malone encouraged me to run both but I was not feeling suicidal and ignored her advice.

I finally rounded the corner where I had seen Habash's car disappear, finding myself in a relatively grungy commercial area. Small office buildings, faded storefronts, a few loading docks. No foot traffic that I could see. Plenty of turn-offs, though, both streets and alleys. Hell, if he was a pro he could be anywhere by now. Even an amateur could get well-lost in the maze I was facing. Damn it.

"Crap," said Malone. "After all that we lost him."

"Probably," I said.

Nevertheless I had to give it a try. I drove cautiously ahead. After ten minutes of inspecting each turn off and intersection as well as the parking lots and loading docks, there was no sign of Habash's vehicle—and little chance that he was still anywhere near the area.

I'd just given up and headed back toward Burnside when my cell phone rang. I punched it on by feel, putting it to my ear without looking at the ID. And heard the well-controlled tenor voice of Daniel Habash: "I hope you had a nice visit with Eleanor."

I almost swerved into the back of a parked semi, then pulled over into a parking area just beyond it. In response to Malone's exclamation, I held the phone up and mouthed the word "Habash."

"Mr. McCall? I know you're there. I'm quite certain this isn't a wrong number. Who is that with you?"

As it happened, I'd hit the speakerphone button just before that last question. Malone bristled and leaned over close to the phone. "It's his partner, asshole."

"Ah," he said, "of course." So he knew about Malone whether

152

Eleanor had told him or not. After a moment, he went on. "Very good that you spotted me following you. Better than I expected."

"You'll find us full of surprises." Malone left the "asshole" unspoken this time, but we could all hear it.

He chuckled. "Perhaps. We'll see."

"Where are you?" I inquired casually.

"On my way back to Eleanor's apartment," he replied. "There's still something I need her to do and I don't want her to lose focus beforehand."

"The audit."

Ever so slight pause. "Ah, she told you about that. Bad girl."

So there was no bug in her apartment, after all. Or he wanted us to think there wasn't one. "It wasn't her fault. I searched her office and found some information that gave it away."

"And have you, in turn, told anyone else?"

Better to be honest, I thought, since he was on his way to Eleanor's and I wasn't. "Not yet. My partner here knows, of course."

"I hope that's true, Mr. McCall. No damage done, if so, since you will both go to your office now and tell no one else."

"Maybe I'll go home and take a nap instead."

"No, you will go to your office."

"Why is that?"

"Because I have your office bugged, of course, and I haven't gotten around to your home yet. I don't mind telling you..." There was that chuckle again. "...because you won't find it or be able to block it."

Which certainly explained how he knew about Malone. I'd have to think about what else it might mean he knew. "So we're supposed to just go sit there and let you listen to us?"

"If you don't cooperate, or if I catch you trying to deceive me, a woman will die."

"Becky Jance?"

"You don't understand how this works, Mr. McCall. I don't do what you say or answer your questions. You do what I say and answer my questions—if I have any. I probably won't. I already know most of the answers."

He hung up.

CHAPTER FORTY-FOUR

I flipped my phone closed. My body was so tight with anger and frustration that I could barely stuff the damned thing back in my pocket.

"Well," announced Malone after a moment of contemplation, "*that* is truly a huge pile of shit."

"No kidding," I responded.

"We need a new plan. For one thing, should we call Eleanor to tell her he's coming?"

I put a hand on her arm. "I suppose he hasn't bugged the car yet, either, huh."

We locked eyes and she didn't say a word, just nodded. We simultaneously opened our doors and bailed out. It happened that I had pulled over in front of a loading dock that wasn't currently being used. It didn't provide much shelter from the chilly and damp February wind, but we huddled together as best we could. The early afternoon light was even more gray than the morning light.

"First off," I said, "I think giving Eleanor a heads up would just piss him off. He's not going to hurt her. He needs her for the audit. Even so, we'd better assume the threat is real that a woman—other than Eleanor—will die if we don't cooperate."

"And that it's Becky Jance."

"Very likely. So we need to appear to cooperate. Second, we'd better assume that Habash is exactly what he told Eleanor he is: a professional spy. There are already plenty of indications it could be true—which would mean he could have access to, and expertise in, all the latest surveillance equipment and methods."

"Thus we don't trust the car or the office or your house, etcetera."

"Exactly," I agreed. "Which means it's going to be very tricky to bring Mike Whitehall, Johnny Crew, and others in on this. Meanwhile, our primary task is to get on top of Habash. I need to be following him rather than the other way around."

"Just you?"

"Since he probably didn't find out about you before bugging the office, he may not have you individually bugged yet. We can thank Eleanor's neglect for that. How about we switch phones and maybe even vehicles?"

She squinted at me. "So he can listen to everything I do instead of everything you do?"

"You go silent until we want Habash to know that he isn't covering me after all; the right time will come to throw him that curve. Get a burner phone in the meantime and work from your apartment when you need to. Surely he hasn't bugged that, yet. Right now, we go back to the office and appear to be cooperating. Think about it: if this guy is *really* good, can we be absolutely certain of anything we think we know? He's almost certainly behind Chet Findley's murder and Libby Jance setting me up for a sexual assault charge, but was he also behind the murder of Heather Lipinski and the kidnapping of Joseph Imeson? If so, how and why? If not, then who? I've got to be out there using the freedom you can give me."

Her fierce squint became an even more fierce frown. "I don't like it."

CHAPTER FORTY-FIVE

Libby Jance awoke slowly, her first coherent thought a hope that at least now she would see her mother. But the vast and dingy room showed no signs of life besides her own. There was enough light from a row of high, small windows to let her see a pile of wooden pallets across the room. That was it.

She wasn't tied up but her body felt tremendously sluggish and she could barely raise herself off the unfinished wooden floor. Definitely a warehouse of some kind and apparently not the first floor. The sound of a truck passing outside and below told her that much.

Libby could vaguely remember Daniel Habash sticking her with a needle and forcing her into a car. Where had he come from? She couldn't remember—and everything after that was a total blank until waking up here.

She didn't know how long it took her to get to her feet, but by then she had a goal. Besides the windows and the pile of pallets there was one other thing she could see: a set of large double doors on one side of the room.

In the process of getting up, she finally noticed that there were a few objects on the floor nearby: a water bottle, a half-dozen small packages, and a bucket. She leaned closer to investigate. The labels on the packages indicated they were some kind of ready-to-eat meals. It seemed that Habash meant for her to be here a while, which probably meant there was no point in trying those doors.

She made her way slowly over to them anyway and was not surprised to find that they wouldn't open. She didn't pound on them or yell. If anyone was on the other side, it would be Daniel himself and she didn't want his attention.

Leaning her back against the doors, she became aware of a faint odor that made her heart beat faster. Her mother's perfume. Her mother *had* been here even if she wasn't now. But...what did that mean? Why would Daniel keep them in two different places? Why did he take them at all? She'd done everything he asked....

The clearer Libby's mind became the more tears streamed down her cheeks. Yes, she'd done everything Daniel Habash had asked. She'd concealed her mother's kidnapping, falsely accused Clint McCall of attempted rape, gone along with everything—with the result that she herself was kidnapped and her mother's fate unknown.

She surveyed the dimly lit room through blurry eyes as she slowly let herself slide down into a sitting position. She'd been a weak and stupid fool. And now all she had was this huge empty warehouse space and a terrible fear that she'd never see her mother again.

CHAPTER FORTY-SIX

Malone was still not liking my plan when we got back to the office but we couldn't continue arguing about it once we got inside. At least we agreed on that much.

We'd barely both sat down when the phone rang. The display showed Mike Whitehall's number at the Justice Center. I gestured to Malone that I'd pick it up and reminded myself that Habash might be able to hear my end of the conversation—so not a good time to arrange that meeting.

Mike Whitehall's voice was about half-an-octave lower than usual, which was worrisome in itself. "Clint?"

"Hey, Mike. How's it going? Anything on Eleanor's case yet? Or Jance?" Meanwhile I was trying to convey to Malone that I didn't want to put him on speaker because I didn't want Habash to hear both sides of the conversation. This time she did push the button for my line and gently picked up her phone, indicating that she would remain quiet.

"Something new on Jance," Whitehall answered meanwhile.

"What?"

"She's missing."

That threw me for a moment. "You mean you've confirmed that the mother is missing?"

"I mean Libby Jance is missing."

The hole in the pit of my stomach couldn't grow any bigger, so I just threw that in with the rest.

"When?" I asked. "Is it certain?"

"Pretty certain. We haven't found anyone who's seen her since you were there yesterday."

"Since I...?"

"We have a witness, the guy who lives in the next apartment. He says he saw you at her door late yesterday morning. He says she opened the door, so we know she was there then. Nothing since.

159

It's not looking good, Clint."

I kept my again-growing frustration and anger under control as best I could. "I guess not."

"What were you doing there?"

"I know it was off limits, but I had to talk to her. That's all. We had a brief conversation and I left."

"Anybody see you leave alone?"

"Not that I know of."

"Have you learned anything that could help us clear you?"

I felt like my head was going to explode. I wanted to blab everything we'd just learned, but Habash could very well be listening. Even if he weren't, he'd know as soon as the cops tried to run with the information—and would probably carry through with his threat to kill Becky Jance (or maybe Libby Jance now). I had no choice.

"Not yet," I answered reluctantly. I *hated* how much our asshole nemesis was probably enjoying this if he really was listening.

"Too bad." He paused.

"You don't...."

"No, I don't think you did it. Otherwise I wouldn't be risking my career to call you like this."

There was something about his tone. "I hear a 'but' in there," I said.

"I talked to the witness. I understand you used my name to get her to open the door."

Oh, shit. "Well, yes. It seemed like a good...."

"We're gonna have some things to talk about, but not now. Now you need to be in the wind. I mean *right* now. As far as I know, they're about to hit your home and office. And there's a bulletin out for your vehicle. You're way past being a person of interest at this point. You're going to be charged."

"That doesn't leave me a lot of choices."

"You can give yourself up, but I don't think a judge will offer bail this time. If you want to have anything to do with clearing

160

yourself...."

"I understand—and I'm sorry about using your name."

"Later." He hung up.

CHAPTER FORTY-SEVEN

I replaced the handset in the cradle and looked across the double desktop at Malone. "Looks like I've got to hit the road," I said.

She hung up as well and at the same time pointed toward the door. I understood. A few moments later we quietly closed the door behind us. Malone glanced around the currently empty hallway.

"You don't suppose he's that smart, do you?"

"Bugging the hallway for when we know we can't talk in the office? I hope to hell not. We've got to chance it. Unless you want to accompany me down to the bathroom."

She grimaced. "I'll pass on sharing a stall with you. What's the plan?"

"Get the hell out of here. Withdraw some money from the nearest ATM before they start to track my banking activity. Get a burner phone of my own—and, come to think of it, I need to keep my regular cell in case Habash calls me. It would be kind of a giveaway if you answered the phone."

She pulled it out of her pocket and handed it to me. "But you still get to use my Jeep, right?"

"Got to get around somehow."

"So, what else?"

"Honestly, I'm not sure yet. I need some time to think it through. I can't stay here. I can't go home. Pretty soon I'll have to avoid being seen by any cops on the street. But in the face of all that it would be nice to find Libby Jance and her mother, foil Daniel Habash, and clear my name."

"It would be nice for *us* to do all that, don't you think?" Arms akimbo, Malone took a step closer so that she was almost in my face. "Are you trying to *protect* me, McCall?"

I took a step back, savoring the hint of cinnamon that I could always smell when she was close enough, this time mixed with the familiar leather smell of her jacket. I wanted to take back that step back. But I didn't. "No!" I said instead, "I wouldn't think of it. So...what's *your* plan?"

Now she smiled triumphantly. "At least I actually have one. I'm going to go chat with our old friend Carl Gunther to see what he knows about international spies running around in his territory."

Carl Gunther, Sr., was more or less the organized crime boss in Portland. He didn't like me much because I'd punched out his son (Carl Gunther, Jr.) in the Home Run across the street. For some reason, probably because she was an attractive female, he did like Malone. It wasn't a bad plan. He usually was on top of any new competition in town.

"That's a good idea," I responded, "but watch yourself. Habash knows you're in this just as much as I am. He'll be working to get you covered just like he has me."

"I'll be careful." She actually reached out and grasped my arm. "You be more careful."

I looked down at her hand and ignored the little tingle from her touch. "I gotta go," I said. "The cops could show up here any minute. You have no idea where I am."

"Of course not. But you let me know as soon as you can. Leave me a message on my home phone. I'll start checking when I have my burner, then we can trade numbers and talk directly again without worrying about Habash."

She let go of my arm and I stepped past her to quietly open the office door. I had to get my jacket and get the hell into the wind, much as I wanted to stay.

I confirmed the Smith and Wesson was snug in its holster, grabbed a couple of extra clips out of the drawer and dumped them in a jacket pocket. I took a quick look around the office, very much aware that I might not be seeing it again for a while, wished my partner luck, and then left her standing in front of the closed office door.

Her last words to my back were, "Take care of my damned vehicle."

CHAPTER FORTY-EIGHT

Just to add insult to injury, I emerged into a damned rainstorm. It can rain heavily in the Pacific Northwest in February—and this was one of those times. The few pedestrians in sight walked fast, head down, looking as if they wished they were carrying umbrellas for once. Me too.

I turned right and headed downtown to get lost, at least for now, among the bustling and shivering weekend shoppers. Maybe I'd buy a warmer jacket while I was at it, maybe even a damned umbrella—if I could get to the nearest ATM before the authorities got to my bank account. I'd have to find a place to stay if I didn't get everything resolved today, which was unlikely.

There was a momentary hitch in my stride as I realized that I hadn't made arrangements for Stella and Maxine. How could I forget them? Once I had a burner I would be calling Colleen to reassure her—again—that the news she was hearing wasn't as bad as it sounded. I could ask her to do it, but I didn't know who might be watching or even hanging around my house. Malone would be better. I'd ask her as soon as we were back in touch.

I have rarely felt as alone as I did hurrying through the downpour toward an ATM that I hoped wouldn't reject my bank card. I'd come to depend on having Devon Malone around and I missed her already. Well, money first. Then burner. Then message on her home phone. We'd go from there.

I passed Malone's Jeep where it was parked on the street rather than in the lot near my vehicle. By the time she joined me in the agency there were no more spots to reserve in my lot, so she had to take her chances every day. Which was just another reason for her to be her grumpy self. I wondered if the Jeep was going to smell like her, cinnamon and leather, and oddly looked forward to finding out. The ATM was just a half-block beyond. Another three steps and my cell phone rang. Only a few people had the number. Maybe it was my daughter. I stopped and flipped it open. The display said "No ID."

Looked like I was about to experience still more insult.

CHAPTER FORTY-NINE

Of course it was Habash's voice I heard when I punched the phone on.

"Very good, Mr. McCall. You didn't say a word, not even to defend yourself to your friend. He is a good friend, isn't he, though I must say not a particularly good police officer."

So much for staying off the speakerphone.

I almost snapped back with some line about the bastard's qualifications to comment on another's honesty and integrity, but I didn't want to sound any more defensive than I already felt—which was substantial. After all, I was fleeing down the sidewalk wearing a medium-weight jacket and no hat in the goddamned freezing rain with a malevolent spy taunting me in my ear. I was cold, sopping wet, and pissed. Life could be better.

"I'm glad you appreciate my efforts," I muttered as I plowed ahead.

The dreaded chuckle. "Feeling testy are we, Mr. McCall? I'm sorry to hear that. I'm feeling quite good, myself, not least because I now have something I can use against Lieutenant Whitehall if you attempt later to enlist his aid."

"Asshole."

"Tsk, tsk. Sticks and stones, Mr. McCall, sticks and stones." His tone shifted. "Well, let's get down to business. I want you to keep this phone because I'll be using it to contact you. However, I should point out that once the Portland police find you're trying to evade them they will undoubtedly attempt to track your phone. Do you know how to shut off your GPS?"

That put another hitch in my stride. I didn't have a clue what he was talking about. "My GPS? My car doesn't have a GPS."

A heavy sigh. "That may be, but your cell phone does. I'll take your response to mean you don't know how to shut it off. Let me see...." There was silence from his end for a moment or two.

167

"There. When our conversation is over and you close your phone, an application will download that disables the GPS signal. You don't need to do anything—which is clearly fortunate."

Shit. All this was making me feel a little out of my league, which was not a good thing to feel under the circumstances. I needed to exercise at least a little control, so I jumped on what sounded to me like a contradiction: "How can you download something after I've disconnected?"

"Flipping your phone shut doesn't necessarily.... Oh, never mind. Take my word for it. The police will not be able to track your phone. I'm surprised it even has a GPS, given that you have to flip the damned thing closed. You need to update your technology, Mr. McCall."

So much for exercising control.

"You'd be well advised to use the phone only when I call you," he went on. "And even better advised to tell no one about me. I will know if the authorities are notified."

I said nothing more and just kept walking.

His voice became insistent. "Do you understand?"

"Yes," I said brusquely, "I understand."

He hung up.

By the time I dropped the phone in the jacket pocket opposite the clips, I'd reached the ATM. Finally some good news. It accepted my card without comment. Next stop would be a clothing store. This rain felt like it was going to turn to snow at any moment.

I was getting really pissed. And *cold*.

CHAPTER FIFTY

The ATM informed me that I had $732.59 in my checking account, which was all I had immediate access to. It wouldn't let me take more than $200 at a time, so I stood there for a few minutes feeling totally exposed as I took $200 three times and then $132. They'd probably slap me with an extra fee for going below the minimum balance but that was the least of my worries.

I stuffed my new-found riches in my wallet and headed for the nearest discount department store as I noted the first flakes of snow in the air. I also noticed one of the display windows I passed had cheery red Valentine's Day decorations. That could not have seemed less appropriate. I checked the date display on my watch. Saturday, February 15. Yesterday was Valentine's Day and I hadn't even noticed. Probably never would have thought of it if this one store wasn't late changing their display.

My next thought was that I didn't get anything for Malone, which was strange because I had no reason to get her something for Valentine's and she probably would have tossed it back in my face if I had.

I put all that weird speculation behind me as I moved on to the department store.

The jacket I'd been wearing all day was both fairly light for these colder temps and typical of what I usually wear when I'm on the street. I needed to be both warmer and less easily identifiable.

The garment that I bought was essentially a cream-colored raincoat with a fake-fur zip-out lining. Not too classy but inexpensive and a good fit over my jacket. I added a dark brown watch cap to cover my thinning hair. Finally I glanced at the umbrellas, scarves and gloves, but couldn't bring myself to indulge in any of them. Just too un-Northwest and I was feeling wimpy enough already.

Thus everything was warm and dry—or, more accurately, drying—as I hurried from the discount store to a nearby hole-in-the-wall coffee shop packed with customers sheltering from the storm.

I ordered a straight coffee and stood in the corner furthest from the plate-glass window, waiting for a place at the counter to open up. I needed to sit down, back to the sidewalk, and think for a while. The hot black liquid felt good in my throat but not so great in my stomach, which seemed to have developed a case of the twitches.

And why shouldn't it? I was on the run from the cops with no access to my office, home, or vehicle. I certainly couldn't go to the Home Run for lunch, as if I was ever going to have an appetite again anyway. Hell, right now I didn't even have a place to take a piss except this coffee shop or some other public restroom.

I was about to add weak knees to the twitchy stomach when a stool was vacated and I managed to get there just ahead of a young female corporate type. This was no time for chivalry; she looked like she probably kicked butt at the office anyway and wouldn't expect politeness from a guy. I occupied the seat and she stepped back without comment.

Which somehow reminded me that Habash had not mentioned Malone at all. Not even a passing reference to my partner. Could he really be leaving her in the clear like that? Maybe, but more likely he just didn't want me thinking about her and what he might do.

Thinking about Devon was something I seemed to be doing a lot lately despite having so many other problems to consider. She, on the other hand, seemed barely resigned to being my partner in the agency—much less anything else. And what else did I have in mind? Did I really want to try to bed Devon Malone? That could be very dangerous. Was I falling in love with her? No, no, that would *not* do. But enough. I had to let it go for now. I didn't need the distraction while trying to dig myself out of this very deep hole.

It took only about five more minutes to get all the coffee down, which left me feeling a little more perky. I turned and looked out the window. The snow was tapering off to a cold drizzle, already turning to dirty slush on the sidewalks and streets. I did a gut-check, literally, and realized my stomach was feeling better. I stood up. Knees ditto. Time to get on the damned move.

I stopped in the bathroom, buttoned up my new coat, and pulled my hat down over my ears. Communication was my first goal, as I'd already decided. Where do you go to buy a burner phone in downtown Portland? Nordstrom? Probably not, but maybe a lower-end department store would do. There was a Target outlet over on Morrison. I stepped outside and headed that way.

I was in luck for once. They had a whole display of cell phones with included talk time and (unadvertised) no traceability. I bought one with 120 minutes on it. According to the directions, it could only be "reloaded" using a credit card, so I'd have to toss it and buy another one at the end of the two hours.

The irony was not lost on me that I—who had so long resisted having a cell phone at all—was now carrying two, one for me and one for the bad guy.

But so what. I badly needed to talk to Malone and now I could.

CHAPTER FIFTY-ONE

Devon Malone ignored the prickling on the nape of her neck as she crossed the lobby toward the bank of elevators. Yes, no question she was going to have to watch her back from now on. But there was very little chance Daniel Habash was monitoring her every move yet and even less chance that he'd try to start in the lobby area of a major downtown office building.

Ever since she'd watched her partner hurry away from their office, she'd been trying to stay focused on her own surroundings rather than worry about how he was doing out in the world without any backup. Without her backup. It was downright irritating how difficult it was to do it, to stay focused.

McCall was in very big trouble and she wished she could do more to get him out of it. Maybe she'd learn something here.

At least one of the elevators was already on the lobby level and in fact the doors opened as she approached—with no one inside. Which was creepy on top of all the other creepy. She forged ahead nevertheless.

As she remembered from the previous visit, it was a very high-class elevator—trimmed in leather with that new vehicle smell. She pressed the button for the twenty-second floor, Gunther Global Import/Export, and just for the hell of it she took advantage of the comfortable bench along one side of the car while she enjoyed the smooth, quiet ascent. She cocked an eye up at the small camera lens and gave it the finger.

Feeling almost cheerful by the time the elevator halted and the doors opened, Malone swung out into the spotlessly clean carpeted hallway and turned right.

She would never admit to McCall that she'd been a little intimidated the last time by the wide corridor of glowing off-white walls hung with modern art, even the air somehow freshened to the point that it felt and smelled more like a meadow than an office building. She was long over that. She knew now that at the end of the corridor lay nothing more than the fancy office of the most powerful gangster in town.

The plush carpet from the hallway continued inside the reception area, as did the fresh-smelling air. Reproductions of old maps were displayed on the walls and a medium-size leather couch sat against the wall to her left.

Behind a highly polished wooden desk sat Mrs. Agnes Pinkerton, Gunther's receptionist and much more—certainly much more than her little old lady appearance would reveal. White hair. A round, cheery face with pink cheeks. Half-glasses over which she gazed at Malone inquiringly. And probably a loaded pistol within easy reach.

"Hello, dearie. Haven't seen you for a while." Even her voice fit perfectly, one of those old-lady breathy but firm voices that can actually make you feel better by saying "there, there."

"The name's Malone, not dearie."

Mrs. Pinkerton nodded. "I remember. You have an appointment that I *don't* remember?"

"No, but I'd like to see him anyway. Is he free?"

"Not even close—but let me check if he has some time." She picked up her phone and pushed a button. "That girl PI, Devon Malone, is here wanting to see you."

She paused, listening, while Malone bristled. *Girl PI?* Could she launch herself across the desk before Pinkerton could come up with a weapon? Probably, but she let the fantasy go when the older woman hung up and nodded toward the door just behind and to her left.

"He'll see you," she said.

Carl Gunther, Sr., stood behind his imposing desk as she entered his office and he leaned a little forward, holding out his hand to shake. "I thought it might be you when I heard about the woman telling our elevator camera to fuck itself."

Malone had to grin as she shook his hand. "You get reports on

174

what's happening in the elevator?"

He sat back down and gestured that she should take one of the visitor chairs. "When they're coming to this floor and acting oddly, yes, I do."

Organized crime meets Big Brother, thought Malone. Gunther certainly looked the part of crime boss, high tech or not.

Expensively dressed in a gray pinstripe suit with dark blue tie. Early fifties probably, a full head of dark brown hair and craggy features. A little over six feet tall carrying much more muscle than fat, a man who was used to getting his way and capable of hurting people who didn't cooperate.

Not that Malone considered him a threat. For some reason, he liked her. Which didn't mean she had to like him.

"So," she said, "what do you know about a new guy in town named Daniel Habash?"

He grinned. "I'm fine. How are you? Would you like some coffee? Are you still playing sidekick to the old guy?"

She shrugged. "I'm good. Nothing to drink, thanks. My partner is, I believe, just about the same age as you. What do you know about Daniel Habash?"

At that he laughed out loud and threw up his hands. "You are something else, Malone. I don't have a clue who Daniel Habash is. Never heard of him. Is he somebody I should be worried about?"

"Maybe. Our information is that he might be a rogue Middle Eastern intelligence agent looking at a major score here in town. Could be embarrassing for you."

He looked down at the desk, momentarily lost in thought. "Ah," he said finally.

"Ah?"

"I didn't have a name yet, but there is word on the street about a foreign national purchasing quite a variety of high tech products off the books, probably not for legal purposes. Could be this Habash character."

"Yes. Yes, it could be. What else have you heard?"

"Not much. Not even his name, as I said. Which tells me that he's very good at staying under the radar."

"Like a spy would be."

Gunther gave her thoughtful look. "About like that, yeah."

"Any idea where we might find him?"

"If I did, he'd be found. What kind of major score?"

"We're just speculating. Some kind of long con, maybe. It's still between us and our client." No way was Malone going to tell Carl Gunther that thirty million dollars was in play right now. He'd probably trample her and McCall both trying to find Habash first. Could get everybody killed. There was nothing more to learn here.

She stood up. "I have places to be," she said.

Gunther kept his seat. "Watch your back, Malone. It's a good-looking back and I'd hate to see anything happen to it."

She gave him a little forefinger salute. "Always, Carl."

She left the office thinking about all those "high tech products" Habash had apparently purchased and how many of them might end up on or about her own person. McCall's back, so far, was in more jeopardy but she'd be watching her own as well. Whatever else happened, she was *not* going to be kidnapped by the bad guy again.

CHAPTER FIFTY-TWO

I needed a warm and unlikely place to make my calls, so I went to the central Multnomah County Library, seven blocks west on Taylor from Pioneer Courthouse Square. I hurried through the entry area, the Willamette Industries Foyer, and the Bill Naito Lobby, then took the stairs—which were apparently not funded by any entity worth naming—to the Mary and Pete Mark Lobby on the second floor. I turned left and settled on a comfortable chair in a far corner of the periodicals reading area. I had a good view of the entrance and the entire space, which currently held only one other occupant—an elderly gentleman on the opposite side of the room who was dozing with an open newspaper on his lap. He wouldn't care if I used my phone quietly.

My first call was to Malone's home number, as agreed, leaving her my new cell number and an assurance that I was okay so far.

My second call was to my daughter Colleen's cell phone.

She answered right away. "Hey, Pops. How's it going?" she inquired with a lively tone.

So she hadn't heard the news yet.

"I'm okay," I said, "but I have to keep this short. You're probably going to have a visit from the cops later today, looking for me."

"Uh oh. Looking for you? Why...?"

"That young woman, Libby Jance, who claimed I tried to assault her? Now she's missing and I'm the prime suspect. I'm going to have to stay off the radar until I can prove I'm innocent."

"They want to arrest you? You can't be serious. Mike wouldn't let them...."

"Mike can't do anything to help me right now. If he contacts you, tell him the same thing I want you to tell the other cops: you haven't heard from me and have no idea where I am."

"All right. Jesus, I can't believe this. Where *will* you be?"

"Actually I have no idea myself, so you won't be lying about

177

that part."

"Well, let me know when you find out. I don't want to have to worry. Any more than I will anyway. Jesus."

"I know, kiddo. I'll keep in touch as best I can."

"What about the cats? Do you want me to take care of Stella and Maxine?"

"No need. Malone's got that covered." Assuming she would agree when next we talked.

She paused just a beat. "Ah ha. Are you two...?"

"I've got to go," I interrupted.

"Ookay. Take care of yourself, Dad. I love you."

"Love you too."

I ended the call. The old man was still snoozing and no one else had joined us, so I punched in Johnny Crew's number. Malone had my back, at least in principle, but just in case somebody needed to have Colleen's back. Habash had to know about her.

Johnny's tone when I identified myself was rather different from Colleen's: "Clint! We were listenin' to the police band and heard your name. What the fuck is goin' on?"

"Libby Jance has disappeared and I was the last person seen with her—so far, anyway."

"Fuck me. When was that?"

"Yesterday afternoon. I went to her apartment to ask her some more questions."

"With the assault charge pending? And then she went missing? Jeez, I hope you got some good info from her."

I almost sighed. "Not a lot, but I've got a better idea what's going on—and not only from her. I'll bring you up to speed as soon as I can."

"So you're on the lam, now? What the fuck are we gonna do? You ain't gonna be alone on this. You need a car?"

"I traded vehicles with Malone."

"Oh. Okay. Of course, she's your backup." He sounded hurt.

"Not just her," I was quick to reply. "What I need you and Hap

178

to do is keep an eye on Colleen."

"Colleen? What's the kid got to do with it? What's the story, Clint?"

"I've got a situation," I replied carefully, making decisions as I talked. "I'm being set up and the person behind it has a lot of leverage right now. Part of it is that he could come after Colleen." I paused and took my own deep breath; they weren't going to like this. "Another part is that I can't tell you any more than that right now."

After a moment: "Shit."

"I'm sorry. That's the way it is."

He wasn't going to let it go so easily. "You're talkin' about the guy who's got the Jance kid. Why's he after you?"

"Like I said. I can't tell you."

"Then when the fuck?" he burst out.

"After I have a handle on it myself," I said. "If there were anything else you could do, I'd tell you, believe me. Right now I need you to be with Colleen. That's important. It will give me some space to do what I have to do. And don't be too obvious about it; I don't want it to look like you're guarding her. Just hanging around. Okay?"

He huffed a bit.

"Okay," he said grumpily. "We'll take care of it."

"Thank you."

"And you take care of you."

"I will," I said.

We left it at that.

CHAPTER FIFTY-THREE

I parked Malone's Jeep a couple of buildings down from Chejung's Northwest Martial Arts on 82nd and watched to see if any suspicious vehicles drove by. None did. Traffic was very light, probably because of the wintry weather, so it was also easy to confirm that no one had pulled over within three blocks behind me. So far so good.

My fourth call had been to the office voicemail system where I found several inquiries from the media, no surprise, and a message from Master Chejung informing me that he'd been "looking deeply" into the death of his student and had some important information he wanted to share. What the hell?

I couldn't imagine what he'd have to offer but decided to see him personally about it rather than try to sort it out over the phone. Certainly the cops wouldn't be looking for me at Chejung's dojo.

It appeared, from what I could see through the street-level plate glass windows, that the Saturday training session was just ending. The impression was confirmed as I pushed open the heavy front door and entered. Two dozen students of all belt levels were just beginning to scatter from the center of the room, chatting, comparing notes on technique, crouching over gym bags along the wall to stow protective gear and retrieve street clothes. Chejung's senior students were gathered around him at the far end of the training area just as they had been when I first visited.

They saw me when I entered, but this time no one came to stop my progress across the dojang.

It wasn't quite the same group as on my first visit. The red-haired black belt who'd been dismissed by Chejung at our dojang was absent, replaced by a chunky blond who actually looked a little like Chet Findley. The other senior student, the one with crew cut dark hair, was still at his master's side with a demeanor about as friendly as the previous times we'd met.

Master Chejung himself looked significantly less hostile than he had when he left the dojang. His expression was neutral, though his massive body still radiated enough energy and strength to be intimidating.

He dipped his head in formal greeting. "Master McCall."

I reciprocated. "Master Chejung."

"This," he said as he gestured at the dark-haired student, "is Terry Goebel. And this," a gesture at the blond, "is David Camp. They are my students." Good so far. At least he was willing to introduce his companions this time.

We all traded bows. "A pleasure to meet you," I said. Then I focused on Chejung. "You said you have information?"

His expression didn't change. "I do."

I think learning cryptic, cut-to-the-chase responses must be part of martial arts master training. "Well," I said, "you called me. Are you planning to share whatever the information is?" (I didn't take that particular class.)

"We have been investigating Chet Findley's death."

What the fuck? Did he think he was running a combo martial arts dojo and detective agency?

"Really?" I responded as neutrally as I could.

He must have picked up on my dismay. His eyebrows actually lifted a millimeter or so. "We are just asking some questions."

"It would be best if you left that for law enforcement professionals," I said as firmly as I could. "It's a far more delicate situation than you know and at least one very dangerous man is involved. You could put innocent people in danger."

"We know about the dangerous man," he replied calmly.

Oh shit. This could be very bad. "What do you know about him?"

He nodded to Terry Goebel. "Go get Jason before he leaves." Goebel hurried off toward the dressing area. Chejung returned his attention to me. "I know that he's violent. He has a record of hurting women. He is a gambler and needs money. Other things."

Violent? Very likely. Record of hurting women? Maybe, but an accessible record? Doubtful. And a gambler? Habash? This was beginning to sound like.... "What's his name?"

"Idris. Martin Idris. He had an interest in your student, Chet's girlfriend. Maybe he got jealous, wanted to hurt Chet."

Relief and curiosity flooded through me in equal measures. "How did you learn about this man?" I asked.

"My students ask Chet's other friends questions about his girlfriend, then ask her friends who she was seeing before, questions like that."

Not bad. He had some of the right instincts, at least. Lucky, too, that he ended up focused on the wrong dangerous man.

Goebel returned with a younger, smaller student in tow; he'd partially changed out of his dobak but was carrying a purple belt, carefully rolling it up as they approached. He finished that task, stopped, bowed to Chejung, and looked from one to the other of us expectantly.

"This is Jason Dominguez," Chejung said to me. "Jason knows much about the Internet."

Aha. Chejung's Eleanor Ivory. Jason and I exchanged a minimal bow.

"This is Clint McCall, a private detective," he said to the new arrival. "Tell him what you have learned of Martin Idris."

Since I did not want to disabuse them of their current suspicions, I listened patiently to Jason Dominguez giving me a watered down version of the same information about Idris's criminal record that Joy Castle had gleaned from her databases.

"Very good work," I said when he'd finished. I was about to leave it at a pat on the back when it occurred to me: Chejung said Idris was a gambler. That was something I hadn't known and Dominguez hadn't mentioned. "What kind of gambling was it?"

Dominguez looked blank. Chejung's eyebrows twitched again. "*That*," he said, "is something we should speak of in private. Thank you, Jason." He nodded in dismissal to all three. "Terry, David." We all bowed and they moved off. Chejung gestured me further into the corner, away from the remaining students.

"Do you know of Korea's national police?" he asked quietly.

"I know a little about them," I replied, more curious all the time. South Korea's National Police Agency was famous in martial arts circles for its officers all being trained in Taekwondo. The Korean system consists of one National Police Headquarters located in Seoul; it has its own chain of command independent of the Army. There are no local municipal police systems or state police departments like those in the U.S. In addition to dealing with criminal activity, the NPA performs a variety of surveillance and intelligence activities for the government.

"My cousin," said Master Chejung, "is the Deputy Commissioner General."

"You don't say," I said.

"They obtained information that Martin Idris is associated with a Russian crime syndicate in the United States. They are still pursuing that connection but assume his gambling is through the syndicate. A very dangerous business, if so."

Interesting that the guy wasn't just a misogynistic jerk but still that was less relevant than Chejung knew. Either the students hadn't come up with Habash's name or he was very good at covering his tracks. I could leave Chejung and crew to pursue their bogus trail but, given his cousin's position, there was a chance he could be of some actual help to me. If the NPA could reach that far down into the Russian mafia, they might be able to confirm whether my new nemesis had been a professional spy.

"Have you come across the name Daniel Habash?" I asked with my fingers metaphorically crossed.

"No one has mentioned that name to me," he replied.

Excellent. Time to lie a little. "I've also been looking into Idris's background," I said, "and I came across Habash's name. He may have some connection to Idris but I can't find any good information about him. He's a mysterious guy. Maybe your cousin could

184

run another background check for you."

"I will contact him. Is there anything you can tell me about this Daniel Habash?"

"I think he's originally from Lebanon," I said, "but that's about it." Shameless.

"My cousin will do what he can."

"Thanks. I'll be in touch." Not wanting to press my luck, I bowed my farewell and started to turn toward the entrance, then thought again about those surprisingly good instincts of Chejung's. I looked back at him. "You weren't by any chance a member of the NPA yourself, were you?"

His face turned even more inscrutable. "I have been in this country for many years," was his only reply—which I took to be a big yes. That's why we were whispering in the damned corner: He didn't want it known among his American students that he'd been part of South Korea's combination FBI, CIA, and National Security Agency. My bet was that he'd be even less eager for them to know *what* part he played.

I left the dojang with some confidence that at least he wouldn't make a ham-handed move to put me, my friends or former clients in further jeopardy.

CHAPTER FIFTY-FOUR

I was scanning the traffic again as I returned to the Jeep. Being a hunted man takes a lot of your attention. I got into the vehicle and scrunched down behind the steering wheel to think.

I looked at my watch. Getting close to five. This had been one hell of a day. Hard to believe it was only this morning I broke into Eleanor's office and learned of the Ecotopia audit. Then Daniel Habash's call. Mike telling me I was nominated for Libby Jance's disappearance. Now Master Chejung and his cousin the South Korean spymaster.... Crap! Time for a little R&R (retreat and re-think). I should be hearing from Malone soon. Maybe she'd learned something that would help.

And just like that my burner phone rang.

"McCall."

"And this is Malone—both of which are kind of a given, under the circumstances, don't you think?"

I ignored the snark. "Are you at the office? Have the cops shown up there yet?"

"I just got back and don't see any sign that they were here while I was gone. But then I probably wouldn't. You're not public enemy number one. Yet."

"If they think I've kidnapped or harmed Libby Jance, I could be getting close."

"The cops that count know who you are, Clint. They know some weird shit is going on and that right now they don't have a choice but to consider you a person of interest, but that's all. That's what I think."

"I hope you're right. I'd like to come out of this still having a detective agency."

"Half a detective agency."

"Right. Were you off talking to Carl Gunther?"

"I was, but all I learned was that he hadn't heard anything

about Habash. On the other hand, he's now going to be listening a lot harder."

"Hmm. I guess that's information of a sort. It means Habash is slick enough to operate without the knowledge of the guy who usually knows everything."

"Yep. Which isn't good news."

"Nope. Anything else?"

"I got a voicemail from Nora Hogan. Apparently she was afraid you wouldn't talk to her."

"What? Reiterating that she'd fired me?"

"Hiring you back, actually."

"Really? What did she say?"

"That she'd been thinking about the good times with Joe Imeson and has decided she still wants you to find out if he's okay— even if he was an unfaithful son of a bitch. Her words. Apparently we are forgiven for letting him disappear from a murder scene. She hopes I can persuade you to continue."

I had to laugh—a short, not very amused laugh. "Isn't that great. We have a current paying client after all. How nice for us. Tell you what: You call her back and let her know that we're happy to stay on the case but at the moment we have to try to expose a major financial scam and save at least three people's lives while avoiding all the cops who think I'm the bad guy and the international spymaster who's watching our every move. Tell her we'll get back to her in a day or two."

Right. I'll call her back and tell her we're on it and will report in a day or two. How about that?"

"Sure. Why not. And who knows? Maybe Habash is somehow mixed up in that, too."

"You never know. I'll give her a call. You doing okay? What are your plans?"

"I'm going to shack up with Reuben."

Silence for a moment. "Now, those are words I never thought I'd hear from you."

"It's not exactly the first place most cops would look. Mike would think of it, but he's not looking."

"Huh. What besides that?"

"I don't know yet. You?"

"I don't know yet, either."

"I do have one thing," I said. "Would you mind feeding the cats?"

I heard a snort. "Oh sure, I got plenty of free time. I'll be happy to feed your kitties. All I need is a key to your house—assuming you don't want me to grocery shop for them as well."

"I'd ask Colleen but I've got Johnny and Hap covering her and I'd just as soon she wasn't moving around town too much."

An outright laugh this time. "But it's okay for me to risk my life stopping by your house to do it."

"I suspect you can handle yourself. There's a spare key around the side taped to the bottom of the phone box."

"Hmm. Well, at least that's more original than under the mat. And now I have a plan. Feed the damned cats."

She sounded oddly light-hearted about it, so I tried to match her spirit. "I move in with a pimp and you take care of my pets. Ain't we a pair?"

Another moment. "I guess that remains to be seen." She hung up.

So much for light-hearted. As is so often the case with Devon Malone, I had not a fucking clue what she meant.

CHAPTER FIFTY-FIVE

I parked on Ash and walked quickly to Reuben's corner apartment building, scanning my surroundings as I went. I took the metal steps two at a time, glancing at my watch again. Ten after five. I hoped he was still home. There was no evening commute on a Saturday but his girls would be out manning their street corners pretty soon, in search of early weekend revelers—and he'd be out there with them or at least nearby, protecting his investment.

I knocked on the door of 2B, waited to be checked out through the peephole, and was relieved to hear the various locks being unlocked. The door opened to reveal the very image of a pimp straight from the seventies. No gym shorts and tank top this time. Reuben was dressed to go out, in full purple velveteen regalia. He did enjoy bucking the latest trends—and probably got a big kick out of all the people who didn't have the guts to comment on his taste. As for me, my eyes went wide and I snorted back a laugh.

He frowned as he looked me up and down. "You wearin' that stupid hat and a piece of shit raincoat with a zip-out fake fur lining and you laughin' at me?" He stood back and motioned for me to come in. "I gotta get you a fashion consultant, man."

I stepped inside and he closed the door behind me, the frown turning to a grin. "But then I guess you wear whatever shit you can find when you on the run."

My, news does travel fast.

I glanced around the small living room, noting that the housekeeper had yet to show up. "You got a police scanner?" I asked.

He shook his head and indicated the small portion of the fold-out couch that was not covered with fast food debris or other detritus. "No, but I got friends who do."

I sat down carefully on the leading edge of the dirty couch cushion and he settled lightly on the arm of an overstuffed chair across from me, clearly not intending the conversation to be a

191

lengthy one. "I ain't heard nothin' about that lady you interested in. She the one you supposed to have kidnapped?"

I looked at him blankly. I didn't recall saying anything about Libby Jance.

"You know," he said. "Hogan? Nora Hogan? You wanted me to listen if she had anything to do with Big's girl that got killed?" An expression that might have been concern crossed his face. "Shit, you don't remember none of this?"

Ah, of course, I had asked him to keep an ear out for that. Back in another life, what, two days ago?

"That's right," I said. "I remember. I've been a little distracted since then."

"So she don't got nothin' to do with why the police is after your ass."

"I don't think so."

"You ain't sure."

I sat back, gingerly, with a sigh. "I'm not sure about anything."

He gave me a long look. "That ain't good. Well, what you want with me today? I got business to tend to."

"I need a place to stay," I said.

He swayed back a little as a grin spread back across his scarred face. "You want to hide out from the cops in my crib? I gonna be harborin' my very own fuckin' fugitive?"

I sighed again. He was having a lot more fun with this than I was. "That's about the size of it," I said. "I need a place to sleep and nobody's going to look for me here."

He had his mouth open to respond, probably with more attempted humor, when there was a sharp series of knocks on the door. We both jumped to our feet and I saw that he had a gun in his hand, a 9mm, 17-round Glock that he must have had stuffed right behind the seat cushion of the chair he was perched on—which probably explained why he was perched rather than seated.

I drew my own weapon, not wanting to feel left out, and he motioned me to stay put. That was fine with me; I had a good line of fire at the door if I needed it. He eased over to the peephole, took a quick look, and stepped back to the side. Our eyes met and I saw that his face was relaxed.

"You sure nobody look for you here?" he asked with a slight smirk.

"Who the hell is it?"

"Big Avenue—and I bet he ain't droppin' by to see how I'm doin'."

Another series of sharp blows hit the door and I lowered the Smith and Wesson, resigned to the fact that my luck just wasn't good right now. On the other hand....

"Well," I said finally, "let him in. He might as well join the party."

CHAPTER FIFTY-SIX

The grin faded. "I got parties to go to, man, but this ain't one of them." He reached for the doorknob. "Don't take no long time with this."

We each held our weapons behind our backs as he slowly opened the door.

It was Big Avenue all right, all six-six, four hundred pounds of him scowling at the two of us. The scowl deepened as he focused on me.

"Just who I was lookin' for," he said. He held his ham-sized hands open, palms out. "I ain't gonna shoot nobody just now, so put your motherfuckin' pieces away. I know you ain't both scratchin' your ass."

I holstered my gun and Reuben stowed his in the waistband of his purple pants.

Big Avenue shoved himself—no other way to put it—through the doorway and into the room, taking a quick and wary look around before frowning down at me. Like Reuben he was attired for the evening's business, only more conservatively in gold-toned pants and matching windbreaker over a brown turtleneck—all of which actually fit. The man must shop at the local Immense and Towering Store.

Reuben had stepped back, giving me the eye. "I meant the *police* wouldn't look for me here," I said to him.

He nodded. "Right."

That got our huge visitor's attention. "What police?" He looked around again as if they might be hiding among the discarded fast food wrappers.

"Don't mind McCall," said Reuben. "He got police on his brain right now. There ain't none here." He paused, then: "What *you* doin' here?"

Big Avenue didn't respond to Reuben, but to me: "I wanna

know who was after that Imeson prick."

I suddenly found myself wondering if maybe Big Avenue had Joseph Imeson. "What makes you think somebody was after him?" I asked. "Is that what he told you?"

"Nah," he replied. "I ain't talked to him. That's what my bitch said. She said somebody took him. That somebody gonna be who killed Brandy—and that's the motherfucker I want."

"Maybe Imeson killed her," I said.

He slowly shook his very large head. "And the other guy took him 'cause he collects killers? I don't think so."

What could I say? I didn't think so, either.

Anyway, it appeared the girl who told Reuben what she witnessed had ended up confessing to Big Avenue as well—probably not willingly since he wasn't supposed to know she was at the motel making money on the side. I thought it was a bad omen he hadn't used her name; it could mean she didn't need one anymore.

"I don't know who took Imeson or why," I said finally, "but"— and here we go again—"I have an idea."

He cocked his bowling ball of a head at me. "What idea is that?"

I paused, needing a moment for my brain to catch up with my mouth; that is, decide whether I really wanted to use Big Avenue the same way I was using Master Chejung. Somehow "Chejung and Avenue" didn't have the same ring as "McCall and Malone." Nevertheless I'd just piqued his curiosity; now I had to satisfy it with something.

And I needed all the help I could get. "Ever heard of a guy named Daniel Habash?" I asked.

Both Reuben and Big Avenue shook their heads. "No," the latter said.

"He's the only suspect I have right now in Imeson's disappearance." Which was actually true. Nora Hogan seemed pretty much eliminated and I didn't have a clue who else it might be. "I don't know much about him," I went on somewhat less truthfully, "but

I've gotten hints" (hah!) "that he's looking to pick up a lot of money from a local bank or maybe some other financial institution. The money's not his own, of course, and the deal is coming down pretty soon."

Big Avenue frowned deeply, probably stumped by some of the words over two syllables. "I ain't heard about nothin' like that," he said.

Which was, unfortunately, not a big surprise. Nevertheless, it was possible that somewhere, somehow, Habash had left some spoor in the lower reaches of Portland, reaches perhaps too low for Carl Gunther's attention. A long shot, but it was all I had.

"You should check around," I said. "See if anybody's heard of Daniel Habash or if there's anything in the air about a lot of money moving. And let me know if there is."

"Why the fuck should I tell you anything?"

"From what I hear, Habash is going to be hard to find. We both want him and we're more likely to get him if we work together."

He squinted at me suspiciously. "You ain't gonna want me to kill him."

Amazing that we'd gone that fast from my hint Habash *might* be involved with Brandy Wine's death to his planned murder. Then again....

"Not before I get what I need from him. After that, I don't care." Or, at least, after that I'd see how I felt. "There is one thing, though...." I had to know, so I asked him outright: "The girl who told you about Imeson.... How bad did you hurt her? She isn't dead, is she?"

The big man shook his head. "Nah. Slapped her around a little, is all. Jus' enough to make her piss herself. She ain't gonna cheat on me again." A little shrug. "Fuckin' dead if she does. And what the fuck do you care?"

"I don't like working with someone who kills his girls."

Another shrug. "I ain't killed that one."

A little chill slithered down my spine, but his answer would have to do. Talk about the bottom of the barrel.

Reuben spoke up. "I think our visit's about done. You got somethin' to do now, Big. Why don't you go do it?"

The huge head turned slowly and deliberately in his direction. "I'll see you again," Big Avenue said so ominously that I almost laughed out loud. He probably had a big-screen high-definition TV and had seen every Arnold Schwarzenegger movie a dozen times. Having established to his own satisfaction that he wasn't leaving because he'd been told to, he left without further comment.

Reuben turned a speculative look on me as soon as we were alone again. "That was a pile of shit that you gave him, right? You ain't dumb enough to have him out tryin' to find somethin' you really need."

I eased back down onto the couch. "More like desperate enough," I said.

He perched himself again on the arm of the chair, transferring his Glock from waistband to seat cushion as he did so. Then he glanced at his watch. "I still got places to go, but I'll hang on a minute to hear about this. You got Big lookin' for somebody named Hashish and you want me to let you stay here, and meanwhile the cops is after your ass. So what *you* gonna be doin' while we out on the street?"

"It's Habash, not Hashish. And, given that you two work the night shift, I'm going to eat something"—I glanced around the littered apartment—"if you have anything to eat, that is, and get some sleep while you're on the street."

He gestured toward the kitchen area. "I got food," he said in an offended tone. "You think I eat take-out shit all the time?"

I again scanned the wrappers, boxes, and bags strewn over furniture and floor. "Yes," I replied.

He took a look himself and snorted somewhat sheepishly. "Well, I got food anyway. You can fucking help yourself."

198

CHAPTER FIFTY-SEVEN

My choices for dinner were beef stroganoff or turkey with dressing—both frozen and packaged with side dish and dessert. Better than stale chips or nothing. I risked a short call to Colleen late in the evening, to confirm that Johnny and Hap were on the job. She was a little grumpy, as always when my work has put her in possible jeopardy; it was her way of covering the fear and we both knew it. I apologized and she wondered how long she needed to worry. I had to say I didn't know but would stay in touch.

I also called Malone but her burner went to voicemail. I tried not to let that worry me and left a message that she should make sure Eleanor was planning to go through with the audit as Habash intended.

I awoke just after five a.m. Sunday morning on the couch, smelling of days-old take-out and other foodstuffs best unidentified. My host had not returned home as yet, apparently still at his night's work of seeing to it that his customers got screwed.

I knew better than to call Malone so early in the morning. I didn't want to continue sitting around the "crib" for very long, either, but I didn't yet know where to go from here.

So I decided to first go nowhere. I could meditate for twenty minutes at least. I try never to miss zazen in the morning, even when surrounded by shit and/or rotting fast food containers. What better time to empty your mind, after all? I drafted one of the ratty cushions from a pile in the corner and settled as best I could. My mind never really stopped buzzing and I missed having Maxine for company, but I counted breaths carefully and ended up feeling somewhat refreshed.

Breakfast was stale balloon bread and slightly rancid peanut butter, followed a half-hour later by Reuben's grumpy return home.

"Fuck!" he shouted as he slammed the door and glared at me.

199

"I forgot you was here." He started toward the bedroom. "I need to sleep. Got stuff to do later."

Damn, he was a worse morning person than my partner.

Speaking of Malone, I had waited long enough. As soon as Reuben had shut his bedroom door behind him, I retrieved my burner phone, went to my call history and called the only incoming number on it.

"It's early," were her first words of greeting and it was a relief to hear them.

"Other than that, how's it going?"

"Well, the cops showed up right after I talked to you—a couple of detectives named Rizzo and Demeter. I guess they know better than to let your best friend lead the chase."

"I don't know them."

"They're okay. Rizzo used to be in Missing Persons and I know him pretty well. Anyway, I lied my ass off as planned and they could find no reason not to believe me. They didn't even go through your desk drawers or confiscate your PC. Like I told you, they have to bring you in if they can but they don't have to believe you're really the guy."

"That's good to hear even though it doesn't help that much. Every cop in town still has my photo and is on the lookout."

"Yep. Maybe a wig and some thick glasses...?"

"Maybe I'll just be careful. Did you talk to Eleanor?"

"I did. She has no plans to vary from what Habash told her to do."

"Good."

"And I talked to Hogan as well, assuring her we were on the case and would be reporting developments soon. She's sending another check."

"Really? Why?"

"Because I asked for another check. No harm in a little cash flow while you're a wanted fugitive."

"Ookay. What else?"

"Not a damned thing. I've mostly been asleep otherwise since we talked last. And I haven't made plans for today yet, though they will probably include trying to get your butt out of all this trouble."

I had to smile. "Well, whatever you can do will be appreciated. I'm going to hang out here at Reuben's for a while longer and then pursue a couple of possibilities of my own."

"Going to share?"

"Well, one thing I'm going to do is check in with Master Chejung again. He's a little more interesting than we originally thought." I settled back on the couch to bring Malone up to date on what I'd learned from and about my fellow martial artist.

CHAPTER FIFTY-EIGHT

After we'd talked out everything we could think of and hung up, I literally sweated out the next two hours: pushups, sit ups, crunches, stretching, anything I could do without awakening Reuben.

I took a quick shower, pleased that the bathroom at least was reasonably clean, and tried Northwest Martial Arts a little before ten—using Reuben's phone to save my own. No answer. Damn, damn, damn. Tried again five minutes later. Five minutes after that.

Finally, at ten twenty-five, I got an answer. Hallelujah. It sounded like Chejung's senior student. What was his name? Terry Goebel.

"This is Clint McCall. Terry?"

"Yes. You wish to speak to Master Chejung?"

Double and triple hallelujah. "Yes, thank you."

"He's just arrived and is dressing. It will be a moment."

"I'll wait. No problem."

No shit no problem. I sat listening to dead air and feeling like one very fortunate private detective. Maybe my luck was turning, but I still had to focus better. I couldn't afford to rely on happenstance like this very often or I'd be *out* of luck.

Chejung came on the line. "Mr. McCall."

"Just checking to see what you've found out," I said, mentally crossing my fingers.

"Nothing new on Idris," he said. "My cousin cannot find any connection between him and this Daniel Habash you asked about."

Of course. At least he'd made the inquiries. "You're sure?" I asked, fishing without wanting to ask outright for the information they did discover.

My luck was holding because Chejung obliged. "Habash was a mid-level agent for Lebanon," he answered. "The NPA is aware of him because he operated briefly in Pyongyang, but mostly he worked in Saudi Arabia and Egypt. Apparently he was considered loose artillery and Lebanese intelligence terminated his employment."

"I think you mean a loose cannon."

"Yes, that's correct. Thank you."

Crap. I got him off track. Why did I care whether he used proper colloquial English? I needed to keep him on Habash without giving away my own interest. Stay focused, McCall. "You're certain Habash didn't get to know Idris after the termination?"

"I cannot be certain, Mr. McCall. Certainty is difficult enough in daily life, much less covert activity. There is no evidence of connection. Habash did come to the U.S. We have information that he was involved in some kind of criminal activity in California and was later behind a smuggling scheme based here in Portland with clients in the Middle East."

"What was he smuggling?"

"Electronics equipment. That's all we know. Neither operation was successful or long-lasting."

I left it at that; I didn't want to get Chejung re-focused from Idris to Habash. I also was not going to follow up on that transition from "the NPA" to "we," but I filed it away. I told him to let me know if he discovered anything more about Idris and we said good-bye.

I sat back on the couch to think over what I'd just learned. I had confirmation that Daniel Habash had been an intelligence agent—but not one of the best, apparently. I already knew from Joy Castle about the California material witness warrant in an identity theft scam. Now I hear he'd earlier been canned by Lebanese intelligence and later failed at a Portland-based smuggling operation.

Clearly he was dangerous, but just as clearly *not* omnipotent.

Better yet, there might be a warehouse or two left over from that smuggling operation. Someplace safe to put hostages, for instance. The day was looking up.

CHAPTER FIFTY-NINE

I got to my feet and headed for the bedroom. Reuben wasn't going to be happy about my interrupting his beauty sleep, but I finally had a lead. A fragile lead, I admit, but it beat sitting around looking at aging fast food wrappers.

I pounded on his door and then stepped to the side. I was quite certain Reuben had a gun next to his bed, if not in it with him, and it's never a good idea to startle an armed man after he's just gone to sleep. I didn't want to be standing in the way of an impulsive bullet.

Instead of a shot, I heard a guttural "Fuck off!" from within.

"Reuben, it's McCall. I've got to talk to you."

"Leave me the fuck alone!"

"Not until you answer a question."

A major groan was the initial reply. Then: "Goddamn it, I just got to sleep. Ask your fucking question and get the fuck away from me."

"I'm coming in."

"Oh *fuck*." Loud sigh. "Okay."

I pushed the door open. He was up on one elbow squinting in my direction. The bedclothes, sheets and a thin blanket, looked like they hadn't been washed within memory. The odor that hit me as I stepped into the room confirmed it.

A second, smaller Glock, otherwise identical to the one in the living room and very similar to Malone's, was within reach on the nightstand. Must be the brand of choice in this household.

Reuben was wearing a dingy white sleeveless undershirt. The rest was mercifully covered by the rumpled blanket. He scratched one of his scars idly. "What you want to know?"

"If I wanted to smuggle electronics gear out of Portland, where would I have my warehouse?"

He sat up straighter. "Shit, you taking this wanted fugitive thing to heart? Figure you might as well go bad?"

205

"It's just hypothetical."

He squinted a little more. "Whatever. I don't know anyways. It's not my thing. Try Big; he got his fat fingers in some of that shit."

I looked at my watch. Nearly eleven. "You got a phone number for him?"

Reuben eased himself down flat on the bed. "Nah, and I don't know where his latest crib is." He glared at a clock on his bedside table. "Later than I thought. He might be down at his club already. Gets up earlier than me. Fucker would rather eat than sleep."

Reuben had to be referring to the Evergreen, a bar out on Columbia near the airport in which Big Avenue had a financial interest. I'd found him there before.

"Even if he ain't there, they can probably tell you where he livin' now. That's the best I can do. Now fuck off." He rolled over and I let him be.

The Sunday I found outside was chilly, gray, and wet. There were no Portland patrol cars in sight as I hurried to Malone's rig, but I'd have to stay alert. I took a deep breath of the damp, clean air as I approached the Jeep.

I was just unlocking the driver's side door when my cell phone rang. No ID.

CHAPTER SIXTY

I punched the answer button and put the phone to my ear, one hand still on the Jeep's door handle and my eyes scanning the surrounding buildings. Surely Habash hadn't found me already.

"Good morning, Mr. McCall."

"It was."

"You're always so testy when we talk. Are you that way with everyone?"

"Only with murderers who kidnap my clients and frame me. Otherwise I'm a pretty mellow guy."

"You could be all wrong about me, you know."

"Knock off the games and tell me what you want," I said as I opened the door and got in the vehicle.

"But I like games."

I almost hung up on him; then a thought suddenly struck me. "Is that why you don't use an alias? You have a record in the Middle East, in California, other places—all as Daniel Habash. In your business, most people would use a variety of names."

He chuckled. "You've been doing a little checking, I see." His tone turned more harsh. "You should realize, then, that I'm not most people. I like credit for my work and it increases the challenge. No point in playing a game that's easily won."

"I had a hunch it was something like that."

"I hope your research didn't involve telling any of the authorities about me. Our game has rules, you know, and penalties for breaking those rules. Penalties like dead people."

At least he didn't know who I'd been talking to. "No law enforcement was involved," I replied. No U.S. law enforcement, anyway.

"Good. I'm sorry you didn't enjoy the comfort of your own bed last night, but I trust you slept well."

This statement was followed by a pregnant pause that I let

come to term. The son of a bitch was trying to get me to reveal where I'd been overnight—because, obviously, he didn't know. Not omniscient, either. Another point in my favor.

"Mr. McCall?"

"Is there some purpose to this call or are you just making sure I have a crappy start to my day?"

I could hear a hint of exasperation in his voice when he replied. "The audit is tomorrow morning. I need to be certain that you'll stay the course."

"I'm on course, don't worry."

"Yes, well, there may be further developments just to ensure that you do." He hung up. Sounded downright snippy there at the end—and more than a little ominous as well. What "further developments" might he have in mind? I had Colleen covered and Malone was more than capable of taking care of herself. He might have as many as three hostages (Libby Jance, her mother, and Joseph Imeson) now, but I couldn't see that harming them would further motivate me to cooperate. We'd all just have to keep watching our backs and see what, if anything, "developed."

I stashed the phone in my jacket and was reaching to turn the ignition when I caught a glimpse of an approaching patrol car in the side mirror. I quickly leaned over as if to open the glove compartment. I held that position until I could see in my peripheral vision that the car had passed and was moving off down the street; then I straightened up with a sigh of relief.

No doubt the reprieve was temporary. Patrol cars are not a rare sight on the streets of Portland, even on Sunday. My only advantage was that the cops didn't know I was driving Malone's Jeep. I started the engine and pulled away from the curb wondering if the bad guys I pursue typically feel this endangered and vulnerable. I could only hope so.

CHAPTER SIXTY-ONE

Normally the drive to the Evergreen would have been a straight shot down Sandy to 82nd, then left to Columbia Boulevard. The major arteries are where you see the most patrol cars, however, so I worked my way northeast on the side streets and didn't pull into the bar's back parking lot until a little after noon. It was already half-full. Quite a few men have "errands" to run after church, making up for excess piety I suppose, which is why a place like the Evergreen opens early seven days a week.

If one of the cars belonged to Big Avenue, he'd either gotten little sleep or was having a *very* long day. I headed for the back door. Maybe I could at least get a lead on his whereabouts here.

I stopped for a moment just inside the door to give my eyes a chance to adjust to the dimly lit interior. There were six pool tables to my left, one of them occupied by two young men dividing their attention between the balls on the table and the small stage at the other end of the bar on my right. Men ranging in age from early twenties to late sixties were scattered among the small round tables covering the area between pool playing and naked dancing. All but one of them sat alone.

That one was Big Avenue. In the far corner, near the stage, he sat with two minimally dressed women who were probably awaiting their turn to make love to the metal pole.

The bartender, a middle-aged bodybuilder-type who could double as the bouncer for the Sunday day-time crowd, looked in-quiringly at me as I started down the length of the bar. I indicated by a hand signal that I was going to Big Avenue's table and he turned his attention back to cleaning a glass.

There seems to be a universal rule about "exotic dance" sets, at least in this type of establishment: near the end of the first song you take off your top, near the end of your second song you take off your bottom, and then you dance the third and final song entirely naked. The current dancer, a lanky black woman with extremely short hair, appeared to be on her third song.

The ladies sitting on either side of the huge Samoan were white, with the same aura of premature aging as the dancer on stage, all three giving the impression of being nineteen going on forty-five. It was something about the eyes and posture. Youth was truly wasted on these young.

The big man himself appeared to be in very good spirits for someone who'd probably been awake most of the last twenty-four hours, waving at me almost jovially as I approached. There were a number of empty beer bottles arrayed in front of him and one half-full in his hand, which probably contributed to his jocularity. He didn't seem to notice that his companions looked depressed and enervated. They smiled, a little, but it didn't come near their eyes.

"It's Spenser," he drawled in a passable imitation of Avery Brooks playing Hawk on the old TV series. "Sit down, have a drink. This here's Scarlett and Crystal." He didn't indicate which was which, so I offered a general hello as I pulled over a rickety wooden chair from the nearest table. "No drink," I said as I sat down. "It's a little early for me."

"Yeah, you workin' days, huh." He chuckled and one of the women made a noise that might have been an attempted giggle. Otherwise they both ignored us, probably well trained that Big's business conversations were not their business.

"You seem to be in a good mood," I said.

"Big score last night. Big score for a Big Avenue. Stayin' up to celebrate a while."

His speech was right on the edge of being slurred. "You find out anything about Daniel Habash?" I asked without a lot of hope. The dancer on Big Avenue's left jumped up and I realized the music had stopped. Her turn to go on stage.

"I heard he was movin' some stuff, fancy electronics, shit like that, but it's history now sounds like. Couldn't connect the Imeson dude to it. Nothin' else."

Not bad. More than I expected.

"Still," I said carefully, "that might be helpful. Do you know where his operation was based?"

He frowned, apparently trying to dredge up a memory. "Nobody said. It was high volume, so maybe somewhere in Southeast." He waved the problem away and took a long swig of beer. "Don't really know."

"Southeast," in this context, would apply to Portland rather than the nation and would be the warehouse district bordered by the Willamette River and Martin Luther King Boulevard, Burnside and Madison. Big's information was fitting very nicely with what Master Chejung had told me.

"I appreciate your efforts," I said as I stood and pushed my chair back to the other table. "Let me know if you hear anything else."

He drained the beer bottle and put it down with a flourish. "You let *me* know, too," he said. "I still want that motherfucker's ass." He glanced over at his remaining companion. "Get on backstage, bitch. I need to go home and get some sleep."

She got, without even a flinch. The woman now on stage was well into her first song.

"Sleep well," I said to Big Avenue with as much sarcasm as I could muster.

It went right past him. "Thanks. You have a good day," he replied as he began unwedging himself from behind the small table.

He was still working on it as I left the bar.

CHAPTER SIXTY-TWO

The full length of Sandy Boulevard, a hundred blocks or more, stretched between me and the warehouse district of which Big Avenue spoke. It was going to take forever on the side streets, but I had a strong urge to be doing *something* that might be useful. I pointed the Jeep in that direction.

It had started to sprinkle as I left the Evergreen and the rain was coming down hard as I finally picked up 7th Avenue, then did a right on Taylor which crossed MLK into the industrial area.

I drove a grid pattern through the area, maybe two dozen square blocks. I wasn't sure what I was looking for. An abandoned warehouse that could be used to conceal hostages, I supposed. Something suspicious showing through a window. A building with "Habash Enterprises" on the front would have been nice.

Most of the properties in the area appeared to be legitimately in use. Not that that told me anything either, because surely Habash was smart enough to make his property look legitimate.

Hell, I had no information even hinting he had actually retained a warehouse—or ever had one in this area at all. I was flailing. *If* he did have at least two hostages, *if* Becky and Libby Jance were still alive, he could have them stashed anywhere—an apartment, a house, a storefront....

There were certainly a lot of warehouses to choose from, none obviously abandoned though there were some possibilities. At the south end of the district there were several square-block, multi-story boxes with covered windows and no signage at all. Under gray skies, through the heavy rain, they looked ominous—and possibly not in use.

Going the other way on 2nd, I came to a dead end, made a wide U-turn through one of the loading dock areas and headed back again. Gritting my teeth in frustration, I glanced up at the rearview mirror.

Through the sheets of rain I could see a blue and white a half-block behind me, matching my speed.

Shit! How long had he been back there? He wouldn't recognize the Jeep but he sure as hell would recognize the pattern of some-one casing the area if he'd been following me for long. It would look especially odd in this goddamned rain storm. Damn! It took all the control I had not to punch the accelerator. No doubt he had my picture even if he didn't already know me by sight. I was toast if he pulled me over.

I locked my eyes straight ahead because at that distance he might see if I kept glancing at him in the rearview. Tricky business, this; I had to be careful but not too careful. I drove straight another two blocks and he maintained distance. I couldn't tell if he was pay-ing particular attention to me or not.

I waited until I was a little closer to the next corner than I should have been (not too careful) before clicking on my left turn signal (careful). I'd see if he followed me out of the warehouse dis-trict to Grand.

I made the turn.

He made the turn as well.

I crossed MLK and was slowing for a red light at Grand when I saw his right turn signal blinking. I held my breath. He disap-peared into the rain, heading south.

I was so busy feeling relieved that I missed the light turning green until I was roused by a honk behind me. Another car had pulled up without my even noticing. I accelerated across Grand and turned left on 6th, looking to again pick my way down the side streets north of Sandy toward Reuben's place.

I was letting cops get behind me, missing other cars coming up, delaying traffic at green lights...running all kinds of unnecessary risks...and all I'd accomplished was a Sunday drive around a ware-house district that might have nothing to do with Daniel Habash or me.

It was only mid-afternoon but I needed to hide out again, at

214

least for a few hours, to see if I could come up with a plan that was worth risking my freedom for.

If I couldn't, people I cared about might soon be in even bigger trouble than they already were. Whatever Habash said now, there was a distinct possibility—in my mind at least—that he would not leave any of the unwilling participants in his scheme alive.

CHAPTER SIXTY-THREE

Devon Malone sat in a corner booth of the Home Run Sports Bar and worked at swallowing the latest bite of her hamburger. It finally went down and she looked with mild dismay at the remainder of her Sunday dinner on the platter in front of her. Half the burger and a pile of fries looked back at her incredulously. How could she have no appetite? She *never* had no appetite, especially when she hadn't snacked since lunch.

On the other hand, she thought, this had been a very unappetizing day. It had started out well enough with a visit to McCall's house to feed the cats. At least she assumed she was feeding both of them. She only saw the one named Stella.

But then, not long after an early lunch she'd prepared for herself at home, Mike Whitehall had requested that she meet him and the two other detectives, Rizzo and Demeter, at the office. This time they did take her partner's PC and most of his files. She'd had to talk fast, backed up by Mike, to keep her own.

That had been the only positive. It was clear that Whitehall was along only on the sufferance of the other two, who were actually the lead, and that they were getting downright grim in their pursuit of evidence McCall might really be the bad guy in all this.

While there, she'd found a number of calls from media types on her voicemail. Now they were after her to comment on McCall's situation, which was very depressing.

She hadn't had the heart to call Clint and tell him—about the confiscation or the media frenzy. There was enough on his plate already. Too much.

She looked down at the table top again. Ditto on her own plate. Unprecedented or not, she had no damned appetite. She inspected the bill, put down enough cash to cover it and a tip, then slipped out of the booth and headed for the front door, still mulling over what she might try next.

She couldn't follow up with Gunther; he wouldn't be in his office on a Sunday evening. Nor would anybody else. Normal people, anyway. She paused inside the front door of the restaurant. She did know some people who kept very irregular "office" hours, her old informants from when she'd been with the Portland PD. Carl Gunther was still the best bet by far but she could try going at it from the bottom up rather than top down. Better than standing here with her thumb up her ass. Who was most likely to know something and be findable on a Sunday? She looked at her watch. At five thirty on a Sunday evening.

Merritt the Ferret, of course. He'd been around longest and done the most business of everyone she knew. There was probably no one in Portland who dealt with illegal goods, selling or fencing, who hadn't dealt with the Ferret. Maybe he'd heard of somebody stocking up on high end spy technology. Hell, he could be this Habash character's retail outlet.

She slowly surveyed the crowded restaurant one more time. On top of everything else, she couldn't shake this feeling that someone was watching her. The hairs on the back of her neck kept tingling and she'd learned long ago to pay attention to her body. But she still saw no one who looked suspicious. Certainly no one who looked like Clint's description of Daniel Habash. Probably just a touch of PTSD, she decided, a flash of herself bound naked on an operating table quickly suppressed.

She stepped outside into a chilly, damp wind and hurried down the sidewalk to the Jeep she had rented to use while McCall had hers. She'd had to go to two different rental places because she wasn't going to settle for anything but another Jeep. This one was a little newer than her own, a little fancier, but she didn't like it as much.

It started right up, however, and she pulled out into the light downtown traffic, keeping her eyes on the rearview and side mirrors as she crossed the Willamette River, picked up Sandy Boulevard and headed northeast. No sign of the plain brown sedan that had been following her and McCall before.

She didn't have to go far. The Ferret actually had his own little storefront a block or so north of Sandy on 28th, almost under the Banfield Freeway. It was basically a junk store, what a Goodwill outlet might look like after it lost all its good will. As far as Malone could tell, the point was to have nothing worth buying on display. Wouldn't want legitimate browsers getting in the way of the criminals.

There was a "barbershop" next door that offered "haircuts" by scantily-clad young women. Otherwise it was basically a light industrial area with little foot traffic, no distractions for those intent on getting rid of their stolen goods or sexual frustrations.

The resident population appeared to be zero on this early Sunday evening, not even any cars parked in the Ferret's block, but Malone knew from previous contacts that he resided illegally in the back rooms of his shop and would very likely be home.

She pulled over to the curb and was out of the vehicle, closing the door, when an ancient and battered Datsun pickup came around the corner from Sandy and headed in her direction. No alarms went off; it was just an old truck. In the dusky light she could just see the driver hunched over the wheel wearing a gimme cap. Somebody on the way somewhere.

Nevertheless, she kept it in her peripheral vision as she stepped around the front of the Jeep and headed for the entrance of the Ferret's shop. It would be locked, of course, but there was a buzzer that she knew sounded in his living quarters and a security camera that actually worked which would show him who was buzzing. Since she used to pay good money for his information, back in the days when she could use the department's slush fund, he would probably answer.

She was just pushing the buzzer as the Datsun disappeared from her peripheral vision directly behind her—and failed to appear on the other side. She spun around, reaching for her weapon, and froze. The Datsun was in the middle of the street, the driver's door open, and a man in classic shooter's stance was pointing a very large handgun at her over the hood. Whoever he was, and she had a hunch, he had moved *very* quickly. He'd even removed the hat before taking his position. Maybe he wanted her to see what a handsome fellow he was with his nicely-styled black hair and middle-Eastern features.

What she wanted was to put a bullet in the middle of that smooth, handsome forehead. But she tamped down the rage that surged through her. No point being angry at him for being so capable or herself for getting caught out, for not considering that he could have switched vehicles. In fact, in the few seconds it took for her situation to really sink in on her, she felt the rage transform to a crystalline focus of concentration on the man and his weapon. The calm of resolution. As she'd already been telling herself, she was not going to be taken off the street by another crazy fuck. She would die, right here and now, before she let that happen.

Better if it was him, though.

Meanwhile he had neither moved nor spoken, though displaying a slight smile as he apparently enjoyed watching her process. "Take the weapon out slowly and drop it on the ground," he said finally in a surprisingly low and cultured voice.

She didn't move, not yet. "Daniel Habash, I presume."

He waggled his gun very slightly. "Your weapon."

He was the width of the sidewalk and the Datsun hood away from her. She didn't see a choice. She pulled her Glock from its holster using just two fingers and dropped it as instructed.

"Turn around, face the door, and clasp your hands behind your head."

Again she did as she was told, all the time coldly calculating what would be her best chance at not getting shot. Clearly if he was going to take her he had to approach her. That would be it. And if he was as good as his reputation, she'd probably be dead. Neither her calm nor her focus wavered. She had to be ready. She'd already seen how fast he could move. She listened intently for the slightest scrape of a shoe on the sidewalk. That was when she had to go for it.

Two seconds later she heard the faint sound she was waiting for and right on top of it she heard "Hey, motherfucker!" shouted from somewhere to her left. Her right foot was already coming up for a straight back kick no matter what.

She connected with a nicely-yielding surface, probably his stomach, and at that same moment her ears rang with the explosion of a shot being fired. She continued the spin to her right that the kick had begun, hoping that adrenaline would keep her going wherever she was hit, and came around to see her would-be captor half doubled over and oddly turned slightly away from her, just pulling his weapon back up in her direction. By then she had both feet down again and aimed a right kick to intercept it, catching it perfectly and sending it flying up over his head.

Then her advantage of surprise ran out and the man stepped inside her right leg that was still in the air and planted a fist square in her solar plexus. He packed a hell of a punch for an elegant-looking guy in nice slacks, shoes, and jacket. That was her last coherent thought for several seconds, her body going essentially paralytic as she tried unsuccessfully to take a breath. She barely felt the impact of his outright haymaker that caught her on the chin and bounced her head off the Ferret's door.

She somehow retained consciousness and even managed to take a shallow breath as her knees gave out and she fell forward into her attacker's arms. She felt him dragging her toward the pickup and she couldn't do much more than scream *no, no, no,* inside her head.

Then she simultaneously heard another shot, seeming from a short distance away, and sirens from even further in the distance. A shout in a language she didn't recognize burst from the man holding her up and she found herself falling helplessly onto her face on the sidewalk. She managed to raise her head in time to see him literally vault over the hood of the pickup, at which point he must have jumped into the driver's seat because the Datsun lurched away with a squeal of tires and disappeared around the nearest corner.

She got to her knees, still woozy, expecting to see one or more police cars appear but the street remained empty. The sirens, in fact, were fading away. Then she heard a familiar voice from off to her right. "A little help here, goddamn it. I've been fucking shot."

She looked over and there was Merritt the Ferret sitting up against the corner of his building with what looked like a single-shot Derringer, of all things, in his left hand and blood streaming down his right arm.

As the Ferret continued to complain, Malone made it to her feet and staggered over to him. He was a little man with sharp features and normally quick, nervous movements. That plus the rhyme made his nickname inevitable. He was currently wearing sweatpants, flip flops and a tee shirt—not the best outfit for a chilly February evening but that was probably the least of his worries at the moment. "How did you know I was in trouble?" she asked as she crouched down to inspect his wound.

"When I saw you turn around and put your hands behind your head I figured maybe you was getting arrested. I just come out to check. If I'd known I was going to have a fucking gunfight I'd have brought along a bigger gun."

"So you didn't call the cops."

"Nah, like I say, I expected to see the cops out here."

She started digging for her cell phone. "Well, I'm going to call them. You need to go to the hospital and I need to report shots fired. Did you hit him, by the way?"

The Ferret looked sourly down at the Derringer. "Are you fucking kidding me? I probably couldn't have hit the building with this fucker." He looked up at Malone. "Who was that asshole, anyway?"

"I think his name is Habash. He's an international spy trying to cover up a thirty million dollar theft."

After a pause of a few seconds, the Ferret grimaced. "Okay. I don't give a fuck who he really is, anyway."

Malone settled against the wall next to her bloody companion and dialed 911, a slight smile playing over her lips even though her head, her stomach, her ribs, and a variety of other body parts hurt like hell.

CHAPTER SIXTY-FOUR

I hunkered down again at Reuben's after my near-miss with the patrol car in the warehouse district, antsy as I've ever been in my life, kicking myself for taking stupid risks and meanwhile not coming up with any better plan. My host was not particularly pleased to see me return, so we pretty much ignored each other until he left for his night of facilitating debauchery. I was in no mood to talk, anyway—nor did I have much occasion to. Habash hadn't called again and several attempts to contact Malone had gone to voice-mail, which was a little worrisome but there wasn't much I could do about it.

I was dozing on the couch when my cell phone finally chirped. I took a bleary glance at my watch as I dug out the phone with the other hand. Quarter to ten. The incoming number was Malone's cell. Relief that it was her mixed with trepidation about the hour. She never called me this late.

I punched on the speakerphone. "What's up?"

"Sorry I haven't gotten back to you sooner. I had a little incident."

That brought me fully awake. "What kind of incident?"

"What did you say Habash looked like?"

"Shit. You saw him? Was he following you?"

"I'm assuming it was him. And, yeah, I saw him all right. Way up close and personal. He tried to take me right off the street a few hours ago."

I was on my feet and grabbing my jacket before she'd finished that last sentence. "Where are you? Downtown at the Justice Center? In the office? What?"

"Actually I'm at Providence Hospital." She must have heard me gasp. "Not for me. I was visiting a source, an old informant, when Habash attacked me and he—the informant, one Merritt the Ferret by name—got himself shot helping me out. I'm here with him."

"You're okay? Did you get Habash?" I was still moving again, in the hallway now and closing Reuben's door behind me. It would take ten or fifteen minutes to get to Providence.

"I'm a little banged up but no big deal. Habash got away, goddamn it. I couldn't even give the responders a license number, just that he was driving a ratty old green Datsun pickup."

"He was?" Already outside, nearing Malone's Jeep.

"That's how he nearly got me. The vehicle was so different from what we saw before it just didn't register in time."

In the driver's seat now. "You can tell me the rest when I get there."

"Whoa! You don't need to come down here. I'm just heading home. I need sleep a lot more than I need company."

I dropped my hand from the ignition key, gritting my teeth a little. "Are you sure? What kind of injuries *do* you have?"

"Bumps and bruises. A headache. No concussion. They checked. That's it. I'm going straight home and to bed. Talk to you again in the morning. Okay?"

Well, crap. I wasn't going to chase the woman all over town, much as I wanted to see for myself that she was all right. "Drive carefully then, and keep an eye out. If he tried once and failed, he'll probably try again."

"I know that. I'll be careful. You too. Talk to you in the morning."

She clicked off and I pounded the steering wheel a couple of times. What the fuck was Habash doing going after Malone like that? How many hostages did he think he needed? Or was he even thinking anymore?

CHAPTER SIXTY-FIVE

My own first thought upon awakening early Monday morning from a restless sleep was that the audit was today and Habash wouldn't need his current hostages *or* Eleanor when the audit was done. That chilly conclusion told me what I had to do: stake out Ecotopia Venture Capital during today's audit, to protect my friend if Habash came after her right away. And try to convince Malone to join me so I could keep an eye on her too.

I looked at my watch: five after seven. Three hours to get everything in place. I rolled off the couch and padded into the bathroom to take a quick shower—for which I would soon compensate by donning the same clothes a third day in a row. Not that stale clothing odor was high on my list of concerns this morning.

I was out of the shower and dressed, just hanging up from assuaging one of those concerns—a check with Johnny Crew to make sure he and Hap still had Colleen covered—when the cell phone sounded the arrival of a call from Malone.

I punched talk. "Good morning."

"Where are you?" was her abrupt question.

"I'm at Reuben's place for another hour or so, then heading downtown." I was already looking for a way to persuade her to join me downtown when she beat me to it.

"I think we should hook up. Where downtown?"

"Actually, I'm planning to stake out Ecotopia's building during Eleanor's audit. Never know what you might see." I pictured that block. "There's a parking garage right across the street from their main entrance, I think. It would be a good spot if we can find parking spaces."

"Sounds like a plan. The audit is scheduled for ten, right?"

"Right."

"So I'll see you there by nine-thirty." She hung up. At least something was going as I'd hoped today. But there was a lot of day left.

By quarter after nine I was downtown. The parking garage was indeed where I'd remembered it and I found a parking spot, the last one apparently, on the second level. I then walked back down the bare stairwell to the first. The stairwell continued on down to parking levels below ground, which had probably been full since before the work day started. The ground level on which I exited the stairwell was the lowest of the open parking floors, actually four or five feet below street level. With any luck, Malone would arrive in time to grab a spot on level three.

There was a metal railing along the adjoining sidewalk, I guess to keep pedestrians from accidentally falling into the parking garage. I found a spot where I could lounge with just my head and shoulders visible, mostly in shadow, and have an excellent view of the entrance to the office building across the street. By then it was nine thirty. I settled down to wait, for both Malone and Eleanor.

It was only about three minutes later that I heard steps coming down the stairwell and then Malone appeared, stopping for just a moment before she picked me out of the shadows and headed in my direction.

She was dressed as always in jeans, leather jacket and boots, her brunette hair nicely tousled and her lithe body moving.... Well, enough about her body. I had enough problems without that preoccupation.

"What are you smiling about?" she asked as she joined me to peer across the adjoining sidewalk at the building across the street.

"Nothing. Just a stray thought."

She stood for a moment looking over the street. We also had an excellent view of the shoes, socks and lower legs of passing pedestrians. "Good spot," she said finally.

"You okay?" I asked softly.

"Sure." She made a show of sniffing the air. "I'll bring you a change of clothes next time."

"Thanks."

"I fed the cats. At least the one that I saw."

"Nobody sees Maxine but me. I'm sure she was there. Thanks again."

Then we were quiet. I knew the confrontation with Habash had to have been scary as hell after her recent experience of being tortured by a serial killer, but I didn't know what else to say or do. She didn't want my sympathy. She certainly didn't want a hug, which is what I really felt like doing. I let it go.

We stood silently together for another little while and then she cocked an eye over at me. "You realize that this Habash guy is completely nuts."

"Yes, that's kind of what I'm thinking. Why are you thinking it? Something about the way he came after you?"

She shrugged. "Not only that. The whole ball of wax. Think about it. He coerces one accountant into helping him steal the money and then another into covering it for him just to buy some extra time. And it might not have been a bad plan, even if a little excessive...if it had worked. But it didn't. Now he's got at least two hostages, maybe three, assuming they're still alive, and trying to take at least one more—namely yours truly. At this point, what good is it even going to do him for Eleanor to follow through and ignore the scheduled transfer? He could have already gone anywhere to wait for the money and thirty mil is enough to hide yourself pretty well without any extra cover. But here he still is, kidnapping people and framing you and whatever the fuck. I think he's lost it, big time."

"Loose artillery," I said.

That brought a full-fledged stare. "What?"

"Just something Chejung said about how Habash had been viewed in the intelligence community. He was a loose cannon."

"Huh. Well, he's even looser now." She sighed and then said in a voice dry as dust, "Gee, it's been months since we've dealt with a deadly dangerous nutfuck. I've missed it."

"Yeah," I replied, matching her tone as best I could, "me too." We settled down to watch.

Promptly at five minutes to ten Eleanor hurried up the sidewalk on the other side of the street, dressed in a conservative gray business suit, hair pulled back, and carrying a shoulder-slung briefcase, eyes front and body erect as if executing a quick-step military march.

"She said this would take no more than two hours, probably less," I said to Malone as I watched Eleanor enter the building. "How about I go get us some coffee?"

"Sounds fine to me. This parking garage have a restroom?"

I chuckled. "I'll look around on the way out. I know the café right down the street does. We can always take the coffee back where it came from."

"Watch yourself, coming and going."

"Will do."

The parking garage did have a public restroom and I was back in about ten minutes with our coffees.

CHAPTER SIXTY-SIX

I have learned long since that it's almost impossible to make small talk with Devon Malone. So, after an hour or so of silently watching pedestrians' feet on this side of the street and building visitors on the other, I pulled out my prepaid cell phone and punched up my office voicemail. Technically my partner could have been retrieving my messages but wouldn't have done it unless I asked—which I hadn't.

It had been about a day-and-a-half since I last checked myself. I doubted the cops could trace a voicemail retrieval, but I'm not exactly a technical expert and hadn't wanted to risk it. For some reason, now that I had company it felt like it was worth the chance.

There were six messages, three of them from fellow black belts in the dojang asking if there were anything they could do to help. No doubt they'd seen media coverage of my problems and probably talked to Mike as well. I deleted their inquiries. No way would I involve amateurs in this one. It was also unlikely I'd be showing up for any workouts until I'd cleared my name.

The first of the other messages was actually from a potential client. I saved it for Malone to follow up later if I were not yet able.

The second was from Mike Whitehall. "Clint. I'm thinking it's safe to leave you a message because the detectives aren't at the point of subpoenaing your voicemail records yet, but you should erase this right away. Nothing new on Libby Jance. You're still the only suspect. If you can't find something soon, you'd better lawyer up and turn yourself in. I don't need to tell you it looks worse all the time you're a fugitive. If you *do* get wind of something, let me know. Take care—even if you are an asshole."

I deleted the recording as requested and went on to the final one, time-stamped just two hours earlier. It was Chejung's senior student Terry Goebel, sounding tense and urgent, telling me to call him at home and leaving a number.

I punched in the number, wondering if something had happened to Master Chejung now. Goebel picked it up before the first ring had completed.

"Mr. McCall?" If anything, he sounded even more keyed up than he had on the voicemail.

"Yes."

"I'm glad you called! I'm not sure I understand what's going on, but I have some information from Master Chejung, about a Daniel Habash. Very important. He told me to find you no matter what and I didn't know what to do but leave a message on your answering machine and then if you weren't checking your messages...."

"But I did check. Here I am. What's the information?"

"Master Chejung said it sounded to him like you thought Daniel Habash was connected to Martin Idris, so he dug deeper into Habash's background. I don't know how; maybe with Jason's help—you know, Jason Dominguez, our purple belt who's a computer geek. Anyway, Master Chejung told me to assure you that there is no connection, no connection at all, and that you should definitely not pursue Habash."

"Why not?"

"I wrote down what Master Chejung said." He took a deep breath and I heard papers rustling. "Habash is much more dangerous than first thought. He wasn't released by his agency because he was incompetent; he was going off on rogue missions of his own and killing interrogation subjects. The Lebanese tried to terminate him, but he killed the agents sent after him and got away. Apparently he's been taunting his former superiors ever since. He's even returned several times to attempt their assassination. Obviously a psychopath."

"Well," I said sounding as calm as I could, "that's very interesting." Ice was surging up and down my back and trickling into my knees. Malone's attention was on me now rather than the building across the street. I must have looked like the news was pretty bad. It was.

Goebel's voice went up a whole register. "I have no idea what it means. I'm just telling you what he said. It all sounds like a spy novel to me, but somehow he found all this out and wanted you to know...."

Really wanted me to know, if he shared even this much with one of his students. "Don't worry about it, Terry," I interrupted. "You're probably right that somebody helped him with an Internet search. You can find anything on the Internet nowadays. Give him my thanks and don't worry about it."

"Okay," he replied, sounding dubious. Maybe he'd figure out that Chejung was, or at least had been, a little more than a martial arts master. Not my problem.

It was impressive that Chejung or his relative had come up with the information. The Lebanese intelligence community would not be wanting to admit they'd lost a homicidal rogue agent. I was sure it took a *lot* of digging to get that kind of background. Thank you indeed, Master Chejung.

"What was that all about?" asked my partner.

"Mike Whitehall wants me to turn myself in and Master Chejung has learned that Daniel Habash lost his job as a spy because he is a murderous psychopath."

She looked at me for a long moment. "Fuck," she said and turned to surveillance of the street again. After another moment: "So, you going to turn yourself in like Mike wants? Sounds like it would be safer."

"Huh. What do you think?" The possibility that Habash would kill everyone involved in his scheme had just become a high probability. It was now even more important to do everything I could to protect Eleanor.

"I think our girl is done early," Malone said and pointed across the street. Eleanor stood in front of the building entrance, looking around as if she expected a ride to appear. An old green pickup truck stopped between us and her. Malone jumped as if she'd just been hit with a cattle prod.

"Shit! Motherfucking shit! That's Habash!"

She took off for the stairwell with me on her heels.

CHAPTER SIXTY-SEVEN

Malone turned at the top of the first flight of stairs and ran straight for her Jeep. She must have scoped out where it was parked on her way down from the third level. She jerked open the driver's side door and held out a hand toward me.

"Keys."

I didn't argue. This was the closer vehicle. It belonged to her. I'd lost Habash when I chased him. Maybe she would do better. I tossed her the keys as I ran around to the passenger side.

The Monday morning downtown traffic was heavy now, approaching the noon hour, made heavier by cars pulling around Habash's pickup. As our vehicle nosed across the sidewalk from the parking garage, Eleanor was just closing the passenger side door of the Datsun. She'd gotten in voluntarily. In fact, she must have been in contact with Habash so that he would know when she was coming out. I hoped she would have a chance to tell me why.

The pickup's tires squeaked as it jumped forward into the traffic flow and Malone floored the Jeep at the same time, cutting across the nearer lane to put us three vehicles behind Habash.

Luck was with us, as it so often seemed to be lately. Bad luck, that is. I heard the single *whup-whup* of a siren behind us. A couple of cars back in the lane Malone had just bulldozed through was a Portland blue and white, red light flashing, uniformed driver staring straight at me.

I looked around to check in front of us as I heard brakes squealing and horns blaring. Good citizens that they were, the drivers around us had all slowed or pulled aside a bit when they heard the siren. My quick-thinking partner was taking advantage and weaving through them like a slalom skier.

Habash meanwhile had turned left onto 4th heading for Burnside. The street was momentarily clear to the corner and Malone took it hard and fast, hopefully ready to hit the brake if that left us nowhere to go on the more heavily traveled street. She made the corner, ignored the brake, and barreled down the center line with me holding a death grip on the nearest handle.

Habash was in the right-hand lane less than a block ahead, currently moving at normal downtown pace as dictated by the traffic that surrounded him. Then he must have seen what Malone was doing because he accelerated toward the center line himself and actually pushed the car ahead out of the way. Oh goodie, I was thinking. We can all die together.

"Go ahead crash into the son of a bitch," I gasped at Malone. "You're going to crash anyway and at least then the cop that's after us will get him too."

She laughed, clearly having a much better time than I was. "The cop's not going to catch us in this traffic," she said. "It's just us and that asshole up ahead."

I looked back and in fact didn't see our erstwhile pursuer. Didn't hear the siren, either. "He'll be calling it in," I said.

"Let him," she said, and didn't slow down.

Neither did Habash as he swung right onto Alder—probably, I thought, going for the Morrison Bridge. If he led us onto the bridge we'd be visible from both sides of the river and easily trapped by any cars responding to the cop we'd left behind.

I saw the green pickup taking the bridge approach as we turned onto Alder. Malone finally took her foot off the accelerator and we slowed. She must have had the same realization I did about our vulnerability on the bridge.

"Shit!" She pounded the steering wheel. "Fucking shit! I'm going to lose him, too! Shit!" She cut the wheel sharp left at the next corner, extricating us from the heavy traffic flow.

"We've got to get off the street," I said. I looked around and registered exactly where we were: three blocks from the office and getting closer every second. Not the best destination at this moment. There was a large parking garage, *not* open to the street, just ahead on our right.

I tapped Malone on the arm and pointed. "Pull in there."

She acquiesced without a word, still obviously pissed, and found a spot in the corner five levels up. She pulled in as far as the Jeep would go and we just sat silently for a few minutes, trying—at least on my part—to regain some sense of equanimity and decide what the hell to do next.

CHAPTER SIXTY-EIGHT

Habash had Eleanor. If that cop downtown had recognized me, the police now had a good idea where I was. So we needed yet another vehicle and then we needed to get a move on.

Malone gave the poor steering wheel another solid shot. "It should have fucking been me."

"What do you mean?" I asked. *And stop cussing so much*, I wanted to say. *It's beginning to get on my nerves.*

She held onto the wheel and took a long, deep breath. "Habash must have been really angry that he failed to take me," she finally said.

It took a moment for me to process. "So you think that's why he took Eleanor? Because he couldn't get you? That's bullshit. Looks to me like he plans to kidnap everybody he's met in Portland before he's done."

Malone looked over at me and then back out the windshield. "Maybe so."

"No maybe. Definitely so."

My cell phone—my own, not the burner—rang at that moment and I jumped so violently that I almost hit my head on the roof of the car. I pulled it out, answering it without even looking at the display. I knew...I knew....

"Not in custody yet, Mr. McCall?" Habash's voice was silky, the texture of victory, and it made me want to throw up.

"You hurt Eleanor and I'll...."

"Do absolutely nothing because you don't know where we are and aren't in any position to find us."

"You son of a...."

"Now, now. It doesn't sound like you're driving, so you must have gone to ground somewhere. Good for you. I would hate to see law enforcement cut our little contest short. Not when you're doing so well. That was very good, covering the audit as you did—

and obviously without telling anyone else. You're abiding by the rules."

I didn't think this was the time to tell him that Malone was along and had in fact been driving. "So no one gets hurt, right?"

He paused much longer than he should have. "I'm afraid that doesn't follow. I'm moving to a new level of the game."

I held my breath. "What do you mean?"

"Are you familiar with the Wood Village exit off the main interstate going east from Portland?"

"Yes."

"There's a large construction project just north of that exit, currently abandoned because the developer has run out of money. I trust you'll be able to acquire new transportation, continue to avoid the police, and get there in a reasonable time."

"Why should I?"

"You'll find a clue there."

"What kind of clue?"

"A dead one."

He hung up.

CHAPTER SIXTY-NINE

I put the phone in my pocket, my pulse racing, and summarized what he'd said for Malone. We agreed there was no time to ask someone to meet us with new wheels. We split up and started down the rows of parked vehicles, looking for an older car (easy to hotwire), with the ticket visible on the dashboard (easy exit from garage) and unlocked (easy access).

You might think such a combination would be almost impossible to find nowadays, but there are still plenty of people who pay no attention to security. Otherwise there'd be very few successful muggings.

Older cars were in adequate supply in my row. Of those, a majority had the ticket sitting on the dash. So all I needed was one driver who didn't lock the car—and I needed him or her fast. My heart was rattling my rib cage, even as I tried not to picture Eleanor or Libby Jance lying dead in a construction site. I imagined that Malone didn't feel any better and I hoped she wouldn't blame herself now for whatever "clue" we were going to find.

I found what we were looking for first, a 1988 light blue Honda Civic. I whistled over at Malone and she joined me in its front passenger seat. I found it; I was driving it.

Offering silent apologies to the greatly inconvenienced owner, I steered our new car—which in fact was drenched in the new car smell that you get from a spray can rather than purchasing an actual new car—down to the exit and handed the ticket, along with a twenty dollar bill, to the attendant. He provided my change without ever looking at me and I pulled onto the street.

I wanted to avoid driving too near the office. It could be staked out—by the cops or whoever the hell else—and I could be recognized even though I wasn't in my own vehicle. I went west to Broadway, then north to Burnside and east across the Burnside bridge where I picked up the Banfield Freeway as instructed. I hit

241

the accelerator and pushed the Honda as fast as it could go in the mid-day metro traffic. Neither Malone nor I said a word, not even about our somewhat unpleasant olfactory environment. She was probably dreading what we would find just as much as I was.

The Wood Village exit is near the eastern edge of Portland a few miles before you enter the Columbia River Gorge on Interstate 84. Gas stations, convenience stores, access to suburbia: nothing special. Looking to my left as I approached, I could see the construction site Habash had described.

I took the exit at nearly forty miles an hour, then slowed for a stop sign. A tenth of a mile later I pulled in among stacks of building materials. There were a couple of green metal outhouses and one elderly backhoe sitting next to the parking area. If Habash was correct that the builder had run out of money, it was either very recently or there was a prospect of more funding becoming available; otherwise the temporary toilets would have moved on.

We both sat for another moment, surveying the scene, and then more or less simultaneously opened our doors to bail out into the whipping February wind. The whole construction area covered an acre or so, probably destined to be condos if the additional funding came through. The work had been stopped at an early stage, with some foundations laid and some utility trenches dug. That was about it. If there were a dead body here, especially one that was intended to be found, it shouldn't be a difficult search.

I headed left, so Malone headed right. The body was in the second trench she checked.

It wasn't Eleanor or either of the Jance women. It was a white male. I realized I'd been breathing very shallowly since we arrived and I let go a deep sigh of relief.

From the position of the body, face down and knees bent with feet skyward, he'd been forced to kneel on the edge of the trench before he was shot execution-style. He was wearing dress slacks and white shirt open at the collar, no coat. Habash, presumably, had put a bullet hole in the back of his head and left him sprawled in several inches of watery mud.

"Watch our backs," I said to Malone and then carefully climbed down for a closer look. It had been a large-caliber gun and there wasn't a lot left of the face. His wallet was still in his back pocket, however. Using my handkerchief to avoid leaving prints, I pulled it out and flipped it open to reveal the driver's license. Joseph Imeson.

I held the ID up to Malone so she could see who it was, then replaced it, slipped the wallet back into his pants, and climbed out of the trench. No doubt I was leaving other forensic evidence at the scene, but I'd already made a decision: while I didn't want to be a suspect in his death, I couldn't just leave him there in the mud either.

I wondered if Nora Hogan would be sad to hear about this. She'd been really angry at her ex-fiancé, but that probably meant she'd been really in love. Certainly she'd been conflicted about whether I should find him or not.

We walked back to the stolen Honda for shelter from the wind. As soon as we settled inside, I used my prepaid cell phone to call Mike Whitehall's direct number at the Justice Center. I glanced at my watch as I listened to it ring. Five minutes after one. He often ate lunch at his desk but this could be one of the exceptions or he could be out working a case. Was I going to be lucky this time?

"Homicide Detail. Whitehall."

So far so good. "Mike, this is Clint."

"Clint, goddamn it. You'd better be calling to give yourself up."

"Not quite, but almost. We need to meet—after you check out a crime scene."

"What crime scene?"

"Malone and I just found a dead body in a utility trench at a construction site north of the Wood Village exit off the Banfield. It's Joseph Imeson, the guy who disappeared while Johnny and Hap were tailing him."

"The suspect in that young hooker's death? And you.... You've really got to give yourself up, Clint. Now. There's way too much explaining to be done."

"Explaining first. Giving up later."

"That's not...."

"There's no other way I'm doing it, Mike. Meet us at the Jantzen Beach Center at three this afternoon." I exchanged a glance with Malone to make sure she was okay with that. "We'll be in the main food court. You should be done with the crime scene by then. I'll trust you not to set me up, but feel free to arrest me if you don't buy what I have to tell you. I'm going to give you the whole story and I'm betting you'll agree I need to stay in the wind."

He took a very deep breath and let it whistle out between his lips. "Shit," he said finally. "You are going to owe me extremely big time. You say this body is near the Wood Village exit?"

I described its location again and gave him the details about what we'd done at the scene, including the shoes we were wearing since we'd left footprints, so the forensics people could take it into account. He wasn't happy to hear I'd climbed down into the trench and looked at the wallet, though he appreciated my not leaving extra fingerprints. I hung up feeling more than fortunate. Only the best of friends would be giving me *any* benefit of the doubt by this point.

CHAPTER SEVENTY

I was stuffing the cell phone back in my pocket when I realized how unusually quiet my partner had been since we'd discovered Imeson's body. I looked over at her and thought she looked both a little pale and more than a little solemn, doing a classic thousand-yard stare out the windshield.

"You okay?" It seemed like I was asking that a lot today.

She took a moment and then, "How long would you say he's been dead?"

"Imeson? I don't know. He wasn't warm, if that's what you mean. We'll have to wait for the ME to get time of death."

She turned to me then and there was something in her eyes. It looked like grief. "You think he was killed after Habash took his shot at me?"

I couldn't help myself; she looked so vulnerable. I reached out and put my arms around her, very awkwardly given the two bucket seats, fully expecting that she would jerk back. But she didn't. She didn't exactly relax against me, either, so I kept my embrace kind of loose. Even as concerned as I was, I reveled a little in the cinnamon and leather of her. I wanted to press my lips to her hair but calculated that that would be going way too far.

"I think he was doomed to die whenever it was," I said, "and has nothing to do with you. Habash is not kidnapping or killing people because he couldn't get you. That wouldn't make any sense."

In response, she did pull back enough to give me a squinty look. "And everything else he's done makes sense?"

I couldn't help laughing. That was more like the Devon Malone I was used to. "Point taken. But blaming yourself doesn't make any *more* sense. He's the bad guy. We're the good guys."

"And you're in a lot more trouble than me. I know." It was as if she suddenly realized we were sitting in the front seat of a car with my arms around her. She pulled back further. I left the one hand on her shoulder just to see what would happen. If anything.

She didn't shake it off, but she did turn further away so she was staring out the windshield again. Still pale but now with that familiar determined expression. "Let's go somewhere."

I lifted my arm from her shoulders, a little regretfully, and started the car. "Where?"

"Anywhere but here."

"You got it," I said. Best not to be here when the police arrived, anyway.

CHAPTER SEVENTY-ONE

We had a little less than two hours to kill before the meet with Mike Whitehall. I used forty-five minutes of it slowly working my way as close as I could to Jantzen Beach on the surface streets, exchanging only desultory words with my companion along the way.

The shopping "super center" covers about a hundred acres on Hayden Island, just on the Oregon side of the state line that runs down the center of the Columbia River between Oregon and Washington; you have to access the island from the freeway. I saw only one cop car on the final leg of my journey, a block to the right as I crossed Killingsworth, but he or she either didn't see me or was not yet on the lookout for a stolen Honda Civic.

I parked on a far edge of the huge parking lot, among what were probably several hundred employee vehicles. We abandoned the Honda there and headed into the mall proper. We'd get a ride from Whitehall after I had confessed all. Either to jail or a destination of our choice. It would be up to him.

In any event, the mall was a good place for this kind of meeting, packed with hundreds of shoppers of all ages, sizes, and styles. We blended right in, pretending to window shop as we slowly worked our way to the food court.

The Jantzen Beach food court is in the center of the mall complex. In the center of the food court is a grand, old-fashioned 72-horse carousel. School had let out for the day and the area was filled with cavorting kids and their parents, everyone enjoying a fine Monday afternoon. We could have been another set of parents, as far as any observer was concerned. I wondered if Malone would agree but I didn't ask her.

We had to wander a bit before I spotted a table near the merry-go-round being cleared by a mother with two toddlers. I nudged Malone, pointed, and we swooped in before it could be captured by anyone else. The tables were the small, round pedestal style that you often see in such spaces. There were three chairs, leaving one empty for Whitehall when he arrived.

"Well," I said as I watched some kids run circles around the turning platform of brightly painted wooden horses, "at least now we know for sure that it was Habash who killed the hooker and took Imeson."

"He still has Libby Jance, her mother, and Eleanor. He must have all three."

"And they're still alive."

"And you know that how?"

"It's what I need to believe."

"Fair enough." She idly rubbed at a spot on the Formica-like table top. "So he took Imeson to distract Johnny and Hap?"

"I guess so. And framed me for sexual assault, then kidnapping, to distract us. Which is working pretty damned well."

"And then tried to take me, just to up the ante I suppose."

"He's fucking nuts. There's no other explanation. Otherwise he'd already be on a beach in Belize waiting for the thirty million to hit his account so he could spend it on spicy drinks with umbrellas and loose women with big tits."

She grimaced. "Now there's a picture."

"And here's Mike," I said as I watched him weaving among the tables, coming in our direction, and looking every inch a plain-clothes cop. I suddenly imagined Habash watching his approach from some other angle, planning the next retribution. Gave me a little shudder, but Mike was looking right at us and if Habash was looking right at him the damage had already been done. I was probably being paranoid, anyway. I hoped. For everyone's sake.

I was glancing around, looking for spy bots or God-knows-what, when Whitehall reached the table and pulled back the other chair. Jerked back the other chair, more like. He seated himself abruptly, nodding first at Malone.

"You aren't surrounded," he announced grimly to me. "You trusted me not to set you up and I haven't. But I need to know everything you two know. I had to leave Nowicki in charge of that crime scene and I want a payoff."

I realized what my uneasiness must have looked like. "It wasn't you," I said. "I was watching out for someone else."

He surveyed the nearby tables, then focused back on me. "You going to tell me who?"

"Yes," I said, and saw him relax a little.

He ran a hand through his short-cropped brown hair. "Good." He looked again at Malone. "How are you, Devon, and what are you doing abetting this fugitive?"

Her mouth twitched almost into a grin. "I'm fine and sometimes I wonder the same thing."

After that I laid it out for him, everything we knew, starting at the beginning, and particularly tried to put my using his name to get into Libby's apartment in context so it wouldn't seem such a betrayal. It took almost half-an-hour, including having to answer the occasional clarifying question and Malone chiming in now and then as well, particularly when we got to the attack on her. During that time, his expression went from attentive to dubious to outright disbelieving and back to dubious.

Given that I was describing an insane plot by a rogue Middle Eastern spy directed at myself, my friends, and at least two clients, I figured that was doing about as well as I could.

"That's quite a story," Mike finally said when he was sure I was finished.

"Yes," I agreed, "it is."

"I don't think I could repeat it to my superiors."

"No, they wouldn't believe it."

He nodded. "That's a fair assessment." Then paused, looking around the food court much as I had been earlier. "But I have to. I can start an investigation of this Habash character, though, without relating it to your case."

"Don't put out a BOLO. It would just make it more likely he kills somebody else."

"I'll be careful." Mike sat back and looked from one of us to the other appraisingly. "It sure is one complicated conspiracy this guy has cooked up."

My good friend still wasn't entirely convinced. I didn't blame him. "It is that," I replied. "From some things Eleanor said, I don't think he originally intended to do any of it except force Libby Jance's mother to transfer the money and Eleanor to give him extra time by ignoring it. But then for some reason he decided I was a threat and he needed extra leverage on Eleanor and then he went after Malone...."

I was trying not to talk too fast; I didn't want to seem desperate, especially since I was. "I'm betting the whole Imeson thing was an impulse, a crime of opportunity, when he found out that I normally use Johnny and Hap as backup. I can't believe he had that planned in advance. He must have been keeping an eye on them while they were following Imeson and just jumped in when he saw a chance; maybe he thought they'd be suspects in the hooker's death. Obviously he likes setting people up—and, after all, he was identified by his Lebanese handlers as a psychopath."

"And you got that last from Master Chejung, whose cousin is head of the South Korean spy agency."

"Yes."

Whitehall leaned back, looking at me for what seemed like a full two minutes but probably wasn't more than thirty seconds. "I think I might check out Chejung as well," he said finally, "just to be on the safe side." Then he sat forward, elbows on table, hands clasped, even more intent, looking from one of us to the other. "I'm going to believe you guys, every word of it, but there's no telling what Habash thinks his goal is now, what he thinks the point of the game is."

"That's true," I admitted.

"Whatever it is," Malone offered, "seems like he's going all in."

"Yeah," agreed Mike. He pushed back his chair. "Which means I'd better get back downtown and get those investigations started," he said as he rose to his full height. "And try to figure out how to get the pressure off you two so you can do your own thing. Otherwise, we might end up with a lot of dead people."

We both stood as well and I offered him my hand. "We appreciate anything you can do, Mike, and thanks for believing me." He shook hands with me and Malone, then started to turn away.

"By the way," I said, "could you drop us off at Reuben's? We don't have a vehicle here."

Whitehall turned back and Malone gave me a glare.

"Really?" asked Mike. "How did you get here? Don't tell me you took a cab."

"No.... Let's just say I borrowed some transportation and it's time to return it."

"Ah," he said with a crooked little smile. "If you happen to know the make, model and current location, I'll see that it gets recovered, er, returned."

"Thanks again."

Malone, meanwhile, was still glaring, arms akimbo. "Reuben's?" she grated. "You want us to hole up in a pimp's apartment? That may be your speed, but it's not mine."

"We aren't going to sleep there. But we need some time and space to plan our next moves. It's not that bad. Well, it *is* that bad but we shouldn't be there for long. Give me a break, Devon."

"Make up your minds," interjected Mike. "I need to get going."

My partner dropped her arms with a huge sigh. "Fuck. Okay. Reuben's it is—but not for long."

We were making our way among the crowded tables toward the exit when I realized that a cell phone was ringing. I could barely hear it under the carousel music and children's cries of excitement. I stopped Mike with a touch on his arm and checked my pockets. It was my own phone. Showing No ID.

Shit.

My eyes were darting over the surrounding shoppers, my heart accelerating wildly, even as I answered the call. Could he know I'm here with Whitehall? What would he do if he thought I'd gone to the police? Shit. Shit. Shit.

"Mr. McCall," came the dreaded voice, "What is that I hear in the background? Music? Children playing? This is no time for a party. You need to concentrate on *my* game. To help you along, there's another clue. Just down the road from the first one, actually. Hope it won't be too long a drive to get back there. I probably should have told you about it at the same time as the first, but that wouldn't have been any fun."

"What...." I could barely get any words out, so much bile was trying to come up in my throat. "What kind of clue is it this time?" I rasped.

"The same kind, of course. You'd better start making some progress before I run out of clues. The game will become really difficult then."

CHAPTER SEVENTY-TWO

"Where exactly is the body?" I asked with even more difficulty, at the same time making eye contact with Malone.

"About a quarter mile beyond the construction project where you found clue number one, there's a road going east-west, paralleling the freeway. Turn left there. You'll find clue number two at the second intersection, hidden in some brush. You should take something for that throat, Mr. McCall. You aren't sounding too good."

"Fuck you."

He laughed, a short, obscene bark, and hung up.

"You are *kidding* me," Mike said as I put the phone away. "Another one? Who?"

I swallowed a couple of times to try to get my voice back. "I don't know who," I said finally. "Let's go. It's near the other crime scene, he said, just down the road."

Malone stopped me with a hand on my arm before we could take a step, her face even more pale than it had been earlier. "Eleanor?" she asked.

I shook my head. "I don't think so. It sounds like this body must have been put in place before he got Eleanor. Could be Libby, her mother, maybe even someone we don't know about." Not that any of those prospects made me feel any better.

"I'll phone it in," Whitehall said, "and drop you guys at Reuben's like you wanted. You can't come out to the scene with me, for Christ's sake. Somebody would recognize you."

I wanted to argue. Hell, I wanted to scream right there in the middle of all the parents and kids with the cheery carousel music blasting away. Instead I just muttered "I'll give you Reuben's number on the way" as we walked together toward the parking lot.

The pale February daylight was already fading as Mike steered his unmarked car back across town. Temperatures were falling with the light and the car heater was blowing hard to keep out the cold.

It was miles out of his way to take us to Reuben's, but he had the crime scene unit alerted to look for the new body and they'd preserve all the evidence until he got there.

Meanwhile, the further we drove from the scene the more my anger grew. Whoever it was, even if a stranger for God knows what reason, I had to take my own life back. I'd been running and hiding and caught off guard about all I could stand. And now Devon Malone was out here with me. We'd go to ground this one last time, but that was *it*.

At least it sounded like Habash didn't know where I was. He'd been surprised to hear the kids and carousel. Which meant he also didn't know who I was with. Plus, if this second body were a reprisal for breaking the rules I'm certain he would have let me know. Nothing the bastard liked better than taunting. Well...maybe torture and killing.

We pulled up in front of Reuben's apartment building just as he was coming down the outside metal staircase.

He was wearing an ankle-length fur coat and Russian-style fur hat, looking like he was heading out to check the girls patrolling Red Square rather than Burnside Avenue. He hit the pavement and registered the unmarked car, pausing with a half-turn as if he might bolt back up the steps. Then he took another look and recognized us. He came stomping over to the car as Whitehall rolled down my passenger side window.

Reuben leaned over and glared past me at Mike. "Hey," he blustered, "I didn't give him no fuckin' permission to go through my stuff! Whatever he says he found, it ain't mine. Somebody planted it! Fuckin' illegal search!"

Any other time I would have been amused. "Calm down, Reuben," I said to him. "We're not here to hassle you. Mike just gave me and Devon a ride."

He finally registered Malone in the back seat, looked at me, looked at Whitehall. "Oh, okay. How you doin', Lieutenant?"

"I'm doing great, Keys. And you?"

"Never better."

"I've got to go," Mike said to me. My partner and I exited the car after one more reassurance I'd get a call as soon as the body was identified. Whitehall drove off, lights and siren going by the time he reached the corner, leaving the three of us standing on the sidewalk. It was nearly full dark and the wind was making me wish I had Reuben's outfit. At least it wasn't raining.

"He's in a big fuckin' hurry," he said. "Thought you was hidin' from the cops."

"I am," I replied, "but Mike's being more of a friend than a cop right now." I pulled my thin jacket closer. "We need to wait inside for a phone call and we need a car, Reuben. Eleanor's in really big trouble now, kidnapped, her life in danger, and we've got to do something about it."

His eyes went wide. "Fuck me! I hope she ain't dead." He pulled a key ring from one of his pockets and stepped under a nearby streetlight to quickly work one of the keys loose. "Here," he said, handing it to me, "a spare key to my place. Go on in and warm up. I'll bring back a car for you soon as I get the girls goin'."

I took the key. "Hurry," I said.

"Do the best I can. I don't show the ladies got some protection, *they* could end up dead. You know how it is."

"I know. We'll be waiting."

He turned, then glanced back. "And don't go through my fuckin' stuff."

CHAPTER SEVENTY-THREE

I opened Reuben's door and stood aside to let Malone enter first. She made it about one foot into the space and stopped. "Yuck," she said.

"I told you, we won't be here long." I gave her a gentle shove, followed her in, and closed the door behind us. "Nobody is going to look for us here."

She continued to survey her surroundings with a deep frown. "Somebody from the Centers for Disease Control might show up any minute."

I walked over to the couch, cleared a space, and sat down. "We'll just tell them to come back when Patient Zero is at home. It shouldn't be more than twenty minutes before we hear from Mike, not with the way he was booking when he left. I have an idea about what to do then."

"Which is?"

"Let's wait and see what Mike says. Find a place to sit."

She leaned back against the wall next to the door. "There *are* no places to sit. I'll stand."

A very long twenty-five minutes later the phone rang. Whitehall's cell number. I held my breath as I picked it up. "Who is it?"

"Not absolutely sure, but it isn't Libby Jance. Caucasian female, late forties, early fifties. No ID on the body, but generally matching the description of Libby's mother. Very likely, it's Becky Jance."

"Execution style, like Imeson?"

"Just like. Preliminary is that it had to be within minutes, one way or the other."

"Anything else? Any hints about Libby or Eleanor?"

"Not yet, but we just started processing the damned scene."

Sigh. "Okay. Keep me posted," I said.

"I'll do that—and meanwhile you stay put."

"Not a chance," I said. "Reuben's getting us another car and then we're out of here."

"Goddamn it, Clint...."

I hung up on him.

Malone straightened up from the wall in the meantime. "So...not Libby or Eleanor. Libby's mom?"

"Probably."

"So that's one you were wrong about."

"Yeah."

"What now?"

I briefly considered trying to hotwire one of the vehicles parked along the street outside, but I knew Reuben would be back soon. He only needed a drive-by of each of his girls to establish that he was out there keeping an eye on them.

"We wait for Reuben to bring us a car. Should be just another few minutes."

Now she was looking pissed. "You're not really answering my question. Why are you being an asshole? You said you had an idea what to do after we heard from Whitehall. We've heard from Whitehall. So what's the fucking plan?"

"We go looking for Habash—and I have an idea where he might be."

CHAPTER SEVENTY-FOUR

It was mid-evening as we sat in our pimp-supplied dark gray 2001 Lincoln Continental at the corner of 2nd and Salmon under a burned-out streetlight. Back in the warehouse district again, surrounded by the oldest and apparently least-used of the buildings. The Lincoln was facing toward MLK, where we could observe several intersections—a couple of which were even illuminated. Certainly we'd see if any other headlights came by. I had a strong hunch there wouldn't be much casual traffic through here after dark; as I'd worked my way through the area to this spot, I'd seen no other moving vehicles and no pedestrians.

"I'll admit this is a shot in the dark, literally," I said to Malone. She leaned away from me against the passenger side door, partially lost in shadow even at such a short distance. "Big Avenue heard Habash was based in the warehouse district and Habash was heading in that general direction across the Morrison Bridge when we last saw him." I looked out at the empty streets. "Of course, he could also have been going almost anywhere else on the planet. A shot in the dark, like I said."

Then we sat and watched.

I called Mike Whitehall a little after seven-thirty and found him still at the Justice Center. He confirmed that the latest body was Becky Jance and inquired where we were. I told him, explaining my reasons why, and he said he'd come down to meet us in an hour or so. I didn't know which he had more in mind, backing up our surveillance or keeping us under surveillance, but I welcomed his offer in either event. It would increase the odds at least a little bit that Habash would be spotted if he entered the warehouse district this evening.

Over the next forty-five minutes three vehicles crossed intersections that I could see. One of them was a police cruiser, but it gave no indication it was doing more than passing by. I even caught a glimpse of a pedestrian a couple of blocks down, shuffling through a pool of light from one of the security lamps, probably a homeless guy with nowhere better to be.

Then Malone nudged me at the same time I saw a familiar-looking sedan nosing slowly across the intersection a block straight ahead of us. Apparently he'd ditched the old truck in favor of his original ride.

"Bing-fucking-o," she said.

I couldn't be positive it was Habash's vehicle, but it looked likely enough to get us out into the chilly night air the second it passed from sight behind the warehouse covering that block.

We each drew our guns, crossed the street, and trotted quietly but quickly down the side of the building behind which the sedan had disappeared. We pulled up and I peeked around the corner—just in time to see the taillights of the now-parked sedan go out. It was on our side of the street, about half-way down the block. My heart was racing. I couldn't believe our luck.

"He's parked," I whispered over my shoulder to Malone. "It has to be Habash."

"Can you see him?"

"No. Still in the car. But it has to be him."

"Anybody ever accuse you of wishful thinking?"

"Shut up."

She punched me and edged around to where she could also see the sedan, but said nothing more. There was no further motion for several minutes and I began to wonder if the driver had been spooked by the pounding in my chest. It sounded loud enough to me. We huddled together flat against the bricks, exposing ourselves just enough to keep tabs.

Then the driver's side door opened and Habash got out. I heard Malone's sharp intake of breath. He closed the door softly, glanced up and down the street, and rounded the front end to cross the sidewalk and enter the very warehouse we were pressed against. He hadn't seen us.

I held up three fingers in front of Malone's face and bent them one by one. On three, we edged together along the wall toward the entrance he'd used, guns at the ready.

The door was wooden with flaking paint and an old-fashioned doorknob and lock just like on my own house. This was a commercial building that had not been refurbished, remodeled—nor, it appeared, even occupied—for quite a few years.

Malone leaned in close, giving me a good dose of her familiar essence, and whispered, "What if he already knows we're here?"

It did give me a moment's pause. The son of a bitch could still have a tracker on us somehow. Still.... "You want to back off?" I whispered back.

A quick shake of the head. "Fuck it. Let's go."

I tried the knob and it turned; Habash had left the door unlocked. *That* set off some alarm bells—in my head, not on the physical premises—and I pulled my hand back for a moment. True, the area was deserted and almost certainly he couldn't have guessed we'd be onto this location...but it didn't feel right that he'd leave such ready access at his back. Nevertheless, it *was* unlocked and I was going to take advantage of that fact.

With a glance at Malone to make sure she was ready, I grabbed the knob again, eased the door open, stepped inside. Malone was right on my heels and closed it softly behind us. Then we stood motionless, listening for any sound and waiting for our eyes to adjust.

After a few moments, I could make out that we were standing on the edge of a cavernous space with windows high up on all four walls. Just enough street light filtered through the dirt on the windows to permit me to see that the area was mostly empty. There were a couple of small office spaces to our right, both visible through large openings that had probably once contained glass. No motion there, nor anywhere else in sight. Otherwise there were just a few forlorn pallets stacked in the middle of the floor, probably damaged and useless. The place smelled of rotting wood and…something else. Tobacco. Cigarettes or cigars had been stored here—for a very long time, given that the smell was still discernible after so many years' abandonment.

Near the offices was a wooden staircase climbing the north wall, leading to the upper floors. My recollection was that the building had seven or eight stories. The present space took care of the first two stories. Above that would be more office spaces or smaller storage rooms. I pointed upward. "You ready for this?" I asked Malone.

"Born ready," she said.

I had to smile. "You are *such* a bad ass."

A little shove. "So move yours."

I moved mine.

The stairs looked firm enough in the dim light. I dug my key chain out of my pocket. On it was a fob Colleen had given me, a tiny but intense flashlight "for sneaking around in the dark," as she had put it. And that was precisely what we were about to do. Thanks, kiddo.

The narrow bright beam revealed no obvious weakness in the steps, so I started carefully upward with Malone a couple of steps back. The staircase, it turned out, was remarkably sturdy for its age. There weren't even any creaks as we climbed the two floors and left the dirty light of the high windows behind. I held my keys tightly to prevent them from jangling.

These stairs ended at the first regular floor. We stepped into a corridor running north-south with open doors on either side. A quick recon revealed all the rooms to be empty. There was a different staircase, this one located midway down the corridor and zigzagging on up.

We had to go even more slowly on this second set of stairs, both because it was impossible to see what was coming just around the next turn and also because it was not so sturdy; every other step had some kind of complaint to make. We could minimize the noise by treading very lightly, but couldn't eliminate it. The situation was getting more iffy all the time. I began to wonder if Whitehall might be showing up soon. Not that I'd exactly left a note telling him where we were.

We found an identical corridor and empty rooms with open doors on the fourth floor. Ditto the fifth.

Just starting upward from the fifth floor, I suddenly paused, uneasy.

"What?" whispered Malone.

"Not sure," I replied softly.

I listened. Nothing. She looked behind us, turned back to me with a shrug. Nothing. I raised my eyes to the landing midway to the sixth floor...and they kept going up to a tiny blinking red light that stood out very clearly against the ceiling in a dark corner. I pointed. So there had been some remodeling of the warehouse, after all: a surveillance camera had been installed.

"Oh, crap," muttered my partner. "If he didn't know before, he knows now."

That was why Habash had left the front door open; he *wanted* to know if anyone were following him. And here we stood on a rickety staircase with no cover.

CHAPTER SEVENTY-FIVE

I thought I heard a faint thump from somewhere above and I clicked off my little flashlight. There was another thump, slightly louder. It sounded like the sounds were coming from the next floor, not too far from the stairwell. Malone and I both ducked lower and remained in a crouch as we inched upward in total darkness now. It was a damned good instinct: about thirty seconds later came the flash and *crack* of a medium-caliber handgun. Wood splintered from the wall apparently quite close to my head. The shot had come from the landing above and we both snapped off shots in return, Malone's no doubt just as blind as mine.

"Shit," muttered Malone. "That was close. You think he's got night vision up there?"

"I hope not," I said, and charged up the stairs. There was no point in trying to go back. We were exposed either way, so might as well make a fight of it. There'd been no time to consult, but apparently Malone agreed because I heard her steps close behind mine.

"I'm right!" I yelled and dived forward onto the sixth floor landing on my left shoulder so that my gun was covering us to the right though I couldn't see a damned thing down what I assumed was another corridor just like the floors below. Malone landed with her back to my back a second later. I heard another shot, not close enough to be Malone firing, on her side. I rolled over and we both scrambled up to press against the wall.

"You hit?" I whispered urgently.

"Missed by a mile," she said quietly. "From the flash it looked like he was in a doorway near the end of the corridor. Twenty or thirty feet."

At the moment, of course, there was absolutely nothing to see in that direction—and I wasn't about to shine my flashlight down there. "We've got to move," I said softly. "You stay low and I'll go high, firing as we go. If we don't hit him maybe we'll at least flush him out or pin him in a room. Either would do."

"That's your plan? You stand up and I crawl while we're both laying down fire moving forward? You think this is a war movie or something? How about we just wait until we hear a noise and then shoot at it?"

"It's dark. If we're stationary when he sees the muzzle flashes, he's got us for sure."

"Huh," she grunted. "What the fuck. Okay, on three."

She was on two and I was braced to rise up shooting when Mike Whitehall's voice came booming from below: "Police! McCall, are you up there?" I looked down the length of my body and could see the glow of lights coming up the stairs.

Right on top of his shout I heard sirens in the distance. Of course, he would have heard the gunfire and called it in. Talk about a timely arrival.

"Hang on!" I yelled back. And quietly to Malone: "Let's move back into the stairwell before Whitehall gets here and lights us up for Habash."

"Much better plan," she agreed and we edged backward together until we were off the landing once again. By then Whitehall and at least one other cop were on the landing below us.

They both shined flashlights up at us, as I'd expected. "You guys okay?" Mike asked softly.

"We're fine," I replied. "Habash is up above us somewhere, in the corridor to the left of the next landing last time we saw a muzzle flash."

I'd barely finished the sentence when I thought I heard faint running footsteps in that direction. "Sounds like he's on the move," I said.

Whitehall and the other cop came up the stairs far enough to join us. The footsteps on the floor above meanwhile seemed to be fading into the distance. Where the hell could he be going?

I pushed myself to my feet with one hand and took a giant stride up to the top step, catapulting my body across the corridor to the opposite wall as I snapped a shot off down the hall in the direction we'd last seen evidence of Habash. Nothing to see. No return fire. No further sound of footsteps.

I motioned the others on up. Malone got there first and, as was her habit when pissed, punched me in the shoulder. "Are you fucking crazy?"

"It sounded like he was getting away," I said. "And ouch, that hurt."

"His blowing your brains out would have hurt more. Though maybe it wouldn't have been a big loss."

Whitehall had joined us by then. "If you two can stop bickering long enough, I'd like to go get the bad guy. What do you think?"

"I think he was in the room near the end, on the left," Malone replied. "That's where I saw the muzzle flash. But I gather he's moved on since then."

"Wherever he went, we've got his ass," Mike replied grimly. "The building ought to be surrounded by now and we should have some help in here in a minute." I realized the sirens had stopped outside meanwhile and no doubt he was correct.

"Habash may want to go down shooting," I cautioned. "The fucker's about as crazy as they come."

"I hear you."

All four of us moved cautiously down the hallway, lights and eyes on that doorway.

As on the other floors, all the doorways in the corridor were open. We glanced into each as we passed and paused just before the one Malone thought Habash had been standing in when he fired. I was closest and pointed both my penlight and my gun around the doorframe, then followed up with my head. The room appeared to be empty but, as I took a slow step forward, I heard a moan from within.

About that time more cops appeared at the top of the stairwell. Whitehall told them to stay put for a moment and moved up beside me. We stepped fully into the room with Malone close on our heels.

There against the right-hand wall was Habash's monitoring equipment, the single screen currently black. Apparently it was set for infra-red since he had seen us. It wasn't much of a set up for such a high-tech guy, it was all he'd needed. And, in the far corner on my right, previously blocked from sight by the door standing open, Libby Jance was lying on the filthy wooden floor, jerking feebly. She was bound hand and foot with duct tape and had another strip of the tape across her mouth.

As I moved to her side, I surveyed the room one more time: no sign of Eleanor or, as expected, Habash. I heard Mike telling the other cops to cover the upper floors thoroughly and carefully.

Libby's eyelids fluttered and then she focused on me, moaning again loudly. I kneeled down beside her and grasped one end of the tape covering her mouth. "This is going to sting," I said, and pulled it off.

She didn't seem to feel it. "Mr. McCall, I'm so sorry, so sorry. I...."

"You've got nothing to apologize for," I interrupted. "Who's been with you here today? Anyone besides Habash?"

She apparently couldn't focus on what I was saying and kept chattering. "...so sorry. He said your name and he was looking at the screen and I knew you must be on the stairs. I hit the floor with my feet, to warn you. He hit me...." She took a breath. "My mother was here, but he took her away. Do you know where my mother is?"

Malone kneeled down with us at that moment and I made eye contact with her. Neither of us wanted to answer the girl's question. I got out a pocket knife and started cutting through the duct tape. "Libby, this is very important: was there anybody else, another woman, here besides your mother?"

"Yes." She was snuffling now. "Just for a few minutes. Daniel brought her in and then took her away again. A blond woman. A few hours ago. I don't know. I lost track of time." She began sobbing openly. "Where is Mom?" she wailed.

I locked eyes with Malone again and it was as if we both took a deep breath at the same time. At least we could do it together.

And then we had to get Habash to tell us where Eleanor was.

CHAPTER SEVENTY-SIX

But it wasn't to be. Not yet.

I'd never been in Homicide Detail in the middle of the night. Though the fluorescent lighting lent a hard edge to all the colorful art and mementos the detectives use to distance themselves from murder, the room still seemed almost cheery against the dark, driving rain beyond the windows of the Justice Center's thirteenth floor.

Malone and I stood together looking out at the lights of downtown, those few that were still lit at one a.m. on a Tuesday morning and visible through the downpour. My body trembled with a combination of exhaustion and stress from the confrontation with Habash in the warehouse; at the same time I felt the easing of great weight because I hadn't been arrested upon my arrival here. I wasn't free and clear yet, not by any stretch, but I wasn't in one of the cells downstairs either.

Habash, on the other hand, had gotten away clean. There was an old dumbwaiter in the building and he had its cables rigged so that he could drop safely to the first floor. Somehow he'd apparently passed right through the cops outside—probably because there had not been nearly sufficient response to create a tight cordon around the building. He could be out there in the night, looking back up at us right now, but probably—hopefully—he'd gone to wherever he was keeping Eleanor. I had to believe he was *keeping* her.

I glanced back over my shoulder at the interview room where Libby Jance had been for the last forty minutes or so. The paramedics had cleared her for interrogation; she'd been in remarkably good shape, physically at least, considering she'd been held captive for three days. Hungry and a little dehydrated, bruised from where he'd hit her after she tried to warn me, but that was it. Emotionally, the girl was not so good after we broke the news of her

271

mother's death. I couldn't imagine that she was being very helpful to her interviewers but Mike was right that there wasn't time to let her rest.

Malone also looked back, then shifted away from the window. "I need to sit down," she said. "It's been a long night already."

"That it has," I agreed.

We wandered over to Whitehall's office where I sat behind his desk and she took one of the visitor chairs. Garfield the cartoon cat kept Mike's PC screen safe, mostly snoozing but occasionally waking up to eat a huge meal of lasagna and donuts. I watched the software cycle.

"You know," I said to Malone, "crazy or not, there is a kind of pattern here."

Eyebrows up a bit. "Yeah?"

"Think about the sequence of victims: First he takes Becky Jance—who, at the time anyway, had nothing to do with us. Then Imeson, the surveillance subject in one of our minor cases. Then Libby, who is by that time a client of ours. Then Eleanor, a friend and essentially part of our agency. Whether he started out to do it or not, he's working his way closer and closer to us."

"He tried to take me before he took Eleanor. That would throw your pattern off."

"Maybe not. Not if I'm the focus rather than us. Eleanor said she never mentioned you to him. He might have thought she was closer to me than you are."

"So he's working his way to you. Why?"

I leaned back and looked up at the ceiling. "That is the stumper, all right." Sat forward again. "Maybe because he thought it was my fault he couldn't seduce Eleanor, that she had a thing for me already? He viewed me as some kind of romantic rival or at least blamed me for his original plan being unworkable?"

Malone grunted. "That could be true, about Eleanor having a thing."

I waved that aside. "Nah. I'm old enough to be her father."

"You're old enough to be *my* father. Almost."

I had to pause and frown at that one. "I don't see the relevance."

"Let's move on."

Okay, another one of those Devon Malone things. I moved on. "Anyway, given that the son of a bitch is totally psychotic, it could work as an explanation. He's become obsessed with me for whatever reason. "So maybe now he'll try to take me—which would be good, because that gives me the best shot at taking him."

Malone did her own survey of the ceiling as she thought that over. "Don't forget family," she said.

"Pardon?"

She lowered her eyes to me. "Family. If he's working his way closer and closer to you, Colleen might come first."

That sent a chill down my back and I determined to check in again with Johnny and Hap first thing in the morning to make sure they were on their toes. Or, given their ages, at least on functional knees.

The door of the interview room opened and Whitehall emerged, followed by the other detectives with Libby Jance. She looked pale and very tired. Mike came in our direction while the others headed out of the Detective Division in a tight group.

I started to get up from his chair as he approached, but he motioned me to stay put and dropped into the other one of his own visitor's chairs.

"You done?" I asked.

He let go a deep sigh and slumped further in the seat. "I'm done. She's done. We're all done." He squinted at his watch. "What the hell time is it?"

I looked at my own watch. "One twenty-two."

"Shit."

"Libby going to remain in custody?"

He nodded. "Protective. The scumbag might go for her again."

"Good plan," I said. "We were just talking about how he's got his game going, his pattern set, and maybe he'll come after me next." I nodded acknowledgement at Malone. "If not a member of my family."

Mike looked at me speculatively. "That could be. You talking about Colleen? Shit, maybe I should get somebody covering her."

"Johnny and Hap are taking care of that part of it." I paused. "Am I going to be free to do my part?"

That brought a wan smile. "Yeah, the girl knew enough to get you off the hook. Apparently our former spy likes to brag, which could be one of the reasons he's 'former.' The BOLO has been cancelled and you are officially no longer a fugitive. Congratulations."

"What did he tell her?" asked Malone.

"Well, he hates Clint's sorry ass, that's for sure. He admitted killing Eleanor's boyfriend, so she's off the hook too...for what that's worth. Libby said he mentioned grabbing someone else on impulse, as a further distraction. That would have to be Imeson. It sounds like he believes the money transfer is safely set but he's hanging around just to make sure and to stick it to Clint here. That's the impression Libby got, anyway. The computer experts are working with the banks to make it look like the money transfer goes through on schedule; it's scheduled for first thing in the morning, I understand. We want to keep Eleanor alive if we can."

"We sure as hell do. Anyway, all that's along the same lines as what we were speculating," I said. "Talk about great karma." I stood up and Malone followed my lead. "Well, if I *can* go home, I will go home. My bed has been missing me."

274

CHAPTER SEVENTY-SEVEN

Maxine and Stella were also happy to see me and even happier to see some fresh food and water in their bowls. That took just about the last of my energy. I barely managed to get my clothes off before collapsing on the bed.

I awoke at eight-thirty, Maxine snugged on top of my legs and Stella against my pillow, my head filled with visions of comfortable zazen in my own spot, a shower, clean clothes, and then breakfast at the Pen and Pastry. Sometime during the night I'd decided it was time to check on my daughter in person and that's likely where she would be this time of morning. Since it was just around the corner and I was famished anyway, it was worth a shot.

Before heading out I called Malone and arranged to meet her there. I would need a ride down to the office whether I caught Colleen at breakfast or not. At least I could drive my own vehicle again when next I needed to go somewhere.

The morning was chilly and gray as I approached the door of the café. Eleanor was still out there, still in desperate trouble if not dead. I hated to indulge myself in any support or sustenance, even another moment of freedom, before I attempted to do something about it. But I'd needed the night's rest and I needed some food and there were other people besides Eleanor who needed at least a few minutes of my time. I opened the door and breathed in the smell of fresh hot pastry.

The dining area was about half full, the late breakfast crowd, and I had only begun to scan the tables when I heard my daughter's voice.

"Dad!"

I saw Colleen standing and waving by one of the back tables. Johnny and Hap were sitting there with her. They all broke into grins as they saw me start across the room; my daughter came to meet me with a big hug. By the time she'd let me go and was escorting me to the table, Malone was coming in the front door behind us.

I took a seat with Colleen on my right, Johnny and Hap to my left, and Malone pulled a chair from another table to squeeze in directly across from me. The small round tables in the Pen and Pastry were really intended for no more than four people. And it didn't help that Hap took up the space of two.

I surveyed our tightly packed group. Colleen looked as if she were waiting for a shoe to drop. Malone looked sleepy. Johnny and Hap's grins had faded and they looked as if they knew some of the news already.

Johnny immediately confirmed my suspicion. "We heard about Joe Imeson," he said.

"We shouldn't have lost him," Hap added mournfully.

"Who's Joe Imeson?" asked Colleen. Obviously the two old detectives had not shared their latest news.

"The guy we lost when that girl got killed at the motel," replied Johnny. He slammed his fist on the table. "He's dead because we fucked up. Excuse my fucking language."

"Oh...okay," she said, clearly a little taken aback by the fierceness of his response.

"It wasn't your fault," I said firmly to the two men. "Put it behind you. We've got even bigger problems than that."

"Uh oh," muttered Hap.

No reason to build up to it. "Libby's mother is dead and Eleanor is missing," I said.

The owner of the café, Veronica Fortune by name, chose that moment to be our waitress and say hello right on top of several gasps, an expletive from guess who, and a squeaky "oh my God" from my daughter.

"Wow!" Veronica said instead of continuing as she'd probably intended. "Do I want to know what I just interrupted?"

I looked up at her and shook my head with a slight smile. "No. You do not."

She was dressed in a loose-fitting caftan that nevertheless hinted at voluptuousness beneath, her long red hair hanging down her back and glowing a little, her arms bedecked with gold bands. The Portland gypsy style today. I was not the only male in the room looking at her. She is remarkably striking for a woman in her middle forties or any age for that matter. We'd known each other quite a while, Veronica and I. She had been my first client, back in the days when she was a working girl on the street rather than a famous restaurateur and author. Long story.

She took a breath. "Okay, then." Whipped out an order pad. "What can I get you guys?"

I ordered a full breakfast and everybody else settled for coffee.

As soon as Veronica had departed, Colleen picked up from where we'd been. "Do you think Eleanor...?"

I cut her off before she could even get there. "I don't think Eleanor is dead, no. But Habash has her." I surveyed my daughter and the two old detectives. "And you guys are going to have to watch your backs. He seems to be working his way closer to me and there's no telling who he might go after next."

"You can count on us," Johnny said.

"And damned if I'm not getting used to it," Colleen announced as she sort of bounced back in her chair. It was, unfortunately, not the first time she'd been in potential jeopardy because a bad guy was pissed at me. Maybe she was getting used to it. I certainly wasn't.

"I heard from Carl Gunther," Malone interjected, referring to the city's dapper crime boss.

"And?"

"He thinks we should check out the warehouse district," she reported dryly.

I felt my shoulders droop. "Oh good. That's very helpful." At least it diverted attention from the possible danger to my daughter.

The rest of the conversation was desultory as I basically wolfed down my food while the others drank their coffee. Malone and I then excused ourselves. I glanced back at Colleen sandwiched between the two old detectives. She was as safe as she could get. They might be retired but they were still tough and would both lay down their lives for her.

The day was turning colder and wetter. "Habash hasn't called," I said to Malone as we stood by her Jeep in front of the café. We hadn't heard from him since he evaded the police at the warehouse. I wanted him to call soon, goading me that he still had Eleanor. A living, breathing Eleanor.

My partner actually patted me on the shoulder. "He's got to taunt you pretty soon." I swear sometimes the woman reads my mind. "It's part of the game. We'll get him." She looked at her hand as if she didn't know why it had done that and dropped it to her side. "Head back to the office?"

"Let's do it," I said. I couldn't remember if anybody had ever patted me on the shoulder before, at least not since I was eight or so.

CHAPTER SEVENTY-EIGHT

I ended up having Malone drop me off at the Justice Center to pick up my cell phone. I'd left it with Mike Whitehall last night so he could have it checked for bugs this morning. I again had my own house and my own vehicle; I wanted to be able to use my own damned phone as well.

He assured me the lab had thoroughly debugged it. I traded it into my pocket for the prepaid phone—with which I executed a perfect free throw into the corner wastebasket. "If that rings," I told Mike, "it's a wrong number."

Then it was just a few minutes' walk to the office. Not exactly a carefree walk, but at least not worrying about a cop driving by.

The office was unlocked but empty. A faint odor of cinnamon hung in the air, so I knew Malone had to be nearby. Maybe she'd gone down the hall to the bathroom. I wouldn't let it worry me—at least for the next minute or two.

I hung up my jacket, got a cup of coffee from the pot that she had already started, stashed the Smith and Wesson in the desk drawer, and saw that the message light on my phone was blinking.

I'd just picked up the phone to check when the door opened and Malone came in. She seemed as relieved to see me as I was to see her, but that could have been my imagination. It occurred to me, not for the first time, that I really enjoyed having a partner in this agency.

"Got your phone?" she asked as she took the chair on her side of the partners desk.

"They debugged it for me like they said they would."

"Mike have anything new?"

"Not a thing."

I punched up my voicemail as she turned to her keyboard and monitor. Two messages. One was from Nora Hogan asking if I'd learned anything more about her erstwhile fiancé. Shit. The authorities hadn't notified her yet? She hadn't seen anything on the news? Well, she wasn't a relative and maybe she didn't watch TV. That was a call I had to return immediately, little as I looked forward to it.

The other message was from Master Chejung, assuring me that he and his students were continuing their investigation of Martin Idris. I'd completely forgotten that I left Chejung to pursue that wild goose; when I got the chance, I'd have to call him off.

But right now, Nora Hogan.

I dialed her number and was debating, as the phone rang, whether I could get away with leaving a voice message, a copout that became moot when she answered.

"Yes?"

"It's Clint McCall, Miss Hogan." I saw Malone stiffen slightly at the name.

"Mr. McCall! I was worried that you never got my messages. Have you found Joe?"

There's no easy way. "I'm afraid I have bad news." At that Malone turned to look at me, apparently just as surprised as I was that Hogan hadn't already been informed.

Meanwhile I heard a quick gasp on the phone. Everyone has heard that phrase about "bad news" a thousand times on TV even if not in their own lives and knows exactly what it means. It isn't said when the person in question is slightly injured. Still, no one ever wants to understand it.

"Is Joe hurt? What's happened?"

"He's dead, Miss Hogan. I'm sorry."

A strangled sob. "Oh my God. Did he...? How did it happen?"

"The police are still investigating, but it appears he was murdered. I can't give you any other details right now, but I imagine they'll be in touch."

She said nothing for a long moment though I could hear more sobbing. "Where is he? Can I see him? Does his family know?"

"I'll tell you what," I said. "You should go ahead and call the police department. Ask for Detective Lieutenant Mike Whitehall.

He'll be able to help you—and you might be able to help him, as well."

"Okay," she said in a small voice. "Thank you, Mr. McCall. Is it all right if we discuss your bill some other time?"

I was amazed and a little embarrassed that she even thought of it. "No problem," I said. "Again, I'm sorry for your loss."

"Thank you. So am I." She hung up. The unexpectedly dead so often leave us bewildered.

"Those are tough," Malone said without looking over from her monitor. "I'm surprised she didn't already know."

"Me too," I agreed as I started to pick up the phone again. Now that I was no longer a fugitive it was time to marshal more resources. I didn't want to pull Johnny and Hap away from their current responsibilities but could use Reuben and his connections, even Chejung if I could get him off his focus on Martin Idris. With all of us, including the cops, looking for Eleanor at least we'd have a chance....

I was just about to lift the handset when the phone rang. I continued the motion and brought to my ear. "McCall."

The voice was a familiar one. "I believe you owe me another life, Mr. McCall."

CHAPTER SEVENTY-NINE

I jerked upright as adrenaline flooded my body. "I want to speak to Eleanor," I said immediately. *That* took Malone's attention away from her monitor. She swung around toward me as if slapped.

"You'll hear from Eleanor soon enough," he said smoothly. "I want to compliment you on tracking me to the warehouse so quickly. You are either smarter or much more lucky than I gave you credit for." His tone grew angry. "*But* you get no extra credit because you didn't follow the rules. You involved the police at the warehouse and, when I tried to call you earlier—much to my surprise—someone in the police lab answered your phone. Trying to trace my calls? Perhaps having them check for tracking or other nefarious devices? Either way, you are *not* playing by the rules. You will pay for that, eventually. Eleanor first. Perhaps others; you never know."

"If you hurt Eleanor...."

"Not *if*, Mr. McCall. How much."

Over the phone I heard a muffled squeal, almost a scream, that went on for several seconds. I felt like it was coming from my own insides.

Habash's voice came back on the line. "You said you wanted to hear from Eleanor. Your wish is my command. If the money transfer doesn't go through in the morning she will die very slowly and painfully—even more slowly and painfully than the fun I'm having in the meantime."

"You motherfucker."

"Obviously you didn't know my mother. Here's the newest twist to our game, Mr. McCall. Assuming all is well you will hear from Eleanor at least one more time, at noon tomorrow. Since she's your good friend, I thought you would want to hear her die. I know I've always felt that way about my good friends."

"What? You just said she wouldn't die if the transfer went through."

A chuckle. "No, I said she would die slowly and painfully if it doesn't go through. If it does, she will die easily and quickly. Either way, I thought you should hear it."

"You don't have to do this. Just come after *me*, you son of a bitch."

"Ah, you *did* know my mother. I'm coming after you, Mr. Mc-Call. I'm coming after you in every way I know—and I know a lot of ways. If you mean I should come and kill you, there will be a time for that. Don't worry. First things first."

I could barely speak from the bile accumulating in my throat. "You'd better kill me," I finally said, "because I'm sure as hell going to kill you if you don't."

"That's the spirit. Do remember the rules in the meantime. If I see any hint of police nearby before noon tomorrow, Eleanor dies at that moment. Oh, by the way, are you absolutely certain a small police lab in Portland, Oregon, can detect every device I might have access to?"

He hung up.

"Habash," said Malone. It wasn't a question. More like an expletive.

It took me a moment to be able to speak. "He says he's going to kill Eleanor tomorrow, with me listening, whether the transfer happens or not. He's torturing her in the meantime."

"We are going to kill that cocksucker, aren't we?"

I stood up. I couldn't sit still even though I had nowhere to go. "We have to do something," I said, hoping—I suppose—that either my partner or the universe would have a suggestion.

Malone also stood. "Let's go scrape the bottom of the barrel again," she said. "Keys, Big Avenue, Gunther.... If there's a lead out there anywhere, it's probably down in the gutter where they live."

We looked at each other across the partners desk. I know I looked like I wasn't holding out much hope and neither did she.

We'd already talked to those three more than once and they were all charged to call us if they learned anything new.... But it was something to do. Being out on the street was better than feeling sick to my stomach here in the office.

"Might as well," I finally said.

CHAPTER EIGHTY

We were at the bottom of the stairs, Malone in the lead, when all at once I heard the high scream of a bullet past my ear, the sound of its impact on the staircase behind me, and the report of a weapon somewhere on the street before us.

Malone disappeared from in front of me and I was pulling my own gun as I dived toward the sidewalk, head up and eyes scanning, hoping she wasn't hit. There was a second shot and this time I saw muzzle flash from a car parked to my left across the street. It was an old Ford or Chevy, greenish-gray, not a vehicle I recognized. I landed with a heavy thump on the concrete and scrambled forward to take up position behind a low-slung sedan on our side of the street where my partner had already taken shelter and appeared to be unhurt.

Another shot ricocheted off its hood and I became aware of screams and the squeal of brakes, seemingly all around us. Tuesday lunch hour on a busy street at the edge of downtown. We were not exactly alone out here.

"What the fuck is that now?" rasped Malone as she twisted upward to risk a quick look over the hood. She dropped back down as one of our cover's headlights exploded and I heard a car engine roar, tires spinning before they gained traction. The shooter apparently had decided it was time to leave.

I took another look and the fleeing car was already disappearing around the corner. I caught a glimpse of the Oregon plate, but didn't have time to register the number.

"He's gone," I said. We slowly stood up, holstering our weapons, and looked around. There were pedestrians peeking around corners and rising from crouches against buildings, drivers sitting frozen behind the wheel or just straightening up from where they'd ducked behind the dash...all of them staring wide-eyed at us and almost all of them with a cell phone in hand. I could already

287

hear sirens approaching.

"No way was that Habash," announced Malone. "No fucking way."

"Agreed. So who the hell was it?"

She gave me a look. "How many people in this town want to shoot you, anyway?"

I pulled an offended expression. "Me? How do you know he was shooting at me? Maybe he was shooting at you."

"And how do you know it was a he? Did you see 'him'? Maybe one of your old girlfriends is looking for revenge."

"Or one of your old boyfriends?"

"Not fucking likely."

"Well, I didn't see him—or her. Did you? Anything?"

"Just the weapon out the car window. Looked like it might have been a Sig."

I stood there for a minute, listening to the sirens getting closer and watching the surrounding pedestrians and drivers recovering from their shock, experiencing a kind of brain-lock. Malone had to be right that that wasn't Habash. A drive-by at this moment didn't fit with his game at all. We didn't even have any other active cases now that Imeson had been found. Why would someone be trying to gun one or both of us down today?

CHAPTER EIGHTY-ONE

Within minutes we were in the back of a squad car, heading for the Justice Center again, Code 2, lights but no siren. I didn't know the patrolman who was driving. He was a big old guy who looked like he'd been on the streets forever.

He escorted us past the front desk, into the elevator, and ultimately to Whitehall's office in the Homicide Detail. We were literally right back where our day had started.

We took our seats in front of his desk. "This is getting to be a habit," he said.

I told him about the phone call from Habash and the drive-by with Malone tossing in some extra detail on the latter.

He looked from one of us to the other. "You didn't recognize the car."

"No," we said together.

"And you didn't catch the plate."

"No." That was just me.

"Didn't see the shooter."

"Nope."

"But you don't think it was Habash."

"Correct."

"Any idea who it was? Either one of you?"

"Not a clue." That was Malone but I nodded agreement.

Mike paused for a moment, then flashed a wry grin. "Well shit, we'll get right on that then."

I groaned aloud. "I know. We can't give you squat. Meanwhile Malone and I have to try to find Eleanor while some fuck-ball is taking potshots at us."

He leaned forward as he lost the grin. "We all have to try to find Eleanor. And we'd better find her in a hurry." He sat back, picking up a well-scribbled notepad from his desk and glancing at it. "Not only because Habash has given you a deadline, but because we have sources telling us he was a sociopathic sadist back when he worked for Lebanese intel."

"I already heard something along those lines from my own sources," I said.

"I know, but listen up anyway." He consulted the notepad again. "It appears that over the course of about five years Daniel Habash went from brand new golden boy of the Lebanese intelligence service to their evil nemesis. He was considered brilliant, innovative, and without peer in his ability to track down people and extract information from them. But after a couple of years his superiors began to notice that everyone he extracted information from was dead, including the ones they didn't want dead. And not just dead, but tortured to death in some pretty brilliant and original ways. Then they began to hear about similarly dead people they hadn't even needed information from. Agent Habash had learned to enjoy his job far too much; he'd begun to do it for fun. Then his superiors started turning up dead when they criticized his methods and tried to rein him in."

Mike put the notepad down as if it weighed too much. "It's safe to say the guy doesn't like to be crossed. I think it may really be true that he's just hanging around to stick it to you, maybe both of you. That sounds crazy but, then again, he's crazy."

"Why didn't they deal with him in Lebanon?" Malone asked.

He shrugged. "Oh, they did their best. Eventually the combined agencies of several Middle Eastern countries were trying to take Habash out. That lasted until he apparently got tired of killing the agents who came after him and moved to the States to put his talents into various get-rich-quick schemes. The Lebanese didn't try to follow him and never notified our government that a homicidally insane agent of theirs might be coming here. Maybe they completely lost track of him. Maybe they were embarrassed."

We looked at each other in silence for a long moment.

"Jesus," I finally said.

"Did you learn *anything* that points to where he might be?"

Malone asked.

"He's probably somewhere within striking distance, but otherwise no clue. Everybody's on the look-out; that's all we can do right now."

I stood up. "I understand. Can we get a ride back to the office? It's a sure bet the media is poised to jump the second we get past the front desk—and somehow I find myself reluctant to walk openly on our city's streets right now, anyway. It would be handy to remain in custody a few more minutes."

He nodded and picked up his phone. "A uniform will meet you at the elevator downstairs. Let me know if you have any luck."

"Definitely."

As the elevator descended, Malone gave me a sour look. "You figure that Roberts chick is down there waiting for us?"

"Yet another drive-by shooting involving the local PI who unfortunately seems to spike her ratings better than anyone else? What do you think?"

Just outside the elevator doors was a very large patrolman. "Follow me," he said, and we proceeded to plow right past Roberts, her cameraman Murray Kravitz, and similar teams from several other stations as if they weren't there. We ignored their shouts and our escort ignored the danger of crushing one of them to death, so there was no problem getting to his patrol car.

The Channel 11 news van was the only one to follow us. One thing you could say for Alison Roberts is that she is a bulldog when it comes to covering yours truly. She was knocking on our office door before we made it to our desk.

I spun around, jerked the door open, looked straight into the camera that Kravitz already had up on his shoulder, said "No comment" as calmly as I could, and shut the door again. This time I locked it.

Malone applauded lightly as I settled on my side of the partners desk. We both ignored the continued knocking.

I looked at my watch. 1:58. "We've got twenty-two hours, at

most," I said.

"And not one new lead."

"We've got the bottom of that barrel we were going to scrape when we were so rudely interrupted. Why don't we try using the phones this time? You call Gunther and emphasize that we're on the clock now. Offer to sleep with him. Whatever it takes. The man should be able to find out something more if he tries hard enough."

"Oh, that's nice. Now you want me to pimp myself out for information?"

"You don't have to actually sleep with him. Just make the offer. And speaking of pimps, I know I can light a fire under Big Avenue and Reuben, especially, by telling them about the latest threat to Eleanor. I hate to do it but I think Johnny needs to get out on the street, too, and see if any of his old informants can tell us anything. Hap can handle Colleen's protection by himself for a while. Then maybe we'll go see Master Chejung again. We need everybody doing everything they can."

She picked up her handset. "Not to worry. We'll get the bad guy and rescue the damsel in distress. It's what we do."

I picked up mine as well. "I hope you're right."

Meanwhile, thank goodness, the knocking had finally stopped.

CHAPTER EIGHTY-TWO

A half-hour later, having made our calls, we were on our way to see Master Chejung. Malone had agreed that he was worth a personal visit because of his unique resources—and because we needed to get him refocused on our real nemesis rather than Martin Idris.

We were speculating yet again about the latest shooting when I pulled up behind a city bus to wait for a red light on Burnside. Which is when I noticed the greenish-gray mid-70s Ford sedan come around the corner several cars behind us.

"Shit," I said. "I think we've got the shooter on our tail as we speak."

Malone twisted around and looked back. "That's the car."

The light changed and I followed the bus across the intersection, mind racing, and immediately saw an opportunity to perhaps turn the tables. The bus in front was pulling over to a bus stop; the two vehicles directly in front of the Ford were delivery vans, making it difficult for the Ford's driver to see my Outback every second. As the bus stopped, I abruptly pulled over to the curb in front of it and backed right up against its bumper.

Seconds later the Ford came by. The driver appeared to be male, but that's all I could tell because his head was turned away as we came parallel. I didn't recognize him. He was looking in the other lane of the one-way street, probably to see if that's where we'd disappeared to. The Ford, I saw now, wasn't really greenish-gray; more like green fading to gray, dented, nearly rusted through in several places.

I bulled my way into the traffic flow right behind him, accompanied by horn blasts from both the bus and the driver I'd cut off. I don't think the Ford's driver even heard them; I could see by his silhouette that he was intent, leaning forward over the steering wheel, scanning through the front windshield.

"Can you tell who it is?" Malone asked.

"I haven't gotten a good look yet."

I stayed right behind him through another block-and-a-half. A light turned red just as he was about to enter the next intersection; the Ford jerked as if he'd thought about jumping the light, then stopped. I could see him sit back, pound the steering wheel once...and finally look straight into the rearview mirror.

Clearly he recognized us. The Ford leaped forward with a wild screech of tires...and traveled perhaps twenty feet before a pickup truck crossing with the green light smashed into its right rear fender. The truck, one of those super-macho 2000-horsepower jobs, kept going almost through the intersection as the sedan spun neatly through 270 degrees and ended up pointing in the direction of the one-way traffic flow on the cross street. I don't think our guy took his foot off the accelerator the whole time and his car's tires kept screaming as it rocketed past the truck that had hit it and disappeared into the distance.

We, meanwhile, were stuck looking at an intersection clogged by all the cars that had stopped because of the accident.

"Fuck me!" exploded Malone.

I looked over at her. "You okay?"

"What? Yeah, I'm okay, but I don't fucking believe it. I got a good look at his face when he was spinning out and I know that guy. That was Martin Idris!"

I could understand her reaction. "Idris? The wild goose? Why the hell would *he* be taking a shot at us?"

Malone gave me a glare. "He doesn't know you. That fucker had to be shooting at me."

I just sat and rested my forehead on the steering wheel for a moment, speculation spinning faster than the Ford had. That was all we needed, somebody else coming out of left field trying to get Malone while Habash was trying to get me.

CHAPTER EIGHT-THREE

There was a parking space right in front of Northwest Martial Arts and as I pulled up I could see a few white dobaks in action through the plate glass front of Chejung's building. At least there'd be a black belt on the premises who'd know how to get in touch with Chejung if he wasn't already there.

I'd given Mike Whitehall a quick heads up while we waited for the traffic to start moving again after the accident. He was just as bewildered as we were about why another one of Eleanor's boyfriends would suddenly be involved. With Mike on the speaker, we all three agreed that we had no clue why Martin Idris would try to shoot us or whether it was somehow related to Habash and his game. We also agreed that Eleanor, if she survived all this, seriously needed to rethink what she was looking for in a boyfriend.

Mike said he'd put out a BOLO for Idris. We hadn't gotten the plate number of his vehicle, so that was all he could do at this point.

I saw Chejung the moment we entered the dojang. He was sitting at a battered desk in a far corner with Terry Goebel standing, arms crossed, nearby. They'd been watching the action out on the floor and both saw us immediately.

It struck me as Malone and I started across the polished wood floor that it was precisely a week ago I'd first visited here. Just as then, there were a small number of students working out on their own or in small groups, almost all brown and black belts. The exception was a group of three women who looked like they were in their early thirties, all with white belts tied sloppily around their waists, gathered before a tall good-looking black belt in the middle of the room. From the subdued giggles I heard as we walked past them, and from my own experience, my guess was that they were trying out training as a lark and at least were quite pleased with their instructor.

Chejung nodded his head and spoke as we came up to the desk. "Good that you are here," he said. "We have much to tell you."

"Oh?" I said as I came to a stop. There were visitor's chairs. Everybody else in the dojo was expected to sit on the floor if they had time to sit at all.

"What?" Malone asked Chejung. Given the latest incident, I could understand she'd be more interested in new information about Idris.

Chejung's eyes tracked slowly from me to her. "We have learned that Martin Idris is not only a gambler through the Russian syndicate. In addition to his job with the storage business, Martin Idris is also employed by the Russians. He deals with the bettors who cannot pay what they've lost."

"So," she said, "he's their muscle."

His eyebrows bounced as if he'd not heard the metaphor before. Or maybe it was that tone from a woman. "Yes, he is their strong arm. We are finding out more. Jason is home doing research on the Internet right now and David is out asking further questions on the street."

Malone frowned. "Jason? David?"

"David Camp," I supplied, "the blond senior student I met on my last visit, and Jason Dominguez, their purple-belt computer geek."

Then it was Chejung's turn to frown. "I don't know this word 'geek' but you will be surprised at what Jason can find," he said to me. "My cousin has provided him some password resources that most computer people do not have."

"Your cousin the Korean spy master," clarified Malone.

Chejung continued as if she had not spoken. "There are indications that Martin Idris may do more than frighten and injure people for his employers. He may kill for them."

Malone and I looked at one another. "Holy crap," I said to her. If we had inadvertently initiated an investigation of a professional hit man, it could certainly explain why he was pissed. And Malone was the one who interviewed him, the one he'd blame for his troubles. "That was a pro hit and you were the target."

Chejung's eyebrows bounced again. "What do you mean?" he inquired politely.

"Just a few hours ago," I said, "Idris took a shot at us downtown."

Goebel spoke up. "David needs to know about this...." Obviously not in the habit of contributing to his master's conversations without invitation, he abruptly stopped, his face reddening. Chejung never flicked a glance in his direction. "Sorry sir," the younger man said.

The master addressed me as if there'd been no interruption, something he was clearly accustomed to doing. "And you believe your companion was the target? Why?"

Malone leaned in on him. "I'm his partner, not his companion. Want to see my gun?"

That got his attention. His head swiveled about one millimeter per second until he locked eyes straight on with Malone. Neither one said a word or even made a sound. I'm not sure they were breathing. If it weren't for the critical nature of the moment, I would have been having a good time. As it was, I was about to interrupt the stare-down when Chejung finally spoke.

"Partner," he said and nodded ever so slightly. "I apologize for my mistake."

Damn. She won.

And so onward. "I believe she's the target because she's the one who actually went to see him and ask questions", I said. "He obviously knows that there's a wider investigation, but Malone is the person he identifies as the source. That's our current theory, anyway.

"But," I continued firmly, "despite any danger from Martin Idris we're more concerned about Daniel Habash. He's the bigger threat here. We *know* he's killed people, including your student, and he just kidnapped a good friend of ours. I'd like you to re-direct your 'resources' to finding Habash. Our friend is in extreme danger and time is running out. In fact, we have until noon tomorrow."

He looked at me, calm, expressionless, for a full thirty seconds. "If that is so," he finally said, "we would be of no help. It has taken time to find out about Idris; it would take time to find out more about Habash. We will continue with the man we know."

I couldn't believe it. "You won't help track down the man who killed one of your students?" I asked in what must have been an almost-plaintive voice. Out of the corner of my eye, I could see that Terry Goebel's face was seriously flushed with the effort to remain still. Malone was almost as expressionless as Chejung.

"It would be an empty gesture," Chejung replied just as calmly as ever. "There is not enough time. We will continue as we are."

There was no arguing with him; I could see that. Perhaps Goebel could persuade him after we'd gone, but I doubted it. I took my leave with a muttered farewell and stomped across the dojang, Malone keeping pace.

CHAPTER EIGHT-FOUR

Outside on the street, whipped by a chill wind and dampened by a light drizzle that hadn't been in the air when we arrived, I looked at my watch. 3:30.

I was about to voice a short but highly obscene rant about Master Chejung being an idiot when Malone punched me in the shoulder. "I don't agree."

I know my mouth dropped open. Surely she couldn't read my mind *that* well. "About what?" I inquired cautiously.

"About putting Idris on the back burner. I think we should deal with him right now."

"Why? Eleanor is the one seriously in jeopardy here, the one with the clock ticking. Idris is a thug who couldn't hit either one of us when he tried. We'll deal with him when we have to."

She stepped away. "Then I'll go take care of him myself."

I took a quick step of my own and grabbed her arm. This was beginning to piss me off. "What is it with you? All of a sudden you're so chicken shit that the threat to you is more important than anything else? You can't go off on your own...."

I thought I was used to Malone punching me; it's what she does. But I was wrong. And very glad she'd just missed my solar plexus or I would have been on the ground in a fetal position.

"Chicken shit? Can't?" She was in my face, nose to nose, and more livid than I'd ever seen her. "Fuck you, McCall. Your partner, your fucking *partner*, volunteers to go take care of threat to both of us and you call her a chicken shit? Tell her she *can't*? Fuck you!"

By that point in her tirade I'd finally managed to pull in enough air to make voice-like noises. "I'm sorry," I croaked, "but we're supposed to have each other's backs...."

She threw up her hands and—I kid you not—spun in a circle so vehemently that I could almost see the sparks flying every direction. "Which is exactly what I'm fucking planning to do, you idiot!"

she shouted as she ended up right back in my face. "I've already gotten people killed! Eleanor's being tortured, for fuck's sake, while we stand here yelling at each other! I'm not going to let you get shot because some asshole is after me!"

"I'm not yelling," I was able to say in an almost normal tone of voice. I was beginning to understand...and I wasn't sure what was happening. I mean, shit, it looked to me like Malone was actually tearing up. Her latest glare was certainly looking shiny. We'd never had a serious fight before, just the incessant bickering, and now suddenly I was literally jerking her around and she was about to cry. On the whole, maybe I was beginning to get more confused. All this within a few split seconds.

I really didn't want her to cry. "You know how it goes with us," I went on. "It never seems to be one thing at a time. Of course when we have less than a day to save Eleanor's life we get some random asshole shooting at us. At the McCall and Malone Detective Agency, that's par for the course. But...."

It really wasn't working. A tear spilled down her cheek as she gave me a shove and started to turn away. "It's not my fault!" she cried, which directly contradicted what she'd been saying up to now but I think we were both past making sense.

That one tear was one too many for me, I guess. I reached out again, caught her arm, turned her back toward me and—to my great surprise—pulled her fully into my arms. I was probably beyond surprised by the time my lips found hers and felt her responding. Right there in the drizzle and chill wind in front of Chejung's dojang, I was kissing the hell out of Devon Malone.

Until she suddenly exploded out of my arms and jumped several steps back, her face pale and breath ragged.

"Oh," she said, in the tone of voice you might use if you discovered a roach on the kitchen floor. "Oh, hell no."

Then she turned and ran.

CHAPTER EIGHT-FIVE

For some reason, as she ran, Devon Malone found herself picturing the partners desk in their office. She imagined sitting there across from McCall on a quiet morning with an interesting but not life-threatening case to talk about over coffee.... And then: *Why the fuck am I running?*

She slowed to a walk but refused to look back. Was he following her, trying to catch up? She didn't hear any footsteps back there. Probably he was as mortified as she. Or embarrassed. Paralyzed. Something.

How were they going to work together now?

McCall *kissed* her, for Christ's sake, right there in front of God and everybody. And she.... Well, she wasn't going to think about that. Abso-fucking-lutely never going to think about that.

Co-workers should never.... Partners couldn't.... Shit, she needed to get focused on something else. She kept walking, already headed in the general direction of the office where she could pick up her Jeep, lucky enough to have gotten a space in the lot this morning. But it was a long walk and there were things to be done. Eleanor was in danger and so was McCall. Habash was out there. And now Idris. What had they been planning to do before...*that* happened?

Crap. They hadn't made a plan yet.

Okay, so she'd make a plan of her own. Give McCall a little time to cool off and realize what a stupid fool he'd made of himself. Then maybe she could forgive him and they could move on. Forgive herself, too, for.... Well, she was *not* for-Christ's-sake going to think about *that*.

And there was a taxi coming her way. She stepped into the street and whistled at it, just like in an old movie. To her amazement, it actually pulled over. She got in and the driver—a young black guy—asked, "Where to?"

301

Which was an excellent question.

On impulse, she gave him the address of Carl Gunther's building. He was her best source. He liked her. He wasn't going to try to kiss her and she'd kill him if he did. Maybe he'd heard something new. Maybe *they* could make a plan. Whatever.

A few minutes later as she strode across the spacious lobby of Gunther's building toward the bank of elevators, she was torn between the likelihood that this was a waste of time and the value of it as a distraction. Gunther had been succinct on the phone; maybe she could come up with more details in person. Probably not. At least Portland's pre-eminent crime boss, no doubt in classic dapper gangster mode as always, would be distracting. If he was in. Shit, she might *really* be wasting her time.

She burst into his reception area so abruptly that Mrs. Pinkerton had jerked open and was reaching into her upper right-hand desk drawer before she recognized Malone and stopped mid-motion.

"Oh, dearie," she said, "you shouldn't startle a person like that."

Malone, who had stopped just as abruptly when she saw the receptionist's reaction, started to laugh. Here was this white-haired little old lady calling her dearie after almost drawing a gun and capping her ass.

Getting herself under control, Malone stepped closer to the desk. "And good day to you, Mrs. Pinkerton. What kind of weapon do you have in there?"

The elderly woman looked down at the closed drawer with a grandmotherly fondness and then smiled up at Malone. "It's a Glock. Very similar to yours, I believe."

"Ah ha. We'll have to talk guns over coffee some time."

"I look forward to it."

"Is the big man here?"

"Yes, and he's free. Just go on in."

That gave Malone pause. "You don't need to, like, get on the intercom and tell him he has a visitor?"

Another grandmotherly smile. "No dear. He already knows you're here. Nobody gets this far without him knowing. Anyway, I have standing instructions that you're welcome any time he isn't in conference."

"Huh. Well, good. I'll go on in then."

Mrs. Pinkerton nodded and turned back to her keyboard as Malone crossed the space to Gunther's office door, knocked once on principle, and then opened it to step inside.

Seated behind his massive desk with its blotter, desk set, phone and not much more, Carl Gunther, Sr., was as usual wearing a gray pinstripe suit—this time with a dark green tie. He didn't stand but did lean forward to offer his hand for a shake.

"You a mind reader now, Malone?" he asked as they shook.

She gave him a frown as she sat in a visitor chair. "No. Why?"

"Because I was about to call you again. Your guy was seen just a few minutes ago."

The frown deepened. "McCall?"

Gunther snorted a laugh. "Is he your guy now? No, I mean that Habash character."

Which immediately over-rode the embarrassment she was about to feel at thinking he'd meant her partner. She jumped right back up. "Where? Where was he seen?"

"Just outside the Mid-Town Motel, on Burnside. On foot. Maybe he has a room there."

It rang a bell. Why did it ring a bell? That was where the hooker was killed and Nora Hogan's fiancé disappeared. Fuck!

"Thanks. Gotta go." Malone literally ran from the office and through the reception area, ignoring the gasp of surprise from Mrs. Pinkerton as she charged by, hoping she didn't get a bullet in the back.

CHAPTER EIGHTY-SIX

Oh shit, what have I done? I thought to myself as I watched Devon Malone's figure shrink in the distance. I couldn't go running after her. In the first place, I had no clue why she was running. And, what could I say? "Sorry about kissing you, there. It was really great that you kissed me back. Not so great that you're running away now. Maybe we should talk."

Maybe we should talk?

Oh, that was good.

I could not deal with this right now. I wasn't getting any closer to Eleanor and all I'd learned recently was that I had bad karma in a big way. Martin Idris had nothing to do with Daniel Habash; we'd simply triggered—as it were—the one by looking for the other. And now I didn't even have my back-up, my partner.

I got into the Subaru, out of the wind and rain, wondering how Malone would get wherever she was going, and punched in Johnny Crew's cell phone number. He answered with, "You ain't found Eleanor yet?"

"No. I'm not getting anywhere yet. I need your help. I want you to reach out to your old informants, find out if any of them know anything we can use—about a big-money operation, the killings, a woman being kidnapped, anything."

"Okay. Probably won't find out shit. They're mostly old farts just like me."

"And, just like you, they've been around a hell of a long time and know a lot about what's going on. Give it a try."

"Oh, I will. As long as Colleen stays put here in the Pen and Pastry, Hap can watch her back by himself. Speakin' of fuckin' backs, you watch yours."

"You can count on it. Talk to you later."

We hung up. I felt sorry for my daughter, semi-imprisoned in a coffee shop by my job. Hell, I felt sorry for me and Devon and everybody at this point. Especially Eleanor.

I hadn't warned Johnny about Idris because there was no indication the idiot was after anyone but Devon. Johnny and Hap didn't know what Idris *or* Habash looked like, anyway; but they'd see a threat coming regardless of its name.

I did, however, want Mike Whitehall to have the new information about Idris even though we were keeping him on the back burner. Or at least I was. In any event, always a good idea to give Homicide the latest scoop on a potential killer. Mike didn't answer his office phone, so I left a voicemail.

I sat for another minute in the car, contemplating what a pain in the ass it was to feel both helpless and alone. I turned the key in the ignition. Might as well go back to the office, wait for some news, deal a few index cards, wrack my brain for something more useful to do. Maybe Malone would be there.

I parked the Outback in the lot, saw that her Jeep was there, hurried across 3rd because it was raining even harder, ignored the mailboxes on my way up the stairs, and found our office empty. No evidence Malone had come and gone recently.

As I hung my jacket on the hook, I could see the message light blinking on my phone. Malone? I dropped the Smith and Wesson in the top right-hand drawer as I sat down. I picked up the phone and hit the message button.

I recognized the voice immediately; it was Big Avenue, speaking rapidly for him, almost a normal rate for regular humans: "That crazy cunt think somethin' else happenin' in that same room. Maybe fuckin' ghosts. I don't know, but I can't get down there right now. I got business. The bitch is goin' fuckin' crazy on me. You wanna check it out, feel fuckin' free." Click.

I put the phone down slowly. What was I supposed to make of that? He didn't even provide a key to the translation.

What the hell was Big Avenue talking about? The "crazy cunt" was probably one of his girls. But what was with the ghosts? And what "same room"? The motel room where Heather

306

Lipinski/Brandy Wine was killed? That had to be what he was talking about, but...was one of his girls telling him it was haunted? It didn't make sense.

And I didn't know how to call him back. Caller ID had not identified his number, so *69 wouldn't work.

Crap. It might not mean anything. Big Avenue was not the brightest pimp in the gutter; I could have simply caught some gibberish. He sounded serious enough, though, and was reasonably intelligible.... Might as well check it out, like he said, rather than sit around here waiting for Malone to maybe never show up.

CHAPTER EIGHTY-SEVEN

I locked the office behind me and approached the bottom of the stairs cautiously. No bullets whizzing by. No thirty-year-old Ford sedans in sight. Ditto no rain, just a chilly breeze.

I called Whitehall's office number again as I walked down Yamhill toward the parking lot. Might as well let him know where I'm going just in case; I had an uneasy feeling. But again there was no answer. Rather than leave a voicemail this time, I opted out to the front desk; they would probably know where he was.

Lieutenant Whitehall was at a scene in North Portland where two dead bodies had been discovered, a man and a woman, probably murder-suicide, the chatty desk sergeant informed me after I identified myself. The medical examiner hadn't even arrived yet, so the lieutenant would probably be tied up for quite a while.

As I was putting the phone away I saw I had a missed call. I checked and it was from Malone—and I had a new voicemail. Which I just didn't want to deal with right now. I could imagine her voice announcing that our partnership was over. What else she might have to say, I honestly couldn't imagine. Later. I'd deal with it later.

So I'd check the motel room with no backup. Used to do that all the time. It was probably nothing anyway. No big deal. Famous last words.

The Mid-Town Motel, where Heather Lipinski's body had been discovered after Joseph Imeson disappeared, was only six blocks from my office—which would, of course, skyrocket the irony level if something were happening there that had to do with Habash.

I parked on Ankeny near the south end of the motel. Even with rush hour traffic, it had taken only a little more than five minutes to get here. I could have walked but I wanted to be able to quickly move on—somewhere—after I failed to find any ghosts, international spies, or damsels in distress.

I climbed out of the Subaru and locked it behind me. I shook my head; I shouldn't be wasting time like this. Still, my gut said to look and I was going to look.

Dusk was already well along and the wind was picking up. I confirmed that the Smith and Wesson was snug in its holster and pulled my jacket tight. I could see a couple of working girls down the block who looked a lot colder than I was. The traffic on Ankeny, even during the evening commute, was light; mostly single males wanting to believe they could warm up the likes of the two who stood waving. I headed toward the motel, alert for anyone on foot within the property.

The room, as I recalled, was about halfway down the single row of units that stretched the width of the block over to Burnside.

The Mid-Town had been sitting on Burnside a few blocks east of the bridge since the late 40s, with very few renovations in the meantime. It consisted of a single row of a dozen small rooms along a one-way drive with angled parking spaces. The entrance and office were on Burnside; the exit on Ankeny. The whole place—walls, doors, trim, sign, everything—was a faded institutional beige. Very few travelers took a room here; the rentals tended to be by the hour.

The room numbering started with 1, next to the office, and ended with 12 next to the exit. As I edged down the walkway, hand resting on the holstered Smith and Wesson, I could see that room 7 would be the one I wanted. There were vehicles parked in front of most of the rooms; none was the sedan I'd seen Habash driving, but he could have traded it off easily enough. All the windows facing the drive were tightly curtained. No one staying at this motel, kidnapper or not, wanted witnesses.

The rooms were designed so that, coming from the direction of the exit, you encountered the window before the door. I stopped at the edge of Room 7's window, confirmed that it too was covered by a closed curtain, and leaned forward to put my ear almost against the glass. Nothing. I waited. Faint, ragged breathing?

Could have been my imagination. Or a conventional use of the room.

With no identifiable vehicle or overt sign of disturbance, I wasn't going to bust in unannounced—nor was I going to simply knock, not until I had a better idea of who was in there, if anyone.

I moved quietly on toward the office at the other end, hoping to find a clerk who could tell me Room 7 was either empty or had been rented ten minutes ago by a hooker. Either way, I'd be able to forget about Big Avenue's message and get on with my business.

I pushed the door to the office open and moved just far enough into the doorway that I could talk to the clerk and still keep an eye on the walkway to the exit on Ankeny.

The guy standing behind the check-in counter was young and skinny with a burr haircut, an earring in his left ear, and a wispy moustache. He looked up, frowned, and yelled "Hey! Close the door, asshole! It's cold enough in here already."

It wasn't the sort of place where you'd expect gracious customer service.

"I need to keep it open while we talk," I said. "Tell me who's in Room 7 and I'll be on my way."

"You a cop?"

"Private," I said.

"Screw you, man. I don't need to give no information to no PI. Our guests like their privacy, if you know what I mean."

The last thing I needed right now was this punk's attitude. I casually brushed my jacket back so that he could see the Smith and Wesson in its holster. "We can do this another way, if you want," I said.

His face visibly paled and he stepped back from the counter. "You're shitting me." He held up his hands, shaking his head. "No way. No way. There's no way you'd shoot me if I don't tell you."

I rested my hand on the butt of the gun. "Want to bet your life on that?"

He hesitated, then took a hop forward to the monitor on one

end of the counter. He attacked the keyboard, squinting first at the screen, then me, then the screen. After a moment he grinned slyly. "Okay, fucker. It's John Smith. That's who's in Room 7. He stays here a lot."

So there was somebody registered. "How long has he been here?" I asked.

He looked at the screen again, the smirk turning to a look of surprise. "Shit. Maybe it's a real tourist. Looks like he's been here since sometime yesterday."

"What does he look like?"

"How should I know? I came on duty at noon today."

"Have you seen anybody coming or going who looks Middle-Eastern?"

His eyes widened. "Crap! You lookin' for a terrorist?"

"Just answer the question."

"I...yeah, just an hour or so ago I saw a raghead-lookin' guy go into one of the rooms."

"Room 7?"

He shrugged. "It was in the middle. Could have been."

I felt like somebody had dropped ice cubes down my back. Sometimes the incredibly unlikely turns out to be the case. This might be one of those times and I found myself really wishing I hadn't kissed Malone. Backup suddenly looked very attractive, but too late now. I couldn't wait for Malone or Whitehall, even if I actually could contact either one, but at least....

"You might want to call the cops," I said to the clerk and let the door close as I stepped fully out onto the walkway and drew my weapon.

CHAPTER EIGHT-EIGHT

I edged back toward Room 7, relieved that there was no one else about. I didn't need someone yelling from the sidewalk that there was a man with a gun. I hoped that the desk clerk would indeed get around to calling the cops. But not too fast.

I paused in front of the window of Room 6, just short of the door to Room 7, running scenarios from a polite "Room service!" knock to kicking the door open. I hadn't yet decided when the decision was taken out of my hands. The door began to open inward, hesitating after just a couple of inches. Daniel Habash's voice came from within: "I'll return in a few minutes, my dear. We can continue then. You needn't worry that I'll abandon you." He laughed—a soft, dry, humorless laugh. "Not while you're alive."

He was right there next to me. The chill down my spine was washed away by a warmth that started in my lower back and climbed to the top of my head. The world slowed down and brightened considerably. It was as though I felt nothing and everything at the same time.

The few seconds that his parting gratuitous cruelty granted me were more than enough time to decide that now, while he was still inside the partially opened door, was the best chance I'd have; more than enough time to take one big stride, turn, and put my entire body weight into a side kick planted six inches to the right of the door knob.

As the door exploded inward, I even had time to reflect that I hadn't seen Daniel Habash up close since I interviewed him in his apartment, back when he was just another name on Eleanor's list of old boyfriends. I was looking forward to it.

I could tell as I lunged forward that the door had hit him, hard, but he was still behind it and there was no way to tell if I'd done any real damage. First I needed to know where Eleanor was in the room; my gun was useless until I knew in what direction it was safe to fire.

Immediately as I crossed the threshold I saw the bed, on my right beyond the door that was now swinging back toward me. I registered the splash of Eleanor's blond hair against the pale bedspread; if Habash appeared around the door with his gun, he'd be right in front of her; I couldn't risk a shot.

I lunged again and threw my shoulder against the door, heard a heavy grunt behind it, and caught a glimpse of what I hoped was a gun flying in the direction of the bed. I stepped to my left, actually saw Habash for the first time, and swung the barrel of the Smith and Wesson down toward him.

Unfortunately, he'd obviously had some martial arts training himself: his right foot shot up as my weapon came down and the toe of his black dress shoe neatly caught the gun butt, tearing it from my hands. He shrieked with rage and came at me with a vicious straight punch to my face, his momentum slamming the door closed.

I ducked back and aimed a roundhouse kick at his lower ribs; he blocked it and tried to plant his foot in my right side that was turned toward him. Again I hopped back, blocking downward with my arm as I moved. He was a little taller than me, wiry and surprisingly agile, not to mention just as quick. I could see I was going to have a hard time getting close enough for a solid hand strike. Even as we exchanged attacks, my peripheral vision had followed the Smith and Wesson to its resting place near the door. I had to maneuver him far enough away to allow the split second that I'd need to lean down and retrieve the gun. The sequence was going to be tricky; it meant moving him *toward* where his own weapon lay.

I deflected his kick and landed a lunging right punch to his solar plexus. The block against his kicking leg threw him slightly off balance and he had to move aside, away from the Smith and Wesson.

I spun into a low left kick that caught him a solid blow on the knee cap, staggering him further back. With each of these moves

I'd been shifting to my right, driving him to the left; I thought I must be just about on top of my gun by now. I could *see* that he was nearly on top of his.

And at that moment the door exploded inward again. Damn! The cops already? My peripheral vision identified a familiar figure in leather jacket and jeans as I dropped my eyes to the floor and went into a crouch, hand reaching out toward the metallic sheen of the Smith and Wesson.

It was just five inches to the right of my extended hand, butt toward me as if I'd planned it that way. I knew Habash was moving, but I'd lost track of him in my brief search and had no idea what Malone was doing. I grabbed the gun and leveled it at him.

He was frozen in a half-crouch against the far wall of the room, hand extended toward his own weapon, eyes blazing at Malone who in turn already had her Glock trained on him. He hadn't made it.

Suddenly the room was dead quiet except for our breathing, hers and his and mine—and then a fourth. A short moan emanated from where Eleanor lay.

"I've got this," Malone said, glancing over at the bed, "if you want to check on her."

"Thanks." Nevertheless, I kept my own gun pointed in Habash's general direction as I eased over to Eleanor's side.

Her bloodshot eyes gazed intently at me above the dirty gag covering her mouth. She was tied spread-eagled on the bed, naked and badly bruised. I saw what looked like cigarette burns on her arms and noticed for the first time the rank smell of tobacco in the air. There was blood on the bedspread.

A hot ball of nausea and rage burgeoned in my gut and chest, threatening to stifle my breath.

I reached down and gently removed the nasty gag. "Hang in there, kiddo," I said. "You'll be okay now."

Her mouth opened and closed but no words came out. Just another moan as her eyes glazed over and she passed out. We needed to get her some medical help very soon, but first....

Habash meanwhile had slowly straightened, his own breath calming and a smile playing about his lips as he looked from Malone to me. He stood with his arms slightly out from his sides, palms open toward me, his short black hair somehow all in place and soft-edged facial features relaxed. From his demeanor, we might have just defeated him in some obscure theological argument rather than a life-and-death struggle.

"Good to see you again, Mr. McCall," he said quietly, apparently planning to ignore the women in the room, "though of course I wish the circumstances were slightly different."

Even as he maintained eye contact with me, I could see the wheels turning, calculating the odds of this move or that. They weren't very good, of course, facing two guns as he was. Still, I kept the Smith and Wesson targeted just above the bridge of his nose. A .38 bullet right there from this distance and the only brains he'd have left would be the bits sticking to the remnants of his skull.

For a moment I couldn't say anything in response, my windpipe constricted with fury. Finally I cleared my throat and managed to croak, "Just don't tempt me."

The smile became manifest. "You are an honorable man, Mr. McCall, an officer of your law. You won't harm me further if I stand quietly. You'll hand me over to the police and"—here his voice dripped with sarcasm—"let justice take its course."

"It's better than you deserve," I managed to get out. I was looking at him but I was seeing the blood and the burns on my unconscious friend. Her dead boyfriend. The bodies left in the dirt of construction sites. The terror and grief in Libby Jance's eyes. Hearing the pain in Nora Hogan's voice.

He actually shrugged. "We'll see. You've been lucky this time, McCall, but you can't stay lucky forever." It really was as if Malone didn't exist for him. "I've been hunted by the best, imprisoned by the best, and here I am. There's nowhere you can put me that I can't escape." He deliberately looked over at Eleanor as if promising that someday he would finish the job.

I thought about all those professional intelligence agencies try-ing to take him out and failing. All those burns and wounds.... It was more than I chose to bear. More than I was willing to risk no matter what Eleanor or Devon might think of me.

"I know one place," I said.

He grinned at me, mocking. "And where is that?"

"Hell." I pulled the trigger.

CHAPTER EIGHT-NINE

The detonation filled the room as brain, blood and skull exploded onto the wall behind Habash's head. His body sprawled backward and down as if it were a rag doll.

It seemed like a very long time before I could take my eyes off him. Couldn't breathe. I'd killed people before, in self-defense, and hated it. But this time.... This was in cold blood and somehow it was very worrisome that I didn't feel a damned thing. Not yet.

I snapped out of it when Malone moved. For a moment I thought she was going to take my gun and perform a citizen's arrest but then I saw that she'd stepped over to Habash's gun and was picking it up using what looked like a handkerchief. Somehow it struck me as odd that she carried a handkerchief. I hadn't known that. She still had her own gun in her right hand.

What was she doing?

She quickly covered the short distance to the body and leaned down, carefully placing the weapon next to his hand. Then she stepped back a yard or two, aimed, and shot the dead body in the chest.

She turned and looked at me for the first time. "He refused to drop his gun and when he raised it we both fired." She took a few steps closer, gazing at me very intently. "That's what happened. Clint? Do you agree? That's what happened."

Sounded like a better plan than being arrested for first-degree murder. "Okay," I said.

"We'd better call it in."

"I'm pretty sure the desk clerk already called." Approaching sirens confirmed my speculation even as I voiced it.

"Good," Malone said and closed the rest of the distance between us. She put her arm around me as if I needed steadying. Maybe I did. "It was a good thing you did. A good thing. The fucker was evil. He'd have gotten free again and more people would have died."

"I know."

She stepped away a little as we heard the first cars pulling up outside. Then something struck me. "How did you happen to be here? I didn't know Habash was actually here. I was just checking out something Big Avenue said one of his girls told him. Were you following me?"

"Hell, no." She made a little *pfft* sound. "I went to see Gunther again and he told me he'd just received a report that Habash had been spotted around here. I called you and if you'd answered you would have known I was on my way. But you didn't. Why was that?"

Ah. Shit. "I guess I wasn't ready to talk."

"Well, next time answer your damned phone."

At which point a voice from outside instructed us to drop our guns and come out with our hands up.

CHAPTER NINETY

Mike Whitehall arrived with the paramedics, soon after the first two uniforms had confirmed to their satisfaction that Malone and I were the good guys. In a manner of speaking, but we didn't address that.

None of us said much while the medics determined that Eleanor had no life-threatening injuries and carefully loaded her into the ambulance. Once she was safely on her way, Mike told the two patrolmen to wait outside, that the Medical Examiner had been called, and they should keep an eye out for his van. They shut the door behind them and he stood for a minute looking down at what was left of Habash.

"You have a problem with what happened?" I inquired finally.

"There's his gun by his hand," he said without looking up at me, "and you two back each other up. Clearly he was going to shoot and you both fired in self-defense." He looked up. "Right?"

"Works for me," I said.

"Exactly what happened," added Malone.

"Excellent," responded Mike. "I'll stay here and make sure our good doctor understands what occurred. You two should go see how Eleanor's doing."

Just then there was a knock on the door. One of the uniforms stuck his head into the room. "There's two guys out here say they have to talk to McCall."

I glanced at Whitehall and I'm sure I looked just as bewildered as he did.

"Who?" he asked.

"Reuben something and Big somebody." The patrolman rolled his eyes. "They're not from the ME's office; I can tell you that. Don't ask me what they want."

Whitehall and I looked at each other. Malone and I looked at each other. She actually chuckled. "I don't believe this," I said.

321

Mike shrugged. "We're done anyway," he said. And they're your problem, he didn't say.

I held his eyes another moment. "Thanks."

"No problem." His mouth twisted in a half-smile. "Just serving and protecting." He looked down at Habash's body. "Now get out of here. Let me know how Eleanor is."

"Will do," I said as Malone and I followed the patrolman out into a chilly early evening, already nearly dark. I looked at my watch. 5:35. More than eighteen hours to spare. Not bad. If Eleanor turned out to be...okay? Well, okay probably wasn't possible, not right away. Not permanently crippled would be good.

The first thing I saw outside was the other uniform standing very near the door, looking quite nervous. The second was the shadowed and looming hulk of Big Avenue standing with Reuben in the motel driveway. I could understand the cop's concern; lit by the small dirty bulbs over the room doorways, Big Avenue looked like he'd stepped out of a bad horror movie.

"It's okay," I said. "We know these guys."

"Good for you," muttered the nervous cop.

I gestured to Reuben and Big. "Let's take a walk, gentlemen, and leave these nice officers to their duty."

"I'll head on to the hospital," Malone said. "These two are your problem."

I acknowledged both her intent and her analysis, then started down the parking drive toward my own vehicle with two pimps in tow. "What are you two doing here?" I asked after we were out of earshot of the patrolmen.

"I come to stomp the motherfucker who killed my cunt," Big Avenue said.

"Big called me. Thought maybe you could use some backup," added Reuben.

"Is the motherfucker here?" Big Avenue asked.

"Consider the motherfucker stomped," I said to Big Avenue. "I appreciate the thought," I said to Reuben.

"Was Eleanor here?" Reuben asked. "Is she okay? What happened?"

By this time we'd reached the Outback. "Eleanor was here. She's alive but pretty beat up," I said as I opened the door and put one foot on the floorboard, "and the man who did it is dead. I've got to go to the hospital and check on her. You two probably want to get on with your night."

Big Avenue looked like he wanted to ask for details about how the motherfucker died, but Reuben punched him on the arm to get his attention. "I gotta go to the hospital, see how my friend is doing. You gotta be on the street. Pretty soon it be prime time."

The big man grudgingly agreed to cover for him and they started to move on; then Reuben stepped back to me just as I was settled into the driver's seat and about to close the door. "I hope Eleanor's okay," he said. "She's a fine...woman."

"Yeah," I said. "I hope so too. See you there."

I spent the next several hours sitting in a hospital waiting room with Malone and Reuben, reassured periodically by various nurses that Eleanor was "doing fine." Not good enough that we could see her, but okay nonetheless. Finally Reuben got too antsy about what Big Avenue might be doing with his girls and left with my assurance that I'd call his cell if there were any new developments.

Meanwhile I had called Johnny and Hap to let them know Colleen was off the hook. I told them where I was and that the word on Eleanor was good.

I didn't tell them that I'd blown an unarmed man's brains all over a motel room wall.

I had no regrets, but no pride in it either. Malone was right: Daniel Habash had been a creature of profound evil and impressive resources; I'd done the world a favor in making sure he'd not be loosed upon it again. So I would live with having committed the unspeakable, maybe seeing the moment of his death in my nightmares for years to come.... All things considered, the price was worth it.

At one point after Reuben had gone I looked over at Malone sitting catty-corner from me, pretending to leaf through an old celebrity magazine, and wondered if she felt the same way. She chose that moment to look up at me, probably mind-reading as usual.

"We were lucky," she said.

Having—as is so often the case—no clue, I replied, "What?"

"That my bullet didn't go through and hit the floor. I tried to angle it just right, but you never know. Would have really fucked our version if it had."

Quick look around. No, no one else in the waiting room or the nearby hall. "About that trajectory...."

"I told them that I fired as Habash was already falling backward. I hated to pretend I was slower than you, but that explained it. Well enough."

"You took a big risk," I said, not quite able to say "thank you." Not yet.

"And you didn't?" She went back to the magazine.

It was clear by eleven p.m. that we weren't going to get any more news about Eleanor; she was sleeping off some heavy medication, recovering from—according to the doctor who finally appeared—an extensive beating, numerous cigarette burns on her arms and stomach, and several minor (but no doubt terrifying) cuts near her jugular. There were no serious internal injuries and he felt reasonably confident she could go home within a day. This hospital's version of "fine," I guess. Her body would recover fully. Her emotional state? He had no opinion about that.

As we trudged through the well-lit hospital parking lot to our vehicles, I reminded Malone to stay alert. Martin Idris was still out there somewhere, apparently determined to shoot one or both of us for unknown reasons.

CHAPTER NINETY-ONE

I sat alone in the Pen and Pastry the next morning, drinking strong black coffee and looking at the huge icing-covered pastry that I shouldn't have ordered because I had no appetite. Surprisingly, I was pretty well-rested. Even though I'd been totally exhausted by the time I got home from the hospital, I'd expected to be awake all night seeing images of brain matter on walls. In fact, I didn't remember going to bed. I may have been unconscious before I got all my clothes off.

Not even the cats were able to rouse me before around six this morning, which I'm sure they attempted to do because I hadn't fed them when I came in last night. So they were busy munching down turkey and cheese shredded bits while I determined that there was nothing in my kitchen I wanted to eat.

Which was why I walked over here for breakfast. I love Veronica Fortune's pastries. Usually. Not this morning, apparently.

Eleanor's condition had continued to improve, according to the hospital when I called earlier. Johnny and Hap were back at home. Colleen was probably sleeping in. Malone was probably up but I hadn't heard from her. And...crap: Alison Roberts was walking in the front door.

She scanned the room, saw me, and headed in my direction. At least she was alone. No microphones or cameras that I could see. So maybe this would be a chance to get past our last encounter when I slammed the door in her face. Irritating as she could be sometimes, Alison was a valuable resource that I didn't want to permanently alienate. I'd rather have made peace later, in my own time, but here she was.

She strode up to my table, pulled out the other chair, and sat down. Apparently not intimidated at all by the slammed doors of the past.

"Sit down," I said. "Have some coffee. Order some breakfast if you haven't eaten yet. My treat."

She gave me a suspicious look. "You seem to be in a better mood," she said. The waitress swung by at that moment. "Just coffee," Roberts told her, then turned her attention back to me. "But you look like shit, to tell the truth. Because you were involved in a shooting last evening, right?"

Nothing like cutting to the chase. I opened my mouth and found that I *really* didn't want to talk about it yet, peacemaking or not. "How did you know I was here? You make me wonder if you've planted a tracker on me."

She shrugged it off. "Not home. Not at the office. Not at the Home Run. This place is number four on my list of likely Clint McCall locations. And here you are. The shooting at the motel? That was you, right?"

"Is that what the media are saying?"

Her eyebrows went up. "Not yet. The official story from the Justice Center is that a woman had been kidnapped and last evening her kidnapper was killed during her rescue at the motel. The police were aided in her rescue by local private investigators. No identities to be released until the investigation concludes, but I know it was you and Devon Malone."

"How do you know that?"

"Because I have better sources at the hospital than my competitors. I know the woman is Eleanor Ivory." She paused, waiting for my reaction. I gave her none. "Given that she's your accountant and friend, what are the chances that some other local private investigators were involved in her rescue?"

Her coffee arrived, and I leaned back as if thinking it all over. She took a sip, then set the cup down firmly. "Come on, McCall," she said with an edge of irritation in her voice. "It had to be you and Malone."

Still didn't want to talk about it. "I'll tell you what," I said. "I'll give you an exclusive but not right this minute."

She sat back, her face flushing with excitement. "An exclusive?"

"Yes," I said. That *is* the magic word if you want to get on a reporter's good side.

She pulled out her cell phone. "I'll get Murray down here," she said and started punching numbers.

"Wait," I said, reaching out and closing my hand over the phone. "I just said, not right now. Later today. Much later. Not here and now."

Her shoulders sagged a bit. "How much later?"

"It will be in time for your newscast. What about late this afternoon, my office?"

"Okay. Three?"

"Four."

She looked like she was going to object, but then she let it go. "It's a date," she said, downed the rest of her coffee, and stood up. "I'll see you then."

I watched her hurry out into the cold February morning. By this point my big, luscious-looking pastry wasn't much warmer than the air coming in the door and I didn't give a shit. I didn't want it anyway.

CHAPTER NINETY-TWO

I picked up my vehicle from the house and swung by the hospital on the way to the office. Eleanor was still asleep, they said, but scheduled to be released later in the day. I looked in on her. She was bruised and battered, but seemed to be resting peacefully.

Traffic was light on the freeway between the hospital and downtown, not only because it was Wednesday mid-morning but also because of drizzle mixed with snow. It had been a long, miserable winter that wasn't eager to let go of the Pacific Northwest.

My parking lot was nearly full, but the pedestrian traffic was just as light as the freeway had been. Most of the people on foot were walking carefully. Even though it snows at least a few times every winter, Portlanders treat the white stuff as exotic and scary. No matter how few flakes fall, people slip and cars slide.

The mailbox was empty, which meant that Malone had been here. Or business was really slow. Or both. The hallway was empty, quiet. The door was unlocked and I opened it to see Malone sitting, tapping away at her keyboard, on her side of the partners desk. She barely glanced up at me and kept tapping.

I hung my jacket on the old hall tree in the corner, feeling oddly awkward about what to say. Between passionately kissing my partner and then coldly killing an unarmed man in front of her, it was a conundrum. I settled for "good morning" as I stowed the Smith and Wesson in the top right-hand drawer and got a pot of fresh coffee started. She must have been here for a while.

No message lights were blinking as I settled into my own chair to await the coffeemaker's conclusion. "Anything new?" I asked.

"A couple of possibilities. We have an appointment with one of them early this afternoon. Suspects her husband of cheating. Surprise, surprise." She actually said all of that to her monitor rather than me. Awkward. "You?" she asked the screen.

"I stopped by to check on Eleanor. She was resting comfortably, as they say, and should be released today. Alison Roberts caught me at breakfast and will be coming by for an exclusive late this afternoon."

"That's good. Eleanor, that is, not Alison."

I was almost reduced to using my "We need to talk line" when the door opened and a man I didn't recognize entered, gun in hand. Which was definitely not an improvement on awkward. Malone and I both froze.

The new arrival did more or less the same, once he'd kicked the door closed behind him. He looked at me, at Malone, back at me. Hadn't made a sound yet. The revolver he kept pointed between us, ready for whoever moved first.

He was a good-looking light-skinned black guy with longish dark hair, probably around forty, athletic build, nicely-dressed in slacks, shirt and leather jacket. If it weren't for the gun, I'd have assumed he was a potential client. The gun pointed me in another direction. The silencer on the gun suggested that it might be a very bad direction, indeed.

I knew Malone would be itching to go for her own weapon, so I sat back slowly, calculating the odds of getting into my top right-hand drawer before our visitor could pull the trigger. Not good at all. But at least my movement directed his attention to me.

"Martin Idris?" I inquired in a neutral tone.

"Got it in one," he said grimly. "Before I kill both of you, I need to know why this bitch has people asking questions about me."

Well, crap. My partner abruptly sat forward and her right hand happened to come to rest just above the drawer where her gun was stashed. "Why would we tell you anything if you're going to kill us anyway?" she asked him belligerently.

I jumped in before she got us immediately killed. "*We* weren't investigating you. Your name came up, that was all, and some people did background checks. You were a person of interest in a case we were working on, one that involved an old girlfriend of yours,

Eleanor Ivory, but that case is closed now. You have nothing to worry about."

Which was of course complete bullshit. He wasn't going to just walk away from a downtown drive-by and threatening us with a gun now. I'm sure he knew that, but I was trying to buy us a little time.

He frowned. "Eleanor? Ivory? The accountant chick? She's the one who put you onto me?"

I was beginning to think that, good-looking and well-dressed or not, Martin Idris was not among the more brilliant people who'd ever pointed a gun in my direction.

"No," I responded as patiently as I could, hoping that Malone would hold fast in the meantime, "Eleanor was in some trouble and we were looking into all her old boyfriends. You were just a name on a list. That was why Malone interviewed you. I was interviewing old boyfriends too. Eleanor's problem turned out to be another guy on the list. You didn't do it."

The frown deepened. "Didn't do what?"

"Wow," Malone muttered, unfortunately loud enough for all to hear, "who wants to be killed by a dumbshit?"

The gun twitched in her direction below a glare from Idris and I was just wondering what I could do now to save her butt when there was a single, sharp knock on the door.

Before any of us had a chance to react, it swung open, almost hitting Idris, to reveal Alison Roberts and Murray Kravitz. She had a big grin and Kravitz had his camera already up on his shoulder. I guess she figured to surprise us by arriving early in the spirit of ambush journalism even when not needed.

She surprised everybody, including herself and her cameraman.

Her expression was just shifting from glee to astonishment as Idris swung halfway around with an explosive "What the fuck!"

I think that Malone and I must have launched ourselves at him at exactly the same time. As far I can tell in retrospect, she slammed into his shoulder just as my hands closed on his gun. I'm glad she

331

didn't make it a split second earlier or I would have missed.

Once I had the gun and Malone had planted her forearm on his windpipe, it took only a few seconds more of wrestling around on the floor to subdue our unwelcome guest. In the end Idris was face down with Malone sitting on his upper back and me sprawled across his legs. Having apparently gotten his breath back in the meantime, he was spewing obscenities at the top of his voice.

I looked up at the doorway to find myself staring straight into Kravitz's camera lens. Beside him, Alison Roberts was literally hopping up and down. "You got that, didn't you, Murray? Tell me you got that."

Malone looked up as well and we all—except Martin Idris—waited with bated breath for Murray's response.

To my dismay, it was that, yes indeed, he got every second of it. Oh well. Another endlessly hyped Alison Roberts exclusive would probably bring in some more clients.

Devon slapped Idris in the back of the head and told him to shut the fuck up, then inquired if Roberts would mind calling the Justice Center.

That's my girl.

CHAPTER NINETY-THREE

A couple of patrolmen appeared shortly. They took everybody's information and seemed satisfied when I told them I'd be in touch with Lieutenant Whitehall concerning the details of what had happened. Then they hauled our last current threat away.

Alison Roberts of course wanted to stick around not only for her promised exclusive but also to get the background on this new one. I told her to come back later when she was supposed to. I told her I thought it was nuts to try to surprise a willing interview subject. I told her that if she did it to us again there would be no more exclusives, ever.

She left quietly, Murray Kravitz in tow.

The next several hours were the first routine time that my partner and I had spent in the office for what seemed like weeks. No one trying to kidnap or kill us. No one threatening clients or loved ones. No one trying to frame me for sexual assault. It felt good. It felt productive.

We caught up on paperwork. We went through all the messages we'd accumulated and started calling potential clients back—several of which were interested enough to make appointments. We compared notes on them and what their cases might involve. We went over to the Home Run at noon and had lunch while we continued to talk business as if nothing had happened between us.

And what all that didn't feel, at least to me, was really routine even though we were trying hard. Because something *had* happened. The kiss. Not to be too fucking melodramatic about it.

I had no clue—as usual—what was going on inside Devon Malone's head and heart, but that moment of passion, if I wanted to call it that (and I did), loomed over me like a massive cloud. A cloud that might dump a terrible storm on my head or part to reveal some sun. I needed to know which, whether she did or not.

So, we were back in the office after lunch and I was once again

333

seriously contemplating my "we need to talk" line when the door opened and Eleanor Ivory limped slowly into the office.

She must have been out of the hospital long enough to stop at home before coming down here, because she wore a long skirt and heavy wrap that I hadn't seen before. She looked like hell, a bandage on the side of her head near her left eye and the rest of her face badly bruised...but she managed a faint smile.

"Hey, guys. I just stopped in for a minute to say thank you."

We both stood up anyway. "It's great to see you," I said, "but you should be home, resting."

Malone started around the desk and reached to steady her, but Eleanor waved her back with a little wince. Probably it was painful to move *any* of her limbs.

I gestured to the closest visitor's chair and reluctantly sat down, as did Malone. "Why in the world did you come down here today?" I asked.

She carefully made her way to the indicated chair and slowly eased down into it.

"I had to check on my office...make sure everything was still here...and like I said, I wanted to thank you. Both of you. I'd be dead right now if you guys hadn't found me. And it probably would have been a slow, really awful death."

"You're welcome," responded Malone, "but you don't have to dwell on how horrible it might have been. It didn't happen. I know it's not easy, but you need to work it through and let it go."

Eleanor smiled, a thin smile. I imagined it was all she could manage without her face hurting. "I understand. I'm working on it and I'll get there."

"I'm sure you will," agreed my partner.

"I'm going back home now," Eleanor said. "I'll get some rest, don't worry, but I'll be back at work soon—and back in the dojang, too."

"One last thing," I said as she started to go.

"Yes?"

"I have to ask: Why the hell did you voluntarily get into Habash's car on Broadway?"

She gave me a wide-eyed look. "What choice did I have? At the time, it seemed like the man was everywhere and knew everything. I felt sure he'd take me anyway if I didn't get in on my own—and then some other people might have gotten hurt." Her mouth twitched, almost a little grin. "Good thing he didn't turn out to be all-powerful." Then she got serious again. "I'm glad you had to kill him, Clint. Really glad. I don't know if I would have ever felt safe with him sharing the same planet."

I was the one who said "You're welcome" this time. It was about all I could say.

Eleanor was again starting to turn toward the door when Malone spoke up.

"I've got one last thing, too. You remember that list of recent boyfriends we went through at the beginning of all this?"

"Yes."

"You do realize that two out of the five turned out to be violent criminals. That's not a good batting average."

A tiny rueful smile. "I do realize that. I've had some time lately to think about my lifestyle. I'm planning a few changes."

"Probably a good thing."

"One of the nurses at the hospital asked me out. I think I might go."

Whoa. Apparently there would be no adjustment in how fast she moved. I had to ask: "Uh, male nurse?"

She looked mildly shocked, then amused. "Yes, of course. I'm not changing my lifestyle *that* much. He's a very quiet, responsible guy who doesn't even like to party." She gave me a look. "Of course, I want to get to know him better, to be sure of all that."

"Of course."

"I don't want to play games anymore."

I thought about the last week or so, all the anguish and blood. "Sounds like a plan to me," I said.

335

Her smile grew broader as she surveyed the two of us sitting on opposite sides of our partners desk. "You know," she said, "maybe you two should stop playing games and think about making some changes."

Whereupon she managed to get out of the office before either of us quite got our mouths closed.

CHAPTER NINETY-FOUR

In the silence following Eleanor's exit, Malone and I looked at each across the expanse of the double desktop. She was frowning, lips pressed firmly together now. I have no idea what my expression was. Then: "Don't ask *me*," she muttered, and turned to her keyboard.

It felt like having a door slammed shut in my face. Not the first time, but it was going to be the first time I kicked the door. I hated to risk our partnership, but....

"Maybe Eleanor is right," I said, with a feeling like you'd have teetering on the edge of a big drop-off.

Malone typed a few more words of whatever she was pretending to work on, then her fingers stilled. She spoke without taking her eyes from the monitor, looking if anything even more grim.

"I don't know what you mean."

Time to take the plunge, I guess. "I would like to have a relationship with you."

Very slowly she turned to look at me, her expression unchanged. "You have a relationship with me."

"I would like to have a romantic relationship with you." Could I sound any more dweeby? Jesus.

That pushed her eyebrows up a bit, but no other change. "A romantic relationship?" She shook her head. "That kind of thing opens the floodgates."

"Floodgates?"

She gestured around us as if I were supposed to see the damned things. "Floodgates. Floodgates, you know, of emotion. Everybody gets all gooey and you end up using the 'l' word."

"Lust?"

"Not that one. That one's okay. The *other* 'l' word."

"Ah ha. What if I promise not to use it?"

She looked down at the surface of the desk for what seemed

337

like a full minute. "You don't know me," she said quietly.

"I know you're my partner. I know you have my back, that I can count on you, that I trust you completely. I know I really enjoy having you around, not to mention kissing you. I know you're an incredibly tough and exasperating woman that I want to know a lot better, on a more personal level."

Big sigh as she met my eyes once more. "Tough and exasperating? You have no idea. This could be a fucking disaster." Another long pause, then, finally, unbelievably, she smiled. Just a little smile. "But I guess you gotta do what you gotta do."

And I thought I saw a door opening.

THE END

ABOUT THE AUTHOR

Glenn Harris lives and writes in the middle of the Columbia Gorge National Scenic Area (Hood River, Oregon). Besides creating detective novels, short stories, and a monthly newspaper column, he acts and directs in community theater.

His former lives include college English teacher, private K-12 school director, graphic design business owner, weekly newspaper managing editor, corporate manager, and taekwondo instructor.

Want more McCall and Malone mysteries? Read *Dying of Desire* next, and be sure to visit Glenn Harris' website (http://www.-glennharris.us) and subscribe to the free e-mail newsletter so you're first in line for new books!